PRAISE FOR THE SERIES

Fifty-Four Pigs

"With Dr. Peter Bannerman, Philipp Schott has created a unique brand of amateur detective, one who is as amiable as he is enigmatic . . . The reader can't help but be entranced and embraced by Schott's charming and saucily unusual first book in what should be a long-running series."

— Anthony Bidulka, author of the
Russell Quant Mystery series

"Deadly and delightful, *Fifty-Four Pigs* is a delicious read with some of the most beautiful descriptions of a prairie winter anywhere."

— Iona Whishaw, author of the
Lane Winslow Mystery series

Six Ostriches

"Schott's second mystery featuring gumshoe veterinarian Peter Bannerman (after 2022's *Fifty-Four Pigs*) combines the soothing sleuthing of *Murder, She Wrote* with the humble charm of *All Creatures Great and Small.*"

— *Publishers Weekly*, starred review

"*Six Ostriches* is both a good introduction to the series and a satisfying follow-up to its predecessor. Whether read individually or together, these books offer lovers of cozy mysteries and animal stories a heartwarming yet stimulating read, with a puzzle that hits the sweet spot between comfortably challenging and brain-buster."

— *New York Journal of Books*

Eleven Huskies

"Wonderful, unique characters (including Peter's sniffer dog, Pippin), a dramatic setting, and a brisk plot all make for an excellent mystery."

— *firstCLUE Reviews*

"Even though the series is cozy — quiet in tone, cast with quirky personalities, including a sleuth-helping pet, and all violence off-stage — there's a lot of humanity to enrichen the plot."

— *The New York Journal Review of Books*

WORKS BY PHILIPP SCHOTT

THE ACCIDENTAL VETERINARIAN SERIES

The Accidental Veterinarian: Tales from a Pet Practice

How to Examine a Wolverine:
More Tales from the Accidental Veterinarian

The Battle Cry of the Siamese Kitten:
Even More Tales from the Accidental Veterinarian

DR. BANNERMAN VET MYSTERIES

Fifty-Four Pigs: A Dr. Bannerman Vet Mystery (#1)

Six Ostriches: A Dr. Bannerman Vet Mystery (#2)

Eleven Huskies: A Dr. Bannerman Vet Mystery (#3)

OTHER

The Willow Wren: A Novel

Heal the Beasts:
A Jaunt Through the Curious History of the Veterinary Arts

THREE *Bengal Kittens*

A DR. BANNERMAN VET MYSTERY

PHILIPP SCHOTT

Published by ECW Press
665 Gerrard Street East
Toronto, Ontario, Canada M4M 1Y2
416-694-3348 / info@ecwpress.com

Cover design: David A. Gee
Cover artwork: © Joey Gao

LIBRARY AND ARCHIVES CANADA CATALOGUING IN PUBLICATION

Title: Three Bengal kittens / Philipp Schott.

Names: Schott, Philipp, author

Series: Schott, Philipp. Dr. Bannerman vet mysteries ; #4.

Description: Series statement: A Dr. Bannerman vet mystery ; #4

Identifiers: Canadiana (print) 20250320223 | Canadiana (ebook) 2025032024X

ISBN 978-1-77041-861-5 (softcover)
ISBN 978-1-77852-547-6 (ePub)
ISBN 978-1-77852-548-3 (PDF)

Subjects: LCGFT: Novels.

Classification: LCC PS8637.C5645 T47 2026 | DDC C813/.6—dc23

This book is funded in part by the Government of Canada. *Ce livre est financé en partie par le gouvernement du Canada.* We acknowledge the support of the Canada Council for the Arts. *Nous remercions le Conseil des arts du Canada de son soutien.* We would like to acknowledge the funding support of the Ontario Arts Council (OAC) and the Government of Ontario for their support. We also acknowledge the support of the Government of Ontario through the Ontario Book Publishing Tax Credit, and through Ontario Creates.

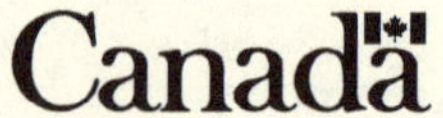

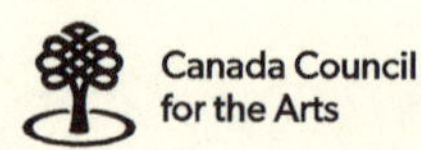

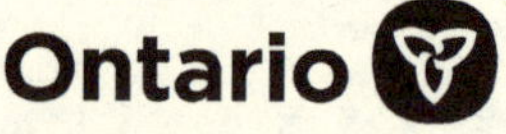

PRINTED AND BOUND IN CANADA

PRINTING: FRIESENS 5 4 3 2 1

For Lorraine

PROLOGUE

They were hungry. Very hungry. Normally the food man filled their bowls two times a day. The first time was after he got out of his bed and made his hot black liquid. They would mew at him and wind around his legs. But he insisted on having his hot black liquid first. Then one morning he did not get out of his bed. They mewed at him and danced on his chest. But he still did not get out of his bed. This had happened a few times before, when the food man had been looking at his noisy light box all through the night. But later, in the middle of the day, he always got out of his bed and filled their bowls. This time he had not been looking at the noisy light box, and now it was the middle of the day, and he still did not get out of his bed. So they stopped mewing and began screaming. They were small, but they could scream loudly. Still the food man did not get out of his bed. And then it was night. It was time for their second feeding. Now they screamed in his face. But he did not move.

It was a terrible night. They were so very hungry, and now they were scared too. What if the food man never got out of his bed again? Who would fill their bowls?

The next morning they heard a knocking at the door. And a ringing. Then more knocking — much louder. Then the door opened, and a new person came in. The new person made loud noises. The new person went to where the food man was lying in bed. Then the new person made even louder noises. They ran up to this new person and rubbed on their legs and mewed. Hopefully this was a new food person.

CHAPTER
One

"He called again," Theresa said. She flashed Peter a smile after she said this, but it was a wry smile, and her tone was sympathetic. "Do you want me to write the message down?"

"Same as before?" Peter asked.

"Pretty much."

"No, that's fine then, Theresa. Thanks. That makes, what? Six times in the last two hours?"

"Only five." Theresa chuckled. She swivelled back and forth on her chair behind the reception counter, absentmindedly petting Cantaloupe. The big orange cat was basking in a bright sunbeam beside Theresa's coffee mug. He had only been named "official clinic cat" for New Selfoss Veterinary Services two weeks before, but he already had assumed regal command of the space.

"I'm sorry he's bothering you," Peter said, sighing, running his hand through his unruly hair. "I'll call him back right away and tell him to stop."

"It's no bother at all. He seems to be in a good mood today. And anyway, it's a slow morning."

It was true. Susan Gislason had cancelled because Dieter, her dachshund, had suddenly started eating again after a mysterious three-day-long hunger strike. And the cat spay had turned into a neuter — a much quicker surgery — when Peter discovered Princess was actually a prince.

"When am I supposed be at Chernov's to look at that bull?"

"Not until one o'clock, and you've only got Michelle Nyquist before then, so you've got plenty of time if Sam's chatty."

"Not if Michelle's chatty too," Peter said.

They both laughed.

Peter stared at the messages on his desk, as if looking at them just the right way might somehow change their content. He stretched his long arms and rolled his head around on his neck a few times. It was a gorgeous late September day out there. His very favourite type of day. Not too warm, not too cold. Aspen and birch glowing. Smell of earth. Crunch of leaves. But he was in here. Waiting for Michelle Nyquist. And avoiding calling his brother back.

Sam Bannerman had returned to Manitoba that summer. His existence as an artist in Toronto, which had always been tenuous, had become unsustainable as rents continued to climb and sales of his paintings continued to dwindle. Sam had confessed to Peter that he hadn't sold a single canvas in two years and was living off a combination of welfare and stretched credit cards, having long since spent the last of the inheritance they had both received from their parents. The only solution was to move back to Manitoba, where it was much cheaper to live. New Selfoss had a tight rental market, and Sam had nothing but scorn for his old hometown and for small-town life in general, so, with Peter and Laura's financial help, he moved to Winnipeg. To a small bachelor suite in the North End, on Burrows Avenue. "This is going to be OK after all," Peter told Laura.

Then the calls started.

Problems with the landlord. Problems with social assistance. Problems with his doctor. Strange noises. Strange smells. Strange thoughts.

Peter picked up the first message. Theresa had numbered them, obviously anticipating multiple calls:

1. *Sam called*
2. *Sam called again — says it's urgent but was polite*
3. *Sam called again — says it's about cats*
4. *Sam asked again nicely but sounds worried*

Something urgent to do with cats. Peter considered that his brother had probably picked up a stray. His North End neighbourhood was full of them. Sam had owned a ferret in Toronto. But after Nosferretu died, in a rare moment of rationality, Sam decided that his apartment wasn't a great place for pets, so he didn't bring home any more. His new place on Burrows was no better, what with the canvases, painting supplies, and garage sale "treasures" stacked floor to ceiling in every available space. He couldn't possibly keep a cat there. *So, what on earth was . . .*

Peter stopped himself.

He was allowing his mind to stumble down a pointless path of speculation. He hated it when he did that. It was a waste of brain power and a waste of time. As always, data was needed to quell the speculation.

He'd have to call Sam.

Sam answered after only one ring. "Hi, what's up?" Peter asked. He forced a cheerful tone to try to conceal the annoyance he felt at having to have this conversation. Today's annoyance was just a thin layer stacked on top of decades of layers. By now, a tower. A skyscraper of irritation.

"I'm sorry, man. I'm really, really sorry to bug you. You know I hate bugging people because I hate it when people bug me. You know? So, I get it. I totally get it. You know that I get it, right?" Sam sucked in a long, ragged breath.

"Yes, I know," Peter said. He suppressed a groan and glanced at his watch. It was going to be one of *those* conversations.

"Cool. That's cool. So, I called — and, again, I'm sorry for calling like a gajillion times because I know you're super busy and all, what with vet stuff and whatever — but anyway I called because there's these cats in the apartment right below me. Don't know the guy's name or anything. Seen him a couple times in the hall. Old and sketchy looking, you know? So, I don't like say 'hey, neighbour' and stuff. But I keep hearing his cats. Like right through the floor. It's like paper. The floor, I mean. Even over my TV I can hear them. And last couple days, they're like extra loud. Extra, extra loud. Like screaming and stuff. So, I've been thinking about talking to the dude, but like I said he's sketchy looking, and I don't want to get into some kind of feud or something. A pissed-off neighbour can make your life hell. Total hell, right? Don't need that. I got enough problems, right? So, I've tried to call the super, but she's not answering. And then —"

Sam cut himself off, and Peter picked up the knocking sound that had interrupted him. "Wonder who that is," Sam said.

"Do you need to get that?" Peter asked. Hoped.

"Nah, probably Mormons or Jehovahs or something. No security system here. I wrote an email to management about that, and they were like —"

Sam was interrupted again, this time by much heavier knocking followed by a loud voice: "Winnipeg Police! Open up!"

CHAPTER *Two*

"You're kidding me," Peter said, reaching for his coffee cup before realizing it was empty and pulling his hand back.

"I am not," Kevin said, and glanced at his watch. "I've got ten more minutes before I have to head to the station, so I have plenty of time to explain to you what the phrase means." He grinned.

"I know what it means, Kev. It's just not something one comes across very often."

Kevin shrugged. "Yeah, I suppose it's rare . . . but not that rare. Brett said they see one every other year or so. But most are by hanging. Plastic bag over the head is unusual."

"Michael Hutchence," Peter said quietly. A waitress approached with a carafe. Peter smiled and shook his head. One cup of Rita's legendary black tar was plenty.

"The INXS guy? That was the rumour, but with a belt, not a bag, and the Aussie police say suicide, not auto-erotic asphyxiation. David Carradine was a clear case. Anyway, it happens." Kevin yawned and stretched his arms out to either side, touching the edges of the booth. He was a large man, with a full red beard. That in combination with his RCMP uniform made him the focus of many glances in the coffee shop. At least half the customers seemed to know him. New Selfoss was a small town after all. There were lots of waves and cheery calls of "Good morning, Corporal Gudmundurson." Kevin always waved and called back. Peter, as the local veterinarian, was equally well known, but although he was very tall, he was not as imposing as his brother-in-law. And he tried to avoid eye contact with any clients who came in unless he knew them really well. He hated small talk, and he always had trouble connecting the client to a specific animal or case when he wasn't in the clinic.

"So, not murder?"

"Nope. Self-inflicted, according to the WPS."

"Good. As I mentioned, Sam is freaking out that there is a murderer prowling his apartment block, picking off the single men."

"Watching too much true crime serial killer stuff?"

"I don't know about that. Mostly he's just the paranoid type. As well being all sorts of other types." Peter chuckled. "Anyway, I really appreciate you checking in with your contact in Winnipeg."

"No worries, Pete. Brett and I go way back. Even dated for a short bit. It was good to catch up with him yesterday. As soon as the family's been contacted, this'll all be public record right away anyway." Kevin pulled a notebook out of his jacket pocket. "Dženan Knezevic. Seventy years old. Born in Sarajevo, Bosnia and Herzegovina. Came over in —"

"Ninety-three?" Peter interrupted.

Kevin put the notebook down and stared at Peter. "How the hell did you know that?"

"Educated guess. Thousands of Bosnians came to Canada that year as refugees from the Yugoslav Wars." Peter shrugged. "Everybody knows that."

Kevin shook his head slowly. "No, not everybody knows that. You are a certified freak. Should we ask around the coffee shop? Take a poll? I will eat this notebook if any of the first ten people we ask knows that."

"You're on," Peter said, grinning. "It's an older crowd. Some will remember."

Kevin waved at Peter and snorted. "Forget it. Not worth the effort. And I've got to get going anyway. But yeah, that's what they know about the dead perv. Also, never married and has lived in that apartment for a long time."

"Occupation?"

Kevin picked up the notebook again and flipped through it. "Doesn't say."

Peter nodded. "OK. Thanks again, Kev. This should help settle Sam down."

"You think?" Kevin arched an eyebrow.

"Not really. Only a solid ten milligrams of lorazepam t.i.d. would settle him down. But I can hope!" Peter laughed.

"Good luck with that," Kevin said with a crooked smile. He stood up and clapped Peter on the shoulder. "Have to dash now — off to fight evildoers and restore justice to the universe. Have a good one. You got my coffee?"

"You bet. See you tomorrow?"

"Hundred percent. I live for Laura's Sunday dinners."

"Before you go, I meant to ask, how's Atlas?"

Kevin smiled. "Atlas is awesome. Adopting him was possibly the best decision I've ever made."

"Glad to hear it. He's due to have his liver rechecked soon, I think."

"Already made the appointment with Theresa."

Peter flashed his brother-in-law a thumbs-up and watched him leave the coffee shop, weaving between the seniors clustered around the till. One of them, a vaguely familiar looking tiny woman with a hooked nose, stopped Kevin and shook his hand. They exchanged a few words. Normally Peter would be trying to figure out what that might be about. His brain was like a radar sweeping the environment for puzzles, no matter how trivial. But he was preoccupied with thoughts of Dženan Knezevic and the dead man's apparent fetish. And his three Bengal kittens.

It presented such a strange mental image, especially in combination with his brother as a neighbour.

Peter briefly contemplated asking for a refill after all but dismissed the notion as unwise. Pleased with his self-discipline, he was just about to get up and leave when a middle-aged man with a big smile and a John Deere cap slid into the booth opposite him, where Kevin had been sitting.

"Good morning, Doc! Don't wanna bother you, but I figured you'd wanna know how Humphrey was getting along."

At least it was a client, and a case, Peter knew well. It was Bill Chernov. Humphrey was his prize-winning Charolais bull.

"Yes, thank you. How is he doing?"

"Fantastic! You'd never know anything was wrong with him."

"Glad to hear that. These usually clear up pretty well on antibiotics. And you're doing the cold water hosing too?"

"You bet," Bill said, and then leaned forward and lowered his voice. "I'd have never guessed a bull would enjoy getting his balls doused in freezing water like that."

Peter chuckled. Back-to-back conversations about auto-erotic asphyxiation and infected testicles. An eavesdropper would begin to wonder about him. "Yes, that must be a relief for the poor guy. The inflammation from orchitis can produce a lot of heat. I'm glad it's working."

"Sure is. Just wanted to let you know. Do you need to see him again?"

"No, not unless there's something you're concerned about."

Bill left to join a group of men in another booth. Peter got up, paid the bill, and stepped outside. It was another magnificent fall day. Manitoba didn't have the famous blazing scarlet sugar maples of the east, but it did have every shade of gold, yellow, orange, and bronze from the aspens, tamaracks, elms, and bur oaks. New Selfoss was well treed. There were also plenty of evergreens to provide contrast to the deciduous trees. And there was red in the understory, especially in the ubiquitous crimson dogwood shrubs. Yellow, green, and red, all of it backlit by the sun's slanting rays. This time of year, near the autumnal equinox, the sun was low enough in the south that the whole day had summer's "golden hour" glow of dawn and dusk.

Peter took a deep breath and considered his options. He had promised to meet Sam for coffee today but had been deliberately vague about when. He had also told Laura that he would help her cut up some of the deadfall for firewood. And Pippin needed a good long walk. He knew that he should get the least pleasant task out of the way first, which was visiting Sam, but he also knew that the weather could change by the afternoon, so it made sense to do the outdoor things first. On the other hand, Sam would be anxious to hear what Kevin had to say. He was probably planning to phone soon — in fact, it was surprising that he hadn't already — so Peter decided to pre-empt that by calling him now to avoid having to field a call from him while he was in the middle of something.

The phone rang three times and went to Sam's voicemail, which now featured dark Gothic music and Sam intoning, "Ph'nglui mglw'nafh Cthulhu R'lyeh wgah'nagl fhtagn." This was followed by an abrupt end to the music and a much brighter, cheerier Sam saying, "Leave a message!"

Peter rolled his eyes. *Cthulhu. What next?*

"Uh, hi. That was cute. Anyway, Kevin's contact at the WPS says it was accidental, self-inflicted. Not murder. I've got a few things to do up here this morning, and then I can meet you at Luda's Deli this afternoon, say two o'clock?"

Peter tucked his phone away and smiled to himself. It was a perfect day, and Laura, Pippin, Merry, and Gandalf were waiting for him. Life was good.

CHAPTER *Three*

The roar of the chainsaw led Peter around the house to the far corner of their property, where Laura was slicing into a large aspen log lying across a battered sawhorse. Freshly cut logs were in a neat stack nearby. It looked like she had already done the majority of the work. Laura's back was to him, and the chainsaw was loud enough that she didn't notice him enter the yard. But Pippin did. In fact, Pippin seemed to expect that Peter, or someone, was coming. He was already bounding across the lawn toward the corner of the house as Peter came around it. There was no car for Pippin to hear as Peter had walked from the café, and the chainsaw was too loud in any case. Smell? Or perhaps some undiscovered sense that people lazily called "instinct"? Peter didn't know, but this sort of thing happened a lot.

"How are you, buddy? How's your morning been?" Peter asked as he bent down to greet his dog by scratching him vigorously behind the ears. He often speculated about how minute differences in the weight of each ear versus the stiffness of its cartilage could lead to one being erect and the other flopped, but these thoughts didn't stop him from being charmed by the effect. He might be a nerd, and he might view emotion with suspicion as an atavistic burden, but he didn't resist feeling joy and love at moments like this. He always bristled at the myth that people on the autism spectrum were unemotional and had difficulty expressing empathy. It was just that understanding how to express these things in the socially prescribed manner was more difficult for people like him. Fortunately, with a dog, the "socially prescribed manner" was very flexible and forgiving. It was usually just what came naturally to Peter, rather than the arbitrary and artificial rules that the dominant human culture had elaborated.

The black and white lab–husky–border collie mix wagged his tail and sniffed Peter's pant leg. The sniffing session was much shorter than it would have been had Peter just come home from the clinic. Post-work pants told far more interesting stories — stories of angry old Pomeranians, sick baby bunnies, and chilled-out fat tabbies. Today's pants-news was just of boring humans, albeit with an intriguing hint of breakfast bacon.

"How's the sawing going?" Peter asked his dog as they walked across the backyard to where Laura was working. Pippin glanced up at Peter when he spoke. He knew very well when he was being spoken to in a way that required him to pay attention versus when he was being spoken to only because someone decided to aim words in his direction. Nonetheless, these speaking modes could change suddenly, sometimes even midsentence, so it behooved Pippin to listen to the blah-blah words regardless.

Laura didn't startle easily, so it wasn't a problem to tap her on the shoulder while she was chainsawing. Peter had learned the hard way that her brother, Kevin, on the other hand, had a hair-trigger internal alarm. He had come into the kitchen once while Kevin was preparing a sandwich and made the mistake of speaking abruptly. Kevin was so startled that he swung around brandishing the knife, his face a caricature of fear and aggression. Peter wondered whether this was a useful trait for an RCMP officer.

"Wow, you're really powering through this," he said.

Laura set the chainsaw down, pushed her safety goggles up onto the top of her head, and turned to face Peter. In almost every respect, she was the physical opposite of her husband. Where he was tall with unruly dark-brown hair, she was short and had bright red hair, a Gudmundurson family trademark, pulled into a neat braid. And where Peter was awkward and a little clumsy, Laura was graceful and dextrous.

"Yeah, you know how it is. Sometimes you get into the flow where your mood and ability and the circumstances perfectly match the task, and sometimes you don't. Today is a flow day. At least so far." She smiled and pecked Peter on the cheek. "What about you? Did you achieve a flow state in your chat with my brother?"

"'Flow' is probably overstating it, but yeah, we had a good talk." Peter went on to summarize what Kevin had told him about Sam's dead neighbour.

"Auto-erotic asphyxiation? Really?" she said, narrowing her eyes.

"That was my response, but Kevin wasn't fazed at all. He didn't accuse me of being naive, but he came close."

"Huh. True crime in the big city, eh?" Laura said.

"Well, not actually a crime if they're right about the auto-erotic asphyxiation. That's an accident. A weird accident, but an accident nonetheless," Peter said.

"*If* they're right? I don't like the sound of that. Haven't you had your fill of murder?"

Peter laughed. "Totally. Three is plenty. Or I suppose it's actually five if I count Dragonfly Lake properly. Anyway, no, I'm not directly questioning the Winnipeg police's conclusion. I have no basis for that. It's just my logic engine automatically kicking in because there hasn't been enough time for a full investigation yet, so the auto-erotic asphyxiation just represents a highly plausible theory based on the immediately available physical evidence."

They both smiled when Peter purposely amped up his already didactic way of speaking: an inside joke.

Pippin sat beside them, looking back and forth as each spoke. The morning was quiet otherwise — no birds, no wind, no traffic.

Laura took off her gloves and looked like she was about to speak when there was a loud bang from the far corner of the yard.

They both turned to look. Pippin let out a soft woof.

It was Gandalf, their white Saanen goat. He had managed to knock over his food trough, apparently by jumping on it.

"What's all that about?" Laura asked, one corner of her mouth turned up in a wry smile.

"Maybe he was bleating at you, and you couldn't hear him over the chainsaw?"

"Did you feed him this morning?"

"I did. But I didn't spend any time with him."

"And you didn't greet him either when you came into the yard."

"True." Peter nodded. "I think he's just bored and lonely. I'll go over and say hi to him now."

"And I'll clean up here. Then maybe a cup of tea?"

"Decaf for me. I just had one of those giant mugs of Rita's coffee. And I'm going to have at least one coffee with Sam at Luda's."

Ten minutes later, they were sitting in the living room, either side of the fireplace, each in their favourite chair. Laura's had a wicker basket of knitting on the floor beside it, whereas Peter's was by a small rosewood end table neatly stacked with books. Pippin lay on the rug between them, while Merry, their tortie cat, lay on the window ledge, fully in the sun. Often, she would seek a lap when Laura or Peter came into the room, but a warm sunbeam held more appeal today.

Peter blew on his tea, a decaf Earl Grey. He had steeped it a little longer than normal, closer to five minutes than his customary four. It was a new high-quality blend, so this did not increase the tannin extraction to an unpleasant degree, but it enhanced the bergamot flavour, which he craved at the moment. Peter was well aware that his mathematical precision with tea brewing, and much else, was considered odd by most people, so he avoided talking about it. Mostly. For him, precision was comforting. Nothing soothed him more when he was stressed than to calculate something, measure something, or analyze something. The jumbled thoughts of stress were replaced by orderly thoughts of math. It was like the peace that came from straightening a bed. Or tidying a sock drawer. Or lining up pencils side by side. At least that's how it was for him.

This time the stress was Sam. The unfortunate death did not appear to be a murder, so that should calm his brother down. In theory. But Peter knew from long experience that Sam's mind worked very differently than his. He would still be frantic. His brother may use the language of logic, but it too often took him down an entirely different path: initially plausible thought leading to slightly less plausible thought, to even less plausible thought, and so on until he landed on something utterly implausible. And that was when Sam was being treated successfully. When he wasn't, his world became a labyrinth of cracked mirrors. "Logic" was an alien notion from a distant planet. Fortunately, he appeared to have found a good psychiatrist in Winnipeg, and his treatment was on track. Nonetheless, Peter was not looking forward to talking to him this afternoon. Maybe he would get a call for an emergency C-section? He normally never hoped for something like that, and he certainly didn't wish ill on an unfortunate labouring cow, but he couldn't help himself but think wishfully. His own logic had failed him.

"You're brooding," Laura said, her voice soft. "Sam?"

"Yes." Peter put his cup down beside the books, looked at his lap, and sighed.

"It'll be fine. He'll talk. You'll listen. An hour or two will go by. And then it will be over, and you can come home."

"This too shall pass," Peter said, smiling now.

"Yes, this too shall pass." Laura smiled back and then glanced into her knitting basket. "But this project shall not pass unless I make some serious progress today."

"That *Matrix* sweater?" Peter asked, grateful for the change of subject. Laura, although trained as a paleobiologist, had through accident and good fortune become one of the foremost knitters of bespoke geek-wear anywhere.

"Yes, but guess what? The red pill, which is in the original design, turns out to be a right-wing dog whistle."

"Yup. Incels reference it to indicate that they have woken up to an alleged hidden truth of men being oppressed."

"Ugh. That's what my client in Atlanta said. She called in a panic. She had picked the design because she had no idea of the possible implications until she mentioned it to a friend. It's supposed to be a gift for her husband's birthday. *The Matrix* is his favourite movie."

"Yikes! So . . . ?"

"So, now I'm going to have to undo three-quarters of it. I can keep the sleeves. They're just plain black. But the red pill design on the front is going to be replaced by those vertical lines of code in acid green on the movie poster."

"That sounds harder." Peter picked up his cup again and took a deep sip.

"Yeah, a lot harder. But I've got the day more or less free, and to be honest, it's kind of fun. I've never tried to knit code before."

"It would be cool if it were real code that, if run, would do something like bring up your website, or install a *Matrix* gif."

"Uh-huh. Cool." Laura rummaged in her basket. "But not happening."

Peter's phone buzzed. He picked it up, glanced at the screen, and groaned.

"Sam?" Laura asked.

"How'd you guess? He texted that he wants me to come right now, and he wants me to bring Pippin."

"To the café? I doubt they allow dogs."

Peter shook his head, ran his fingers through his hair, and groaned again. "I'll ask him what's up."

Peter tapped out the message. He put the phone down on the end table and picked it up again three times, checking for a reply, before Laura asked him to stop.

"Drink your tea. I'm sure it's nothing. Don't let him get under your skin."

Another minute passed, and then Peter's phone buzzed again.

He grabbed it. His brows furrowed in puzzlement. He showed Laura the screen:

mr bingley escaped — urgent urgent

CHAPTER *Four*

This new place was exceptionally interesting.

This had been a good choice. His brothers were going to regret not having joined him. But they were asleep when second food man left the door open a moment too long. Second food man didn't even notice him leave. And then the young man who was not a food man and who was carrying stuff didn't see him slip out the next door either. Humans are so blind and clumsy and dumb. It's a good thing they have the food. Otherwise, there would be no reason for them to exist. Though his brothers seemed to like warm laps and pats from humans, he didn't care for those.

But anyway, it was the perfect escape. Well, not really escape. He was going to go back when he was done exploring. Blind, clumsy, and dumb, or not, second food man did his food job well. And his place was interesting. Lots to smell. Lots to look at. Lots of places to nap. First food man had been more boring.

This was not boring. Freedom was the most un-boring thing he had ever experienced. Every few steps there was a new sound, a new smell, a new sight. Even the rough, dirty surface he was walking on felt different. And the ceiling! The ceiling of this massive room was not flat and low and white but was extremely high with bumpy white blotches on blue. The blotches might even be moving, but he only glanced at them because he was focused on the incredible size of the room. It seemed like it had no doors or proper walls, just gigantic boxes the size of dozens of the food men's rooms. Really gigantic. The largest things he had ever seen. By far. These boxes had windows and doors leading into them. As if there were rooms inside of rooms inside this room. It threatened to blow his mind, so he stopped thinking about it and concentrated on the smells and sounds and sights immediately around him.

It occurred to him that maybe he should be scared. Of what, exactly, he didn't know. He just had this faint, buzzy sensation inside of him that curiosity was keeping at bay. So far.

But curiosity was gradually being replaced by another sensation. Not fear, but hunger. And sadly, none of these many smells was appetizing.

Maybe it was time to go back to second food man. He could always return to this endless room after second breakfast.

He turned around but was startled that he didn't recognize anything. He hadn't memorized the sequence of giant boxes. And the smells, so helpful in food man's room, were all mixed up here. The air was moving in some weird way that also ruffled his fur unpleasantly and made him feel cold. Facing this way, it moved right into his eyes, which he hated. And it made smells come and go really quickly.

This was stupid. He didn't like this room after all.

And then, suddenly, there was a loud noise that made him jump a little. His heart began to race. He looked around.

A large, shiny object was moving toward him. It was very noisy. It was attached to the ground by large, round black objects that rolled like some of his toys. It had windows.

He had no idea what to do. He considered bolting for cover behind one of the large plastic bins nearby.

Just then the object stopped rolling and became quieter. It still made noise, but not as horribly loud.

A door opened. He was startled that it had doors. That was unexpected.

And then there was a human voice. A quiet, friendly human voice.

A female human got out and crouched down beside him. She was still quiet and friendly. She knew how to talk to cats.

Was he going to have a food lady now?

What about his brothers? He'd miss them, he supposed, but mostly he was hungry.

CHAPTER *Five*

Normally Peter enjoyed the drive into Winnipeg. He was indifferent to the vehicle itself and quickly became bored when the guys at the darts club got into "car talk" — hemi this, camshaft that; Dwayne Lautermilch was a particularly egregious offender — but he loved the illusion of freedom driving gave him. And he loved the solitude, Pippin's frequent presence notwithstanding. Normally this freedom and solitude allowed his mind to meander over a vast terrain of ideas, questions, and concepts. He would muse on the absurdity of the blueness of the sky. Or on the math hidden in the complexity of Glenn Gould's *Goldberg Variations*. Or on the likely thoughts in the minds of the Canada geese as they gathered in multitudes in the fields on either side of the highway.

Not today.

Today the sky, the music, and the geese were crowded out by rage. Rage at his brother. Rage at the idiotic decisions he was capable of making. Normally Peter tempered this rage with the understanding that when Sam did something, sometimes it was not a "decision" in the same way a mentally sound person chose to do something.

Still.

This was so stupid. And the stupidity was going to mess up Peter's day.

Sam's reply to Peter's multiple question marks after the Mr. Bingley text kept looping through his brain, like a train shunted onto a circular track:

hes one of the kittens — dead guys
kittens . . . humane society came to
take them — i said i promised him to look
after them if something happened to him

spur of the moment white lie —
dont know the guy

called em mr bingley, barry, flinders —
all boys i think — cute!!!

but mr bingley got out

come now!!! with pippin for tracking

urgent urgent

Peter had written and deleted multiple replies before simply sending an OK. Any other answer would just delay the inevitable. Short of disowning his brother and cutting off all communication, he'd have to drive into the city now, with Pippin, and sort this out in person.

But three kittens?

There was no way Sam was in a position to look after one kitten, let alone three. No way. And then what? This would end up somehow becoming Peter's problem. He just knew it.

Peter tried to take three deep breaths.

There was no point in arguing. He really wanted to, but it would end up wasting even more time. He could not control Sam's actions. He could only control his response to those actions.

Usually.

Right now, he didn't feel like he was completely in control of his response.

He gripped the steering wheel like he was strangling it until he noticed he was doing that and consciously relaxed his fingers again.

Deep breaths, Peter. Deep breaths.

It was a good thing that it was over an hour's drive to Sam's place. Peter expected that he would be calmer by the time he reached the Perimeter Highway. And if not, well, maybe taking Pippin for a walk first would help. Burrows Avenue and nearby Main Street weren't ideal for dog walking, but Pippin would find it interesting. However, Sam would have calculated exactly how long it would take Peter to get to his place, and any delay would result in another deluge of rage-inducing texts.

Peter pulled up in front of the Lady Alice apartment block. The sign was in block wooden letters, painted in peeling pale green. The *Y* and *A* were missing, so it now read *LAD LICE.* It was a two-storey, eight-unit building, probably dating from the 1940s or '50s. There were a hundred like it in Winnipeg. He had been there once before, shortly after Sam moved in. They had met at the front door and gone to Luda's Deli for coffee because Sam had said that the apartment wasn't ready for visitors yet. Peter wasn't clear on whether he would be let in this time or not.

The building didn't have an intercom or security system, so Peter texted Sam.

I'm here.

Sam replied immediately.

Peter and Pippin waited at the glass front door between the yellowed stacks of flyers piled up on either side of the stoop, looking out on landscaping that consisted of low shrub festooned with an array of empty Big Gulp cups, cigarette packages, and assorted receipts and other scraps of paper. As they had approached, Peter noticed that the side of the Lady Alice had been tagged with the inscrutable white glyph of some local street gang. He had noted that the building across the street, the three-storey Bardwell Towers, was in better shape. No doubt the rent reflected that. What one could afford on what was optimistically called "employment and income assistance" was only the very bottom of the market, if not below it.

After a minute, Sam appeared, breathing heavily from having run the full length of a hall and down the stairs. He fumbled with the lock for a moment and then flung the front door open.

"Don't know how it happened! One second Mr. Bingley is right there in his favourite spot, perched on top of the speaker — you know that big Klipsch I got from Greg what's his face? And the next he's not!"

Typical Sam — no hello, no thank you for coming, no preliminary pleasantries.

"Um, OK. So, he could still be in the apartment? Hiding somewhere?"

"No, no, no!" Sam shook his head vigorously. "There was this weird sound in the hall, you know, kind of like a scraping and squishing at the same time. Like a corpse being dragged."

Oh boy, here we go, Peter thought.

"So I grab my katana —"

"You have a samurai sword?"

Sam shot him an exasperated look that seemed to say, of course, doesn't everyone?

"So, *like I said*, I grab my katana and put my phone in my shirt pocket with the camera facing out and the video on, just like the cops and their body cams," Sam said, and tapped his temple, apparently to indicate that this idea was the product of an especially clever line of thought. "And I open the door real slow and quiet." Sam stopped and cocked his head as if listening. "And nothing. No scrapy squishy draggy sound no more. Silence. Nobody and nothing in the hall. Nothing. Except some box in front of number five, but it's been there for days. I walk up and down, careful and slow. But nothing. Pretty creepy, if you ask me."

Not anywhere near as creepy as you stalking the halls with a samurai sword, Peter thought. "So, you think the kitten slipped out while you were doing that?" Peter asked, trying to bring the conversation back to the practical details.

"Hundred percent. Hundred and one, even." Sam nodded emphatically. "Little pecker high-tailed it. He's the adventurous one. Barry's totally mellow. Like Manilow, right? Get it? But what's hilarious, totally hilarious, is that it's a coincidence! I actually named him Barrie after Barrie, Ontario, because I liked a girl on Tinder from there, but then when I found out how mellow he was, I changed the *i-e* to a *y*! And then Flinders is the intellectual of the bunch. Like earlier this morning when I was —"

"Let's stay on track. I gather you think Bingley —"

"Mr. Bingley."

". . . *Mr.* Bingley not only escaped the apartment but got out of the building too. How would that happen?"

"I don't know for sure for sure, but I got my theories. Top one, numero uno, is the meth-heads who live downstairs. They're in and out all the time like it's a friggin revolving door. They wouldn't notice Mr. Bingley. Or if they did, they wouldn't care."

"But you've searched the building, and he's nowhere?"

"Ha! Searched the building? Two hallways. One set of stairs. That's it. That's all. Yeah, I searched every square inch of it. And I knocked on every friggin door and asked. All seven. Good way to meet the neighbours, by the way. Bunch of whack jobs, like those meth-heads, and this sketchy thrash metal drummer, and a weirdo religious couple I'd never seen before, blond-haired, blue-eyed, pale like they never see the sun. Friggin ghosts. They never leave the building. Because I watch and pay attention, you know? But anyways, I called his name and everything. Mr. Bingley, I mean. Even if he's hiding in the, I don't know, ceiling or ducts or something, or the cultists snatched him, he always meows when I call his name. And let me tell you, a Bengal meow is a friggin feline foghorn. No, he's outside somewhere. That's why I asked you to bring Pippin. So, let's stop wasting time!"

Peter considered asking which of the two of them was wasting more time but let it slide. "OK," he said, "but first Pippin needs to get a scent to work from. One of the other kittens should do the trick."

Sam nodded. "Right. Yeah, that makes sense. Sense, scents, get it? Ha ha. I'll snag Barry. Like I said, he's the ultra-chill one. He won't be scared of Pippin or want to try to make a break for it or anything."

"Can we do this inside? Is Pippin allowed in?"

"Yeah, sure. Everything is friggin allowed here. Or not enforced anyways."

Sam held the door open for them and then bounded up the stairs, taking them two at a time to his apartment in the back right corner of the second floor. At six foot five, he was exactly as tall as Peter, yet his legs and arms seemed even longer, like a Tim Burton character's. His nose was longer too, and his hair was long and straggly. Sometimes he put it in a greasy ponytail that Laura called his Patented Girl-Repellant.

While he waited, Peter looked at the door to the last apartment on the right. A man had died there, yet it looked like any door. He wondered how many deaths had occurred, peaceful and violent, behind other doors here at other times. Closed doors conceal so much.

Then the door to the first apartment on the left opened and a woman stepped out. She appeared to be in late middle age and was wearing an ankle-length green dress. To Peter's unpractised eye it looked elegant, mostly because it was sparkly. She smiled at Peter and then looked down at Pippin and smiled even more broadly.

"Good day," she said in a European accent Peter couldn't place. "And who is this handsome fellow?"

"This is Pippin," Peter said.

Pippin cautiously sniffed the woman's proffered hand, wagging his tail slowly.

"May I scratch your ears, Pippin? I used to have a dog very much like you."

"He would be delighted to have his ears scratched. It's one of his favourite things."

Sam reappeared, holding a kitten. As he had predicted, it was remarkably placid. It hung from his arms, its back legs dangling, just staring straight ahead with its emerald eyes. It didn't appear to register Peter, Pippin, or the woman.

"This is Barry," Sam said, facing Peter and ignoring the woman.

"So, not the missing Mr. Bingley?" the woman asked.

"No," Sam said with a sideways glance at her.

"Well, he's lovely," the woman said. She glanced back and forth between Sam and Peter. "Are you two brothers?"

"Yes, we are," Peter said.

The woman smiled. "I must be off. Good luck finding the other little one." She turned her attention back to Pippin. "I hope you're here to help?"

"He is," Peter said. "He's a Western Canadian champion sniffer." He generally looked for the quickest way to end a conversation with a stranger, but bragging about Pippin was an exception.

"Are you now?" she asked Pippin. "How clever of you!" She gave him another scratch behind the ears before leaving.

"Don't be fooled," Sam said, after the door closed. "She's as whacked as the rest of them."

"Oh? She seemed pretty normal to me."

"Ed, from across the hall, has some pretty crazy stories about her."

"Mm hmm. Well, let's get started, shall we?" Peter asked, eager not to allow Sam to get sidetracked again. "Show Barry to Pippin. Let him have a good sniff."

Barry continued to hang passively as Sam lowered him to the level of Pippin's nose. Peter didn't need to give Pippin a command to sniff the kitten. Sniffing was no different for him than looking was for a human. It was as automatic as a person simply keeping their eyes open. He flared his nostrils, moving air in and out in short, rapid cycles, barely perceptible to anyone who wasn't paying close attention.

When he was done, Peter bent down, lightly touched the kitten, and said "seek!" to Pippin.

Sam furrowed his brow and frowned. "He's not going to seek just any cat? The neighbourhood is lousy with them."

"Maybe, but related individuals have specific scents in common. He'll probably be briefly distracted by other cat smells, but he's trained to follow the scent trail of whatever most closely matches the presented sample. So, if there are 20 cat scents out there, but one of them is Mr. Bingley, and Mr. Bingley's is more similar to Barry than any of the others, he'll follow that one."

"Huh. That's like an alien power. If dogs came down in UFOs and showed us what they could do with their noses, we'd be amazed and treat them like gods. But because they've been around us forever, we treat them like shit."

"Some people treat them like gods," Peter replied, but Sam was already heading back up the stairs with Barry.

Peter and Pippin looked out the door while they waited for Sam to return. Peter heard an indistinct sound behind him. He turned around just in time to see the edge of someone's head disappear and the door close behind them. Long black hair was all he could see. Last room on the left. Without consciously deciding to, Peter immediately generated a mental floor plan of the building:

Unit 1, main floor, front left: "Green Dress Woman."

Unit 3, main floor, back left: "Black Hair Person." Likely one of the meth users. He might have considered the drummer as an option, but Sam had said that the "meth-heads" live downstairs.

Unit 2, main floor, front right: "Ed."

Unit 4, main floor, back right: dead guy, Dženan Knezevic.

Unit 8, top floor, back right: Sam.

That left three rooms upstairs unaccounted for, but one would contain the drummer, and one would contain the religious couple, leaving only one that he knew nothing about at all. Not that any of this mattered. But this sort of analysis was as automatic for Peter as sniffing was for Pippin.

Low fast-moving clouds had slid in from the northwest. The wind had picked up. It was noticeably colder than it had been just 15 minutes prior. Sam muttered and hunched his shoulders, but Peter didn't mind. Moderate cold, the kind that produced apple cheeks, made him more alert, which might be useful. Pippin was also unconcerned about the temperature change. His nose was down within a centimetre or two of the ground. He swung it slowly from side to side, taking one step at a time away from the door toward the sidewalk. Then he stopped and doubled back, first sniffing the shrubs and dead grass to the left of the door and then to the right.

Something there caught his interest. Suddenly he picked up his pace and started trotting to the right, tail up, nose still down.

Peter signalled to Sam, who was stamping his feet theatrically and blowing on his hands.

Pippin disappeared around the corner. Peter was right behind him, followed by Sam. They found themselves in a narrow space between the Lady Alice and the neighbouring Lady Beatrice. They appeared to be twin buildings, with the Beatrice in slightly better condition. The space between was remarkably clean. Peter wondered whether the Beatrice had a resident superintendent, unlike the Alice.

Pippin slowed down to carefully sniff along the edge of the Beatrice.

"Beet rice," Sam muttered.

"Pardon?" Peter asked.

"Beet rice. That's what Ed calls it. Not Bee-ah-triss. Not sure if he really doesn't know or if he thinks he's being funny. He used to live there."

Peter nodded and was about to comment, but Pippin was suddenly on the move again, trotting very quickly toward the back lane. Without pausing he turned right and was gone behind the Beatrice, headed west. Peter and Sam ran to catch up with him. Pippin had stopped, just out of sight, evidently waiting for them. As soon as they were close, he started again, nose still down, furiously sniffing. The lane was paved, but the pavement was cracked and potholed, with weeds filling every gap, still green despite the advanced season, albeit a muted, tired green. Past the Lady Beatrice, small wooden houses backed onto the lane on both sides. Most had fences, some of which were chain-link, some nicely painted wood, and some decayed and half-collapsed. One reddish-brown wooden fence leaned into the lane, only prevented from falling over by a large garbage bin. Pippin stopped there.

The lane was quiet and empty. The wind had shifted so that it was coming directly at them, out of the west. A Big Mac wrapper tumbled by.

"Is that it? Does he think Mr. Bingley is there, in the house behind that fence?" Sam asked, hunching his shoulders more and jamming his hands deeper into the pockets of his stained blue parka.

"It's too early to say. The kitten may have just stopped there and left extra scent, or Pippin might be trying to figure out something that is confusing him."

Peter suddenly had the sense that they were being watched. He turned around.

Nothing. Just the Big Mac wrapper continuing its erratic eastward progress.

A crow swooped down from behind a house and landed on the lane to peck at something. Then it took off again.

Pippin was still sniffing the same spot under the leaning fence.

Peter walked up to him and crouched down. "What's here, buddy? Did the kitten stay here for a while? Is he nearby?" He knew that asking his dog questions was pointless and illogical, but despite his fervent belief in the centrality of logic to a correctly lived life, he couldn't help himself.

"I wouldn't hang around there for too long, if I was you," a voice said from behind them.

Peter jumped up and banged his head on the fence.

Sam yelped, "Jesus!" and whirled around to face the source of the voice.

Pippin kept sniffing.

An old man in a wheelchair was in one of the unfenced yards, farther along the lane, diagonally across from where they were. Peter was astonished that they hadn't noticed him before.

"Sorry. I didn't mean to spook you guys." The old man smiled and held up his hands, palms out, in apology or mock surrender. He was wearing an oversized white Winnipeg Jets jersey and a Day-Glo orange toque. The legs of his faded jeans dangled and flapped in the wind. He had a bulbous red nose and pockmarked cheeks, but his expression was open and friendly.

"It's OK. Just didn't see you there," Peter said.

Sam glowered at the old man.

"Yeah, they call me the stealth roller!" The old man laughed. "But seriously, I'd step back from that fence. They've got cameras."

"They?" Peter asked. He noticed the surveillance cameras now — one at each upper back corner of the house.

"Gang. Don't know which one, and don't care to know. But everyone around here steers clear." He paused and moved his mouth briefly as if chewing something. "What you guys looking for anyway?"

Peter glanced at his brother, expecting him to answer, but Sam was still glaring at the man, his eyes narrowed to slits, lips set tight.

"Lost cat. A kitten. Golden-brown with dark stripes."

"Oh no. I hope you find him. And I hope he didn't go there." The man nodded toward the house behind the fence.

"Thanks. I doubt he did," Peter said. "My dog Pippin here is indicating that the scent trail stops at the fence. If the kitten climbed over the fence or went around it to the house, Pippin would show us."

"So, he vanished?" Sam said, turning to face Peter.

"Probably picked up by someone in a car. Pippin would still be able to track him for a bit if someone picked him up and walked away with him, but in a car, he'd lose the scent right away."

"I'd tell you if I saw someone driving down here, because I watch, but I was at the Tim's this morning," the old man said. "Sorry."

"Thanks. We'll call the Humane Society and Animal Services, and we'll put up some posters and get the word out on social media," Peter said, not immediately noticing the rapid facial expression changes moving across Sam's face. It finally settled on angry.

"You mean, some moron catnapped Mr. Bingley?!" he shouted.

"Not . . . catnapped. Picked up. He would look like a lost stray kitten. Probably some Good Samaritan did it."

"Good friggin Samaritan my ass. Mr. Bingley's a valuable purebred. He's going on the dark web to be sold to the highest bidder."

The old man watched this exchange. "Well, good luck, fellows. I have fresh doughnuts and today's *Free Press* waiting for me." He turned around and wheeled back toward his house.

"I can't friggin believe it!" Sam said, clenching and unclenching his fists.

"It'll be OK. I'm sure we'll find him," Peter said. Telling soothing white lies was a skill he was trying to cultivate. He had learned the hard way that rigorous truth-telling didn't always produce the desired results.

"What about that whack-job in the wheelchair? That's kind of like a car. He's redirecting, I bet. Messing with us. We should get a warrant and have his place searched!" Sam was getting worked up. Each word was louder and more strident.

Peter suppressed a sigh. He made an effort to keep his tone calm and matter-of-fact. "Pippin would still be able to track Mr. Bingley carried in a wheelchair because it's not enclosed like a car."

Sam looked at the ground and shook his head. "Whatever. Let's go back. Barry and Flinders will be wondering what's up."

They walked back to the Lady Alice in silence. The wind had stopped, and the clouds loosened, allowing sunshine to pour into the lane. Peter noted that this made even the trash look more cheerful. But Sam's mood appeared to be darkening still. He walked with his arms crossed over his chest, and he muttered steadily under his breath.

They emerged from the space between the apartment blocks to see a police cruiser parked in front of the Lady Alice. Two officers were just coming out of the building.

One of them, a younger woman, approached them and asked, "Do either of you live here?"

"I do," Sam answered.

"Do you know a Samuel Bannerman, who lives in unit 8?"

"That's me. I'm Sam. Samuel Bannerman," Sam said, his voice flat.

The officer pursed her lips and nodded. "Good. Mr. Bannerman, we would like to ask you a few questions. Could you please accompany us to the station?"

Sam's eyes widened. "Am I under arrest?"

"No, sir, you are not under arrest at this point. But we are requesting your cooperation in our investigation regarding the homicide of your neighbour, Mr. Dženan Knezevic."

Sam's eyes widened even further. "Homicide . . . ?"

CHAPTER *Six*

"Yes, sir, his death is being treated as a homicide."

Sam's mouth started working as if he was trying to formulate a response, but no sounds were coming out. Peter felt a stab of panic that Sam was going to say that Kevin had a contact in the force who had assured them that it was an accident. But instead, Sam turned to Peter, his face ashen, while rummaging in his parka pocket.

"You're going to have to look after Barry and Flinders. I don't know how long I'm going to be at the cop shop —"

"It won't take long," the officer said.

Sam ignored her. "— and they haven't had their second breakfast yet. And Flinders expects cuddles around this time too. As a vet you know how important routines are, and they haven't lived with me long, so it's extra important now. And then you can go back out and keep looking for Mr. Bingley. And at three o'clock it's tea time for kittens. Except they don't get tea. They get a little treat and a few drops of cream in a saucer. And if it goes later . . ." Sam stopped and turned to face the officer. "But I'll get my phone call, right? My one phone call? So, I can save it to let my brother know what to do next if I'm still there?" In the meantime, he had found what he was looking for in his pocket and handed Peter a set of keys on a tiki keychain.

The officer looked like she was trying to stop herself from smiling. "You're not under arrest, Mr. Bannerman. Within reason, there is no limit on the number of phone calls. And if you cooperate fully, you'll be back home in no time."

"You can't ask the questions here?" Sam shuffled his feet and glanced back and forth between the two officers.

"We can, but we would prefer doing this at the station so we can take a formal statement."

"A *formal statement*?" This came out in a squeak. Sam's eyes widened again.

"Standard procedure, sir. Nothing to be alarmed about."

The second officer opened the back door of the squad car and gestured to Sam to climb in.

Peter took a deep breath as he unlocked the door to Sam's apartment. He had some idea of what to expect, yet his brother never failed to surprise him. He could hear the kittens yelling. Peter smiled to himself, thinking that Sam was right about the second breakfast.

The door only opened 45 degrees, its full swing blocked by something hard and immovable. Two kittens immediately swarmed Peter's legs, one attempting to climb each, yelling constantly. Pippin gave them each a sniff. He spent more time on the one clambering up Peter's left leg, so he assumed that must be Flinders, as Barry would be familiar to Pippin. They looked identical to Peter. Two tawny coloured little cats with prominent symmetrical black stripes and with wide open pink mouths.

"OK, OK, guys! Second breakfast is coming. Just let me get oriented here."

He leaned down and plucked the kittens off his legs, first Barry, then Flinders, and tucked one against each side of his chest. He stepped inside and pushed the door shut with his heel.

Peter sucked his breath in through his teeth.

It was worse than he imagined.

And he had imagined something quite bad. Sam's apartment in Toronto had been larger, so they had talked about downsizing his possessions before the move. Clearly, this had not happened. In fact, it looked like Sam had acquired even more stuff in his short time in Winnipeg. Among its many titles, Winnipeg laid claim to being the "Garage Sale Capital of Canada." It would seem Sam had somehow managed to take full advantage of that, even though he didn't have a car.

It was like looking at a 3D Jackson Pollock painting — every imaginable colour, and every imaginable shape, with no blank space and no discernible pattern. Floor to ceiling, wall to wall. Narrow paths led between the immense piles of . . . stuff. Peter had expected a lot of U-Haul boxes, but none were visible. Evidently, everything had been unpacked. Peter was unsure whether Sam considered this to be an intermediate step before properly organizing it all, or whether this was the desired end result, that reflected some bizarre version, or, more accurately, perversion, of organization.

The kittens squirmed in Peter's arms.

Pippin sniffed about cautiously, sticking to Peter's side.

The smell was the next thing Peter noticed. At first, he couldn't place it, but then it hit him.

Oil paint. He's been painting in here somewhere!

Peter couldn't imagine how that was possible in this crammed-full bachelor suite. He supposed he should be grateful because the paint smell was likely masking any more obnoxious smells that might be present. Having thought that, he admonished himself. Sam might be a hoarder, but he had always been as fastidious about hygiene as his circumstances would permit. Whatever else Peter might find in the apartment, he knew that at least he was unlikely to find mouldy bananas or filthy litter boxes.

He switched his focus to the sound. Quiet music was coming from somewhere beyond the Himalayan stacks of books and VHS tapes, mixed with an oddment of broken plastic toys, several backgammon sets, and what looked like a collection of Russian fur hats. It was Indian sitar music, like Ravi Shankar or similar. Peter grinned and wondered whether his brother thought that Bengal kittens preferred music from Bengal. He wouldn't put it past him.

The kittens squirmed harder, and then Flinders got loose and jumped to the floor. He ran off down the path to the right. Pippin followed, with Peter right behind. He let Barry go, who took off after Flinders, darting between Pippin's legs. The path led between heaps of old textbooks and VHS tapes on one side, and alarmingly precarious-looking towers of antique cookie tins, stacked on small appliances, stacked on battered furniture, with assorted sporting goods inserted into the spaces on the other side. So, not completely random after all. Each category of item seemed to be clustered together. There were simply too many categories (Russian fur hats? backgammon sets? antique cookie tins?) and too many items in far too little space. Sam needed a small aircraft hangar.

They arrived at what appeared to be the kitchen. Any cupboards that might be present were obscured by heaps of magazines and newspapers, but the visible portion of the floor had transitioned from hardwood to linoleum, and there was a small table in the corner with a toaster oven, an electric kettle, and a jumble of chipped Victorian teacups. Tea drinking was a family trait. That, and a youth spent playing Dungeons & Dragons, were two strong threads that connected their otherwise disconnected lives. Three ceramic food bowls were lined up under the table, one green, one blue, and one red, as well as a large stainless-steel water dish. These were all spotlessly clean.

The kittens were already sitting by their bowls, yelling.

Peter looked around for cat food. He couldn't find it until Pippin woofed softly at an ice cream pail in the corner.

Kittens fed and water topped up, Peter sat down at the table and looked through Sam's collection of teas, which were in the broken hull of a plastic toy boat, possibly a Playmobil pirate ship. It was only bagged tea — Peter preferred loose leaf — and it looked like it had all been scavenged from free tea services in various waiting rooms. Peter settled on a PG Tips black tea blend and waited for the water to boil.

In the meantime, he tried to call Kevin to ask if he had any idea how this could have suddenly turned from a weird accident into a murder investigation, but he got his voicemail.

But that was OK. It was time to take some deep breaths and think.

The kittens curled up in a plastic laundry basket, and Pippin laid down by his feet. The muffled sitar music was soothing. Other than occasional soft thumps from next door and distant sirens, it was quiet. When Peter wanted to think through something, his preference was to do it while walking, or to write out his thoughts in a special bison-hide-bound book he had at home, but sometimes talking it out with Pippin worked too. Obviously, Pippin would not understand anything, so it was objectively a silly thing to do. Pippin was smart and knew a lot of words, but he was not preternaturally smart. It was more a matter of being able to articulate thoughts as if the listener understood, without the inconvenience and social awkwardness of trying to find a human willing to be monologued at. Laura was willing sometimes, and Kevin sometimes too, although he had the irritating habit of interrupting and trying to turn everything into a joke. His friend Darryl was OK . . . but no, Pippin was the best audience for thinking out loud. The best by far.

"What do you think, buddy?" Peter said, looking down at his dog and smiling.

Pippin perked one ear and half opened his eyes. He knew the drill. Certain words said in certain tones were meant for him to act on, but otherwise his duty was just to show some semblance of listening.

"Are they genuinely just getting information from Sam, and have done the same with all the other tenants? Or is he a suspect?"

Pippin closed his eyes again but kept the ear up.

"The latter seems more likely because Sam didn't say anything about anyone else in the building being taken in for questioning, and he claims that he sees all the comings and goings."

Peter paused to fill his teacup. He selected one with pink roses and gold trim.

"And if he is a suspect, why? From the looks of the place, there's no way they've searched in here, and anyway Sam would have said so if they did, so they must have found evidence in Knezevic's apartment."

Peter checked his watch. He didn't want the tea to steep too long. The cheap blends could quickly become too tannic.

"Do you think Sam's telling the truth? He claimed that he didn't know the guy at all, but he seemed almost too adamant about that, didn't he? I have an inkling of doubt."

He took the teabag out and took a small sip. He grimaced and sighed.

Pippin looked up at him.

"Don't get me wrong. It's not that I think he murdered this guy. In fact, there's no way." Peter paused. "Don't look at me that way. I know I've been wrong about people before, but not my brother."

Pippin was still looking at him. Not staring, just passively watching.

"But anyway, now I've got to wonder whether he lied about not knowing this guy. Maybe Sam was even in his apartment at some point. He's much more social than I am. Maybe he panicked when Knezevic turned up dead, and he started making up these stories."

Peter paused again and took an absentminded sip of the tea. "Ugh," he said softly and pushed the cup away so he wouldn't accidentally pick it up again. "But you know what? Now that I'm thinking about it, Sam told me that he didn't know Knezevic when he called about the kittens screaming, before he knew he was dead. So not just a panic lie. The whole thing is strange."

Pippin suddenly sprang to his feet and stared at the wall behind Peter. It was the wall that separated Sam's apartment from number six next door.

There was a loud bang, as if something heavy had been dropped from a height, followed by a piercing scream and a shout:

"Oh my god!" It was a young woman's voice.

CHAPTER *Seven*

Peter froze.

He knew he should shout back through the wall, something like, "Are you OK?" But he never shouted — it was just not something he did — and it felt weird to communicate with people he had never even seen. Yet he couldn't ignore this either.

Without further analysis of the problem, he hustled back through the apartment, Pippin at his heels, and went out into the hall, making sure the kittens didn't get out before closing the door behind him. He paused briefly at the door to unit 6 before knocking loudly.

A short, slender girl with long purple hair opened the door a long minute later. Her skin was so pale it seemed translucent. Her expression was wary.

Cultist, or the meth addict? Peter thought. *But the cultists were blond, Sam said. So, meth addict. But hang on, he said the meth addicts lived downstairs. Drummer, then?*

"I'm looking after my brother's cats next door and heard the big thump and the scream and wondered if you needed help," Peter said in a rush, the words piling into each other like a chain reaction freeway accident.

The girl's expression softened a fraction. "Thanks," she said. "My boyfriend fell. He'll be OK."

Peter considered that this boyfriend must be very large. Or must have been standing on something very high when he fell. Or both. Over the girl's shoulder, Peter could see a sparsely furnished apartment.

"OK, good to hear." Peter chuckled. "It sounded bad."

"Oh, yeah, I'm sure it did. Sorry to disturb you, sir." The girl began to close the door.

Sir? Am I already at that age?

"No trouble at all," he said, but the door had clicked shut before he could finish that sentence.

Returning to Sam's apartment, Peter considered two odd things about this brief encounter. The first was that the alleged boyfriend wasn't visible or audible anywhere. In his experience, usually the other person in a small apartment will call out, "Who's at the door?" But this was by no means consistent. It was just so quiet in there. The second odd thing was that she didn't comment on Pippin, who was right beside Peter. She didn't even look at him. People always comment on Pippin. But she was probably preoccupied.

These were admittedly trifling oddities that both had plausible innocent explanations, but it reinforced the notion in Peter's mind that either drugs or strange religion was involved, rather than drumming.

Whether any of this mattered or not was another question entirely. And the answer to that question was no, it did not matter. What mattered was that Sam come home soon so that Peter could go back to enjoying his Saturday. Pippin really needed a walk, and Peter really wanted a walk. The aspens were at their peak colours.

But, knowing that he had no influence over when Sam came home, Peter decided to push all that out of his mind and make the best of his time in Sam's apartment by looking around a little.

"It's not snooping," he said to Pippin. "'Snooping' has a pejorative connotation, implying that one is looking through someone else's things for personal gain or to satisfy prurient curiosity."

Pippin stopped to deeply sniff an eyeless teddy bear propped up against a broken electric guitar in the corner.

"In contrast, I'm doing this to help my brother. I'm proactively looking for evidence that might help exonerate him if he ends up accused of being involved in this case."

Peter stopped and picked up a dusty yellow hardcover entitled *The Stanley Complete Step-by-Step Book of Home Improvement and Repair*. He chuckled at the irony and put it back down.

"I know, I know — the probability of finding something useful for that in this, um, *collection*, is extremely low. But it's not zero, and we should stay until the kittens' tea time at three, as ridiculous as that sounds to a sensible dog like you. I don't want to have to deal with Sam freaking out if we don't follow his instructions. He's going to be on edge already anyway. And Sam freaking out is different than a regular person freaking out. Worse different. Much worse." Peter sucked his breath in. "Anyway, we're stuck here until then, or when Sam comes home, whatever's first, so we may as well do something vaguely productive."

Peter turned around and, stepping over a stack of novelty beer mugs, opened what he assumed was the bathroom door.

"Ah, this is where he's painting," he called over his shoulder to Pippin, who was still sniffing the teddy.

There was an easel in the bathtub with a canvas on it, besides stacks of other, smaller canvases also in the tub. There were piles of painting supplies and mysterious bins and boxes on the vanity and on most of the available floor space. The painting looked half-finished. At first Peter couldn't tell what he was looking at, thinking that perhaps Sam had gone into abstracts. Previously, he had done mostly figurative work. Then Peter recognized what looked a lot like a gallbladder. And possibly a bit of liver. And definitely stomach and intestines. Now that he saw it, he couldn't unsee it. These abdominal contents were all jumbled up, and they were depicted in lurid colours. The gallbladder was acid green, the liver burnt orange, and the bowels a sickly lilac.

Before he could process this, his phone vibrated. It was Kevin.

"Hey, Pete! You called?"

"Yes, thanks. I'm at Sam's. Did you hear the news about the case?"

"I'm off, and it's Saturday. We were just out for a walk with Atlas. So, no, I didn't hear the news. What's up?"

"Winnipeg police are calling it murder now. And they picked up Sam for questioning."

"Wait. What? That old perv — so he didn't off himself while getting off?"

"That's what the officer said: homicide investigation. This friend of yours on the force, I didn't ask, is he in traffic or something that he didn't know this?" Peter immediately regretted his irritated tone, but he couldn't help himself.

"Ah, no. General patrol. I talked to Brett yesterday, and his information was probably a day old by then, so two days old now. A lot can change in 48 hours, especially when the autopsy report comes in. You'd never guess the kind of surprises the coroners turn up. You think you've got your case wrapped, and suddenly, bango, there's a tiny but very deep penetrating wound in the armpit, or a massive brain bleed, or a dead hamster in the rectum."

"What?"

"True story. Sort of. But anyway, don't worry about Sam. Routine stuff. Now that it's a murder investigation, they're going to talk to everyone in a lot more depth than they did before."

"Yeah, I get that, but it seemed like they had a special interest in Sam," Peter said, gingerly stepping back over the beer mugs to see what Pippin was up to. He had stopped sniffing the teddy, but now he was lying beside it, staring at it.

"Well, no offence, Pete, but your brother would be pretty high on my list of suspects as well if I didn't know him."

"Oh?"

"Come on. Male. Mentally ill. Loner. Objectively speaking, if you didn't know him, what would you think? I'm not saying first degree, but maybe a manslaughter type situation? Again, 'cause I know more about Sam than they do, he would be lower on my list. But, for the Winnipeg cops, it's a different story."

"No, you're right, Kev. Funny that you're the logical one this time." Peter bent down to pick up the teddy.

"I'll try not to take that the wrong way. But listen, I've gotta run. Stuart and I have to make a special pickup in Headingley. Don't ask me what because it's a surprise. A big surprise." Kevin paused, evidently hoping that Peter would press him for details, but Peter was preoccupied with looking at the teddy, holding it up to the light in his free hand. It was large, but not heavy. And it didn't rattle when he shook it. He detected something odd and un-teddy-like when he sniffed it. The scent was faint, though, and he couldn't identify it.

"Anyway, you'll find out tomorrow at dinner," Kevin continued.

"Right. Tomorrow's Sunday. I'm losing track of time. OK, thanks, Kev. See you then."

Peter tucked his phone away, and now with two hands free, he turned the teddy over and examined him more carefully. Pippin watched him intently.

"I wonder what you're smelling, Pippin," Peter said softly. "Hang on, there's a tiny zipper here, buried in the fur."

Peter fumbled with the zipper for a moment and then pulled it open. All he could see was dense white cottony stuffing. He pushed his fingers through the stuffing. It was barely a centimetre thick, and under it he could feel a large number of firm, flat objects, roughly the size of quarters. They had a gritty texture.

Peter fished one out.

It was a black, elongated disc, and it was coated in white crystals, like salt or sugar. It was marked with the letter S. He squeezed it. It was rubbery. He brought it to his nose and sniffed it.

That's it! Licorice! But why inside a beat-up old teddy bear?

Peter cautiously put it in his mouth. It was definitely licorice. Salty licorice. Not bad, but extremely strong. And chewy like a gummi.

He pulled another out and took a photo of it with Google Lens. It identified it as Salt Skum, a popular, notoriously strong, salted Swedish licorice. The "Skum" in the name turned out to be Swedish for foam, referring to this type of soft, rubbery candy.

"My brother is a very strange person," Peter said to Pippin, who was now smiling a big doggie smile and wagging his tail, apparently pleased that Peter had taken the hint and investigated the unusually scented bear.

"But that's not news to either of us, is it?"

Peter zipped the bear back up and set it down. He put his hands on his hips and surveyed the appalling chaos around him. The total cubic volume of his and Laura's living room in New Selfoss was perhaps 10 percent objects, including furniture, and 90 percent air. This was at least 70 percent objects and only 30 percent air. There was a bit of open space between some of the piles and the ceiling, there was the space in the paths between the piles, and then there was some space between the objects as they weren't stacked particularly efficiently. Yes, 70 percent solid matter was about right. He figured he could be off by 5 percent either way, though.

The visual noise of it all was starting to get to him. His autistic brain couldn't just blur away the details. It was constantly trying to make sense of all the input, seeking patterns, seeking explanations, seeking connections. It was like standing in the midst of a noisy crowd and trying to sort out and understand all the conversations swirling around you.

"You know what, Pippin?"

The dog looked up at him, noting a tone that was more oriented toward him than just the usual thinking out loud.

"I'm going to check on the kittens and then we're going to get out of here for a bit. It's too much, isn't it?"

Pippin wagged his tail.

"How about a walk in the forest?" Peter peered toward the window. The sky was completely blue now. "The Assiniboine?"

Pippin wagged his tail harder.

CHAPTER *Eight*

The Assiniboine Forest was the perfect antidote to Sam's apartment. The aspens created regular patterns of vertical white lines with black spots, and their shadows produced horizontal lines across the paths that looked like bar codes. The canopy was a stained-glass wonder of bright golds, pale yellows, and dark greens, backlit by the intense Prairie sun. Peter loved this beauty. Nature's magnificent cathedral. And he loved the smell too. An aspen woodland in the autumn smelled of rich loamy earth, offset by a higher astringent note from the fallen leaves. Apparently, that astringency, or sharpness, was related to a compound that had anti-inflammatory properties, but Peter had no interest in chewing the leaves. Only admiring their appearance and smell.

Populus tremuloides, Peter repeated to himself, enjoying the way the Latin made him feel. Calmer. More in touch with reality. More in control. Trembling aspen in English, or sometimes quaking aspen, or most commonly on the Prairies, poplar. Poplar was confusing, though, as it was also used for balsam poplar, *Populus balsamifera*, which, while in the same genus, was a very different tree.

The sounds of the forest were limited to the twitter of a few chickadees and the low hum of traffic. They were still in a big city after all, although this was a large enough oasis that if they kept walking straight in, they would soon no longer be able to hear the cars. Peter knew the trails well and knew how to quickly access the lesser-used ones, the ones not marked on any maps. On a sunny September Saturday, people and their dogs thronged the main paths. Peter wanted no part of that. The main problem was that so many people wanted to stop and say hi to Pippin, and then they would usually praise his appearance and good behaviour. This would then make Peter feel obliged to return the compliment to whatever dog they had, even if it was obviously less good-looking and less well mannered. He hated these false social niceties. It felt extremely awkward to him, and he was sure that people could tell that he was insincere. So, he just avoided the whole mess.

Pippin didn't seem to care. He was happy to meet people and other dogs, but he was also happy to just trot along and sniff the potpourri of scents left behind by previous dogs, as well as the wildlife. The forest was becoming known for coyotes. Normally they avoided people, but recently some had reportedly become bolder. People even said "aggressive," but Peter couldn't help but assume that these were panicky people. Should they happen to cross paths with such a coyote, Peter's plan was to open and close his jacket rapidly, spreading it wide as if flashing the animal. He was confident this would work.

They ambled along in splendid quiet companionship for a good 15 minutes before encountering the first person. Often, there would be nobody at all in this section of the forest, but it was a busy day. The person was walking directly toward Peter and Pippin with a golden retriever. The dog was off leash, which irritated Peter because it was illegal in the forest, and a bad idea, especially given the wildlife.

The person, a middle-aged man with a round red face and a grey brush cut, looked vaguely familiar.

"Dr. Bannerman!"

Uh-oh.

"Fancy seeing you here! Look, Lucas, it's your doctor!"

Lucas, Lucas, Lucas . . . Peter tried to place the name, and while it rang a bell, he was unable to remember anything about the dog. He looked to be in the peak of health, so perhaps he was just an annual vaccine patient rather than one who had been memorably ill.

"Hi," Peter said. "You've come down into the city too?" he added, feeling inane as he did so.

"Yup. Visiting the in-laws. My wife's taken the twins shopping at Polo Park first, so Lucas and I decided to go for a walk. And you?"

The two dogs sniffed each other cautiously at first, and then more enthusiastically when they determined that neither was a threat. They circled slowly, each nose to hind-end of the other. A woodpecker loudly hammered a nearby tree.

"Similar, I guess. Visiting my brother. But he's . . . unexpectedly detained for a bit, so we came here."

"And this must be the famous Pepper?" the man asked.

"Pippin. Yes, this is he."

"Well, Pippin, you should be proud of your dad. He saved Lucas's life! Cost an arm and a leg. I think we paid for a whole wing of the hospital! But I'm not complaining. Worth every penny. Right, Lucas?" The man laughed.

Peter took a deep breath and forced a smile. If New Selfoss Veterinary Services had a new wing for every time someone claimed to have paid for it, it would be the size of the Mayo Clinic by now. And it was always the clients he could barely remember, never the ones who were in regularly and actually spent the most. And anyway, vet clinics didn't have "wings." Oh well, people were strange and irrational. He knew this well enough that it shouldn't irritate him, yet it did.

"I'm glad I could help. He looks great now." Peter bent down and gave the golden retriever a scratch behind his ear. The two dogs had settled into sitting, facing each other, both smiling and panting lightly.

"Did I ever tell you about the cocker spaniel I had growing up?" the man asked.

Peter took another deep breath.

Just then his phone rang. He always had it on vibrate, but he had turned on the ringer — a clear bell tone — to make sure he didn't miss a call from Sam.

Saved by the bell, literally, he thought, and smiled.

"I'm sorry, I've got to take this call," he said.

"No worries! Nice to see you. Catch you later."

It was Sam. As Lucas and the man walked on, Peter spoke quietly into the phone, "Hi. I've been waiting for your call."

"It's my first chance," Sam said. His voice quavered. "They . . . they're going to lay charges."

"What?!" Peter spoke much louder now. Pippin looked up at him.

"I'm under arrest, Peter. First-degree murder." Sam was very quiet, and in contrast to his normal chaotic, rapid-fire speaking style, his words came out in a monotone.

"But why? What's the evidence?"

"I had to confess that I knew him and had been in his apartment the day he died. The time of death was later in the evening, but I was the last person to be with him."

Peter paused, taking this in. He had wondered about that. Sam's denials that he knew the victim had been too vociferous and were contradicted by his statement that he promised to look after the kittens. *And yet . . .*

"That's quite a leap to murder. They must have something else."

"They say he was suffocated, but probably drugged first."

"But that doesn't implicate *you*. None of this makes sense. You need a lawyer."

"I don't know anyone." Still the monotone. It was freaking Peter out a little to hear Sam sound like that.

"I'll figure it out. Where are you right now?"

"Still at the station. But they're transferring me to remand right now, as soon as I get off the phone."

"OK, I'll make some calls, and then I'll come visit."

"Thank you."

Peter put his phone away and stood quietly for a moment. Unbelievable. Yet, also believable. He could see why the police might be suspicious of Sam, but there was no way he could be guilty of murdering someone, and certainly not in a premeditated way. He winced at the memory of when he had been wrong with this kind of assessment before, but this was different. This was his brother. A kook for sure, but a completely harmless kook. An accidental killing might be possible. Peter supposed anyone could accidentally kill someone. Even that seemed unlikely. But there was no point getting worked up in his head about this now. There was far too little solid information to go on. Far too little data.

He pulled his phone back out and called Kevin, expecting to get voicemail again, but not immediately knowing what else to do next.

Pippin sat patiently beside him, sniffing the air.

Kevin answered immediately. "Hey, Pete, how's it going?"

Peter could hear a commotion in the background. Indistinct animal noises and people laughing. "Not good," he said. "Thanks for picking up. Sam's been arrested."

"Oh yeah? What charge?"

"First-degree murder."

Kevin sucked his breath in. "Hang on a sec." The noises became quieter as he seemed to be moving away. "OK, that sucks. Any details?"

"Well, Sam confessed to having been in the victim's apartment, and the investigators think that Knezevic was drugged and suffocated. But that's it. No idea why they think they have enough evidence for a murder charge, let alone premeditated."

"Huh. I gotta say, they're professionals. They make mistakes, for sure, but not many. Sorry, Pete." He did sound genuinely sorry.

"I'm sure that's true. But 'not many' mistakes still means they make some."

"Fair enough. But if you're asking me to check in with Brett again to get more info, then . . . I'm sorry, I can't do that now. I'm sure you get that, right?"

"Yeah, of course. It was different before your brother-in-law's brother was charged. No, I'm not calling to ask you that. I'm calling to see if you can recommend a criminal defence lawyer."

"Oh, sure." Kevin paused. Peter heard faint barking in the background and the murmur of voices. "Off the cuff, I'd say give Dave Kostakis a call. Otherwise, Len McSweeney. But try Dave first. Good guy. Not shockingly expensive."

"OK, thanks. Kostakis or McSweeney," Peter repeated.

"That's it. I gotta go now. But Pete, good luck. I mean it. I know this is going to be rough no matter how it goes."

"Thanks, I appreciate it. One more quick thing, Kev. What's the deal with visiting at the remand centre? Can I just show up?"

"No, you need to make an appointment. The number should be easy to find online. Usually 24-hours' notice is required, but tell them your brother is mentally ill and they might make an exception."

Peter thanked him again and tucked his phone into his jacket pocket. He crouched down and gave Pippin a vigorous scratch. He wasn't a hugger, but he really felt like hugging his dog. However, he knew that dogs don't like being hugged, so he didn't. They'll tolerate it, but they'll usually go rigid and adopt a facial expression that clearly says, "Fine, but let's just get this over with, shall we?"

"OK, we'll restart our walk right away, buddy. I'm just going to text Laura and update her, and I'm going to call remand. I doubt they allow dogs, so I may have to leave you back at Sam's apartment for a short bit. You can hang out with the kittens."

An hour later, Peter was in front of an angular glass building on Kennedy Street, downtown. He had never taken note of the Winnipeg Remand Centre before. It looked like the collision between several large, mirrored, blue glass cubes. The reception area was small. The guard told Peter to take a seat on one of the two plastic chairs in the hall. A young woman was sitting in the other one, doing something on her phone. She didn't look up at Peter. Other than the buzzy hum of the ventilation system, it was quiet. Peter wasn't fond of waiting or of white noise, so he hoped this would go quickly. He pulled out his phone to glance at the time and then tucked it back in his pocket again.

After a few minutes, the guard, who had disappeared through a door marked *Authorized Personnel Only*, returned.

"He's still being processed. Half an hour maybe?"

Peter nodded. "OK if I go for a walk and come back then?"

The guard shrugged in a suit-yourself sort of way.

Peter rarely visited downtown, so he looked forward to seeing what was new. He was somewhat familiar with Portage Avenue because when he did come, it was usually to go to the Mountain Equipment Co-op at Portage and Donald, so he decided to head east instead of north, and follow York past the Convention Centre. Once he reached Main Street, which should take just under 15 minutes, he would decide whether to turn left and circle back left, passing the Millennium Library, or right, going by the Fort Garry Hotel. That should be almost exactly 30 minutes. Peter's map sense rarely failed him, but he checked his phone to make sure he had it right. He did. Either loop was listed as 29 minutes. He was amused to see that the Winnipeg Remand Centre had a Google rating of 2.1 stars based on 34 reviews. He wondered who did the reviewing, the inmates or the visitors? And he wondered what would be required of the remand centre to achieve a five-star rating? It brought very funny mental images to mind.

Twenty-nine minutes later, he was back at the remand centre. The young woman was gone.

The guard glanced at the clock on the wall. "Ten more minutes, and then I can bring you through," the guard said.

This is just like in the movies, Peter thought as he saw the row of booths in the visiting room. Each one had an old-fashioned-looking phone, but without a dial, and each one had a pane of glass separating it from a mirror-image booth on the prisoners' side of the room. He didn't know what he'd been expecting, but not this. He supposed he assumed that there was some more modernized way of doing non-contact visits. The girl from the waiting area was there, talking quietly to someone Peter couldn't see from his angle. He was shown to the first booth on the left. Sam was already sitting on the other side, holding the phone handset. He was wearing a simple grey T-shirt. Peter wasn't sure whether it was his or issued by the institution. He couldn't recall what Sam had been wearing that morning. He had expected to see him in an orange jumpsuit here, so this was one aspect, at least, that differed from the movies.

Peter sat down and picked up the phone. "How are you doing?" he said, not knowing what else to say first.

Sam drew his breath in dramatically and said, "Shitty. Pretty damned shitty. You wouldn't believe what they do to you. All the searching and stuff. And that passive aggressive politeness. 'Stand here, please. Stand there, please. Bend over, please. Cough, please.' I was going to say something, but you know what —"

"That sounds terrible. I'm sorry. Did you hear from the lawyer yet?" Peter asked. He knew he was going to have to interrupt his brother constantly. Visits were limited to half an hour.

"Um, yeah. Greek name. Kista, Kosta, Kusta something. Just called before you came. Seems OK, but he didn't have time to talk much. He'll come later, he said. But you know, with lawyers —"

No thank-you for arranging it. But Peter didn't really expect one. "Did he say anything about bail?" he interrupted again.

"Oh yeah, about that. He said he'll apply, but not to get my hopes up. Not with it being a first-degree charge and not with . . ." This time Sam paused. He looked at the table for a moment and then looked back up, but seemingly at a spot over Peter's left shoulder. ". . . not with my prior. Now, don't get mad or anything, but —"

"Prior? What? Like a prior conviction? What are you talking about?"

"It was a bullshit charge and conviction, but yeah, I have a prior in Ontario. Couple years ago, for uttering threats, but —"

"Uttering threats?" Peter's mind was reeling. This was completely unexpected. They had only been in loose contact for long periods, but, surely, he would have somehow heard about something that big.

"Yeah, yeah. Uttering threats. A neighbour of mine kept beaking off at me. A real weirdo, that guy. Wore these green corduroy coveralls all the time and had like a giant blond 'fro, kinda like Art Garfunkel, you know? And anyways, he was always on about the paint smells from my place and how he had allergies and sensitivities and shit, and how he was going to get me evicted. So, anyways, one day he gives me a shove in the chest when he claims I stepped into his personal space when I was arguing back at him that he was the one who smelled, and so I shove him back, and then I like trip or something and fall, and he starts laughing, the loser. God. So, I lose it. Anyone would, right? You know? And then I may have said some stuff about murdering his ass and shit, which is whatever, but then that nosy bitch down the hall, she shows up and says she heard everything and is calling the cops. Calling them on me! Can you friggin believe it? So anyways, next thing I know I'm in the cop shop and charged and —"

Peter snapped out of the daze that sometimes developed when Sam spoke in this kind of onrush of nonstop words. "And you were convicted. You said. What was the sentence?"

"The judge gave me a suspended sentence. Two years' probation with a requirement to see my psychiatrist regularly. Which I did. Samuel Bannerman, model citizen and —"

The girl in the other booth began screaming a torrent of swear words at what Peter assumed to be her boyfriend on the other side of the glass. She stood up and kicked her chair over. The guard quickly removed her. She was still screaming. Another guard, on the other side of the barrier, escorted the boyfriend out of the room, walking behind Sam. The boyfriend, a tall guy with a dragon neck tattoo, was smirking.

"Wow," Peter said.

"Yeah, I've only been here an hour, and I can already tell it's going to be a laugh a minute. A real fun fair, this place. A veritable pleasure dome. A garden of infinite delights. But listen, Pete, no more interruptions. I've got stuff I have to talk to you about before we run out of time. So, listen up. Like I said, no more interruptions."

Peter clenched and unclenched his fists on his lap while he considered that the glass was likely there more to protect the prisoners from the visitors than the other way around. *Deep breaths, Peter, deep breaths.* He forced a smile and nodded.

"Three things. First one is a question, the second is a request, and the third is another question. The first question is, where's Mr. Bingley?"

Mr. Bingley? Peter blanked out for the briefest moment.

Mr. Bingley! Right. That Mr. Bingley.

"Don't worry about him, Sam. I haven't precisely located him yet, but I've called all the agencies and rescues, I'm working on the posters, and I have a search plan ready." Peter figured that this white lie was preferable to the bald truth, especially when that bald truth might cause Sam distress. Distress was OK if it led to concrete rational action, but Sam had no recourse to such actions, so it was better for him to remain happily in the dark for now. Plus, in Sam's case, "distress" was usually manifested as freaking out, something for which the guards evidently had a low tolerance.

Sam scowled. "That's disappointing. You've had lots of time to find him. But if it's catnappers, they won't be easy to find. You didn't mention checking the dark web for suspicious kitten sales. Get on that right away. We have no time to lose."

"OK, will do."

"Next, my request is for you to spend the night at the apartment. The kittens are going to start screaming if they're left alone for more than a few hours. They will scream all night long. That's what they did before, those poor little guys, because you know you can't blame them, they've had such a rough start in life, and I sure don't blame them, but the whiners in the building won't understand. No empathy or understanding there, you know? And they will complain. You bet they'll whine and complain. They'll get the friggin Humane Society to come and take the kittens, and I'll get evicted. Out on the street with winter coming. The crying kittens would have gotten Dženan evicted if he hadn't been dead."

First name basis with the victim, now? Peter thought before scrambling to formulate an answer. "Um . . . I don't know, Sam, that's —"

"Come on, Peter, I never ask you for anything."

Not even remotely true.

Before Peter could think of how to respond to that one, Sam went on. "Do you want me to beg? Here's me begging." Sam put the receiver down and pressed his palms together in a prayer position and mouthed, "Please."

Peter looked down at his lap and stifled a sigh. He took three deep breaths and then looked back up at his brother. "I've got to check with Laura first. And it'd be just one night. What happens tomorrow night? I can't take them home. Merry does not like other cats. I suppose I could keep them at the clinic for a little while.

Come to think of it, I could even do that tonight." Peter was pleased with himself for having thought of this solution just in time. *Whew.*

But Sam shook his head vigorously. "No cages. I'm not institutionalizing them. How could you be so insensitive? Look at where I am, buddy!" Sam waved his free hand around. "Ed's back tomorrow, and he and I made a deal where if anything ever happened to me, he'd look after the kittens, and if anything ever happened to him, I'd take care of his fish. He's an animal lover. Took to the kittens right away yesterday when I introduced them. Bonded with Mr. Bingley especially. And I don't mind his fish. Some kind of fancy little eel things. Don't remember what they're called, something that starts with an *L*, but not leeches. Ha ha! Definitely not leeches. So anyways, he's visiting his sister in Gimli today, and if the weather's nice . . ."

Peter began tuning Sam out. He glanced at the clock on the wall. Time was running out, and he had questions of his own.

". . . and Ed always says . . . Hey, Peter? Are you even listening?"

Peter flushed. Was it that obvious? "Just tired, sorry. But I heard everything. Ed. Fish. Gimli. Tomorrow. Got it." He grinned in what he hoped was a disarming way, although why he thought it was important to remain in his brother's good graces was beyond him.

Sam grunted. "Fine, whatever. You're looking after the boys tonight, and Ed's got 'em from tomorrow until I get out of here. I hope that lawyer you dug up is good."

Peter gritted his teeth. "You had another question?"

Sam nodded and cleared his throat. Then he leaned in close to the glass, cleared his throat once more for good measure, and whispered into the phone, "Can Pippin smell ghosts?"

CHAPTER *Nine*

"What do you mean, ghosts?"

"Ghosts. Spirits, spectres, phantoms, apparitions, spooks. Ghosts! What do you think I mean?"

"I know what ghosts *are*. What I don't know is how they relate to anything we're talking about." Peter could feel his blood pressure rising again. He knew that Sam sometimes had trouble with the commonly agreed upon boundaries around reality, but this was ridiculous. He had to quell the urge to get up and leave. Go collect Pippin. Head home to Laura. Let Sam sort all this out himself.

He took an especially deep breath and briefly closed his eyes. This helped a little, but only a little.

"I'll explain as soon as you answer the question," Sam said, also clearly irked. This was the reason they didn't see each other very often. Most conversations ended up veering into feedback loops of mutual irritation.

"Can Pippin smell ghosts?" Peter took another deep breath. "Well, despite his formidable powers, he cannot smell things that don't exist, so the answer is no, I'm afraid. I fear I might regret hearing the answer, but why do you ask?"

"I'm going to rebut your usual science-centric ideological statement first, and then I'll answer your question." Sam squared his shoulders and looked Peter directly in the eyes. He cleared his throat. "'There are more things in heaven and earth, Horatio, than are dreamt of in your philosophy.' Kinda says it all, doesn't it? I could try to top the immortal Bard, but I won't. What your type don't get is that science is like a bubble of light in the darkness. It has no way of knowing what might be out there in the darkness beyond the bubble, let alone describing it or comprehending how vast and full the darkness is." Sam wedged the telephone receiver between his chin and shoulder. He cupped a small imaginary bubble between the palms of his hands. "But the bubble keeps expanding —" he started very slowly moving his hands apart "— so what science thought was impossible 200 years ago is boring and routine now." Sam grabbed the phone again and pointed at it dramatically. "Like this, for instance."

"Yeah, I get it. Fine. But we're running out of time. Why does this matter?"

Another woman was escorted in, accompanied by a nervous-looking little boy. The boy clutched a large green plush dinosaur. They were shown to the booth the angry young woman had been in.

Sam had been speaking louder and louder, but he now lowered his voice again. "Dženan told me that ghosts were going to kill him. They used to harass him when he lived in Bosnia. It had something to do with a place called Todorovo, in the far west of the country. He told me there was a specific reason, but he didn't tell me what it was. We didn't know each other that well yet, but I knew he wanted to tell me, and if he had lived a little longer, and those ghosts hadn't gotten to him, I would have found out. But anyways, he had peace in Canada for a few years, but then they found him. The ghosts reappeared. They messed with his stuff and moved it around. He knew this was a warning. He was terrified. He didn't have any close friends or family here to support him. They broke things. Left messages. I never saw them or any of that when I was at his place, but I totally believed him. Very sincere and serious guy. Very smart, like reality smart, not school smart."

"You think ghosts killed him, and that if Pippin can find the ghosts, you will be proven innocent?" Peter struggled to keep his tone neutral and flat.

"Yes, that's what I said, isn't it? It's the only explanation that makes sense. He kept his apartment double-latched from the inside. Nobody could get in there. He told me that the landlord ordered him to remove the latches for fire safety reasons, but he just put them back on after. A human killer couldn't put the latches back on from outside the door after leaving. That's why the cops stuck with that weird sex accident theory until they found out he had been strangled, but —"

"Ghosts can strangle people?"

Sam rolled his eyes. "I won't dignify that with an answer. We're wasting time. Pippin is the key. My mistake was asking whether he could smell ghosts. Of course, he can. I know you've seen him staring at shit you can't see, right? The kittens do it all the time, and they're not even trained sniffers. Just take him around the building and see if he picks up something unusual, OK? Not too much to ask, is it?"

"But even if he did, how would that constitute proof of murderous ghosts? I mean, Sam, I want —"

Sam held up his hand to cut Peter off. "Just do it. Be open to what's outside your bubble." He snorted with what Peter took to be irritation. Peter pictured himself strangling his brother. Just a little.

A guard appeared behind Sam and tapped him on the shoulder.

"Time's up. Shit. OK, you know what to do." He began counting off on his fingers. "One: find Mr. Bingley. Two: stay with the kittens until Ed gets back. And" — he glanced at the guard and lowered his voice again — "three: get Pippin working on the ghost detection plan."

With that, Sam stood up and allowed the guard to usher him out of the room. No good-byes. No thank-yous. Just absurd instructions. And no chance for Peter to ask the questions he wanted to ask. How well did Sam know Dženan? What did they do together? How did the police explain Sam getting into and out of a locked and latched apartment to allegedly commit this murder? What possible motive did they think Sam had? And, what was up with the licorice in the teddy bear?

Peter waited until he was back in the car to phone Laura. He explained everything in detail. There was a long pause before Laura said anything.

"Wow. Hard to know where to begin with that. Prior conviction. Ghosts. Sleepover . . ." Peter heard her take a sip of what he assumed was her afternoon tea. "I guess he's right about the kittens yelling, though. That would be a problem. Can you sleep there? I mean, what kind of state is it in? Maybe you can sneak them to the clinic after all, and just not tell Sam. From the sounds of things, he's not getting out right away, so how would he know?"

"No, I'll stay there tonight. Sam's really fragile right now, and if he somehow found out I had put the kittens in cages at the clinic, it could tip him over the edge. Which would not help his case. And regardless, I should have a better look around his apartment for anything that might help his lawyer defend him. God, I can only imagine how Kostakis will react if Sam starts going off on his ghost theory."

"OK. But just one night, no matter what happens with this Ed guy."

"Agreed."

"I can help. This *Matrix* sweater is still driving me crazy. I need a break. I'll call the rescues about Bingley —"

"*Mister* Bingley, if you please!" Peter chuckled.

"Ha! Sorry. *Mr. Bingley*, and I can also put up the posts on the various lost pet social media sites."

"Thanks, that would help a lot. And Sam wanted physical posters on lampposts and stuff too. And for me to search for black market kitten sales."

"Right. Black market kitten sales. Got it." Peter could hear the smile in Laura's voice. He didn't often think about how lucky he was. But at that moment, he did.

"Changing the subject to something hopefully more pleasant, any idea what Kevin and Stuart's surprise is?" Peter asked.

"No," Laura said. "But he's making a pretty big deal about it. I would have guessed an engagement announcement, but he said he had to pick up the surprise in Headingley. I don't think there are any jewellery stores out there."

"I don't even want to guess."

Peter could hear the kittens crying as soon as he and Pippin reached the second-floor hallway. Sam was right about one thing, at least. Peter had stopped on the way to pick up some groceries for dinner and breakfast for him and Pippin, so it seemed they had been gone long enough to make the kittens anxious.

Entering the Lady Alice, it suddenly occurred to him that Sam's apartment might be sealed by the police. He wasn't sure how quickly search warrants were issued or how soon they would act on one.

Approaching the door, he was relieved not to see any police tape. He assumed they had enough evidence from what Sam told them and from their other investigations that they weren't in a blazing hurry to immediately search his apartment. But it could happen at any time. Looking after the kittens was a good reason for Peter to be there, so he wasn't worried about explaining his presence to the police, if they suddenly showed up.

While Peter fumbled for the keys, balancing the grocery bags in one arm, he heard a door open and then quickly close somewhere behind him.

He turned and looked. Nothing.

He assumed it had been apartment 7, right behind him across the hall, but now he wasn't so sure. Then he thought he heard a security latch slide at 5, but it was hard to tell with the kittens screaming. Definitely not 6, though, where the short pale girl with the clumsy boyfriend lived. Didn't matter anyway. People opened and closed doors all the time. With a murder in the building, everyone was probably on edge.

The kittens climbed up Peter's pant legs as soon as he stepped into the apartment.

"Whoa guys! Whoa! I was just gone a couple hours. Abandonment issues? Separation anxiety?" This was a real diagnosis. Peter saw it all the time in his practice, although much more commonly in dogs.

He set the groceries down and gently unpeeled the kittens from his legs, holding each up to his face, cooing, "It's going to be OK." The kittens were unpersuaded. They still meowed pitifully, but maybe a tiny bit more quietly.

"What do you think, Pippin? It can't be mealtime for them again. Maybe I just need to sit with them and give them some attention."

Pippin looked up at Peter and cocked his head to the side.

"It's not like we have a heavy agenda. Do you want your dinner now, though? It's just about five thirty."

Pippin ran into the kitchen, assuming that he'd be fed in the same place as the kittens.

This done, and tea brewed with the new decaf Taylors Yorkshire he had bought, Peter sat down in the only available chair, a dining chair with a ripped rattan lattice back and a thin green velvet seat cushion. Sam also had a red leather armchair, but it had several precarious-looking towers of books stacked on it. And Sam's single bed in the corner, while clear of clutter, did not look inviting for this purpose. Peter preferred rigid and firm furniture to cushy anyway. "Straight back, straight thoughts," someone had once said, although he couldn't recall who.

The kittens immediately leapt onto his lap and began kneading with their paws and purring far louder than seemed possible for such tiny creatures. Peter couldn't tell which one was Flinders and which was Barry, but it didn't matter.

He looked around him and sipped his tea. Spending the night here was a distinctly unappealing prospect, but he may as well make the best of it and use the time to try to find evidence that would help Sam's defence. But what kind of evidence? It was always difficult to prove a negative. This came up all the time at work. For example, Peter could definitively diagnose the presence of cancer with tests, but there were no tests that conclusively proved its absence, that it was not lurking somewhere. In this situation, it was easier to prove that someone was a murderer than to prove that they were not, unless they had a solid alibi. Peter did not know whether the time of death had been confirmed, but even if it had, it was very unlikely that Sam would have an alibi, as he very rarely left his apartment.

So, rather than trying to prove Sam innocent, maybe it was more logical to try to find evidence of someone else's involvement. That theoretical person was probably one of the other residents. Not certainly, but probably; a supposition arrived at by assessing the odds given the locked front door, Dženan's apparently solitary existence, and the fact that the great majority of victims know their killer. And the residents of the building were far easier to investigate than the 800,000 other people in Winnipeg. So, probably good enough for now.

But how to find such evidence? He couldn't enter the dead man's apartment, nor did he have the investigative skills to do anything useful in there. But maybe he could talk to the other residents? Of course, the police would have interviewed all of them, but some people, especially those living on the margins of society, can be nervous talking to authorities. Peter had at times been accused of interfering in police business, but this would definitely not be the case here. He was merely being a helpful, vigilant citizen, doing what the police had difficulty doing effectively, through no fault of their own. Although the girl in 6 had ignored Pippin, he was otherwise often an excellent icebreaker. Much more of an icebreaker than an intimidating person in uniform!

Now all he had to think of was what he could say or ask that might prompt people to reveal useful information. And what innocent excuse he had for going door to door.

Then he remembered.

Mr. Bingley.

CHAPTER *Ten*

Peter's sense of order dictated that they go downstairs and start at apartment 1, the first unit on the left, or, as Peter liked to think of it, the northeast corner. Before knocking, he mentally rehearsed what he was going to say. He would tell her that he knew that Sam had already asked, but now they were offering a reward. And then he'd try to slide in a question about whether she knew anything that might help Sam's case.

The woman in the green dress answered the door immediately after he knocked.

"The man with the lovely dog! How can I help you?" she said, smiling and reaching down to let Pippin sniff her hand. The accent now seemed Slavic. Maybe. A Ukrainian refugee perhaps? But there were at least a dozen Slavic languages, from Belarusian to Bosnian. Peter prided himself on figuring out accents, but he couldn't pin this one down any further. He heard what sounded like CBC Radio coming from her apartment and smelled jasmine tea. Most people wouldn't have picked that out, but to Peter, it was distinctive. A tea lover. That was a pleasant surprise, but did that tell him anything? Nothing that came immediately to mind.

"Sam is desperate to find that lost kitten he spoke to you about before, so I'm going around to announce that we're now offering a $500 reward for any information that leads to his safe return."

"Oh my. That is a lot of money for a little kitten. I was keeping my eyes open anyway, but I will be especially sure to do so now. Thank you." She began to close the door. Peter noticed that she was wearing a gold fleur-de-lys on a necklace. Her accent definitely was not French or Québécoise. He was certain of that.

He quickly turned his attention back to the closing door and raised his hand to stop her. "Oh, and I guess I also wanted to . . ." Peter fumbled for the words. This was not going how he had planned. He would have to modify his script.

"Yes?" The woman arched her eyebrows and smiled again.

"I'm sorry, but as you might know, Sam has been accused of killing the man in apartment 4 and is in jail, which is why I am here looking for Mr. Bingley and not him. It might seem like a low priority given the situation, but it would do so much to help cheer him up. I should add that he is, of course, completely innocent. Not knowing what's happened to Mr. Bingley is . . ." Peter realized he was babbling. He hated babbling. He hated it when others did it, notably Sam, but hated it even more when he lost his own focus and verbal discipline. "It is, well, really distracting him at a time when he needs to be able to think clearly."

The woman nodded. "I can understand that." Her eyebrows were still arched, clearly waiting for Peter to spit out what he seemed to be wanting to say.

"So also, in addition to keeping an eye out for Mr. Bingley, I wonder if I could impose on you to try to recall if there's anything, anything at all, that you saw or heard that I can pass on to Sam's lawyer that might help prove his innocence?" Peter felt a little foolish as he said this. It had sounded like a more reasonable question inside his head.

The woman didn't seem put out, though. "As I told the police, I wish I could help as he seemed like a nice man, but I really did not hear or see anything unusual. I do know that he and your brother were friendly with each other, but the police know that already. And it hardly helps you. I'm sorry."

Peter knew that he had always been terrible at reading people, but he was working hard on improving that. He had recently read the latest scientific research on how to detect lying. He was keen to try it out. No doubt the police knew these tricks too, but the liar may be less on guard with an awkward vet and his cute dog than with a cop. The probability of success was low, but certainly not zero. But in the moment, Peter blanked on several of the cues that someone might be lying. He did remember that they frequently made little grooming gestures, like hair smoothing, which she didn't, and that the speed or pitch of their answers changed midway, which wasn't the case here either. So, there was some evidence that she was telling the truth.

"OK, thanks. I didn't think it hurt to ask." He paused, and was about to say goodbye and move on, when a thought occurred to him. "You say the victim seemed like a nice man . . . Did you know him well?"

"Just passing in the hall, like any of the neighbours. He was always courteous and always smiling," she said.

After thanking her again and saying goodbye, Peter wondered whether he should have asked for her name. It would have seemed awkward, though. It was a shame that the mailboxes at the front had only numbers on them. Not that he had any specific reason for knowing the residents' names, but somehow it felt like it might help.

Jasmine tea. Slavic accent. Fleur-de-lys necklace. No obvious lies. That's what he could file away for now.

Number 2, in the northwest corner, should be Ed's and should be empty, but he knocked on it anyway. Maybe Ed was home early. He could have sworn he heard a scraping noise in there, but nothing else. He waited a moment and looked around. There were marks beside the door where stickers had been removed. He also noticed an odd smell that he couldn't place that seemed to be coming from the apartment. Vaguely chemical? He knocked again. Silence now. No more scraping, or any other sound. Peter reasoned that the scraping could have been from the apartment above instead. The one with the strange girl. Scraping noises can be difficult to localize.

On to apartment 3, southeast. This was where he had gotten a fleeting glimpse of black hair the other day. He could hear music and voices through the door. The voices stopped when he knocked. It took several long seconds before the door opened to reveal a young man with shoulder-length black hair and tattoos on his forehead and neck. He was wearing a black hoodie with something written on it in an illegible font. Was the first word "opal"? *Strange.*

Peter said his bit, feeling a little more confident this time. While he was talking, Pippin sniffed the door jamb intensively, tail slowly wagging. The young man didn't appear to notice this or care. He listened to Peter, looking at him with heavy-lidded eyes. His response to the reward was, "Cool." But to the request for information to help Sam, it was, "Sorry, bro, I'm not getting involved." Before Peter could think of a different angle to try, the young man said, "Hope you find the cat." And he closed the door.

Not getting involved, Peter thought, repeating the phrase a few times in his head, trying to parse something from the inflection and the facial expression. Did this imply he knew something but was afraid to say? If he didn't know anything, why wouldn't he just say that, like the green dress lady did? But it might just be a turn of phrase, and possibly a more effective way to cut off further inquiry so Peter wouldn't ask things like when he last saw the victim or what he knew about him. He wished he had paid more attention to the tattoos and the writing on the hoodie, but these doorstop visits went far too quickly to catch many visual details. One neck tattoo was of a snake, he was pretty sure, but there were various symbols, objects, and words that he didn't take in properly. And Peter didn't get a chance to practise his new lie detection skills. Given their content, none of the young man's three brief statements could be lies, unless he didn't hope that Mr. Bingley would be found. But who would feel that way, or lie about it?

Peter sighed.

Apartment 4, southwest, was Dženan Knezevic's. The hall light was burned out at this end of the hall. Peter wondered how long that had been the case. He looked at the door, not knowing what he expected to see. Pippin sniffed along the battered baseboard beside the door in the dark corner.

"Anything there, buddy?" Peter whispered.

He bent down and took out his phone to illuminate where Pippin was sniffing. Peter couldn't see anything of interest there, but as he stood up, his phone's flashlight caught something written in dark red ink or paint on the cream-coloured wall. The hallway walls were badly scuffed and marked up throughout, but this was definitely deliberate. It was at eye level, about a metre to the left of the door, but had been hard to see in the dark.

It was a kind of eight-pointed star. The top, bottom, and two sides featured typical points, and in between each were rounded loops, all of it drawn with three parallel continuous lines. He supposed it was vaguely like a Celtic knot with a big open area in the middle for what appeared to be the letter *U*.

How bizarre. Presumably, the police had taken note of this, whatever it meant. Maybe it had something to do with the guy across the hall. Peter cursed himself again for not having looked at the tattoos more carefully, although he wasn't sure how he would have been able to do that without seeming even weirder.

He took a picture of the symbol, planning to see if Google Lens came up with anything when he got back to the apartment.

Then Peter carefully inspected the rest of the walls at that end of the corridor, including back across the hall, beside apartment 3.

He was just finishing his examination when he heard a noise from the other side of the door, like a throat clearing or a cough. Coincidentally near the door? Or preparing to leave the apartment? Peter didn't want to take the chance, so he signalled Pippin and they walked quickly toward the stairs.

Apartment 5, in the upstairs northeast corner, had a small welcome mat in front of it that Peter hadn't noticed before. It was one of those tan coir fibre ones. In black cartoon letters it declared, *Visitors Must Be Approved by the Cat*, beside a silhouette of a cat with its tail up, looking toward the presumptive visitor.

This is a good sign! Peter thought. At least the person was more likely to be receptive to talking to him. Although it struck him as odd that Sam hadn't mentioned other cats in the building.

Pippin gave the mat a brief sniff and then looked up at Peter as if to say, "nothing to report."

Peter knocked. No response. He waited a moment and knocked again. Still nothing.

"Oh well," he said quietly to Pippin. "Can't expect everybody to be home."

He mildly dreaded knocking on the door at apartment 6, given his less than enthusiastic reception last time, but postponing it just made the anticipation worse. *Get it over with,* he told himself. *Eat the frog.* This was Laura's favourite encouragement. If you know you have to eat a frog — or do anything really unpleasant — sometime today, just gulp it down now rather than eating it in your mind over and over again in advance.

But did he really have to?

He paused.

No, he had told himself he was going to be thorough, and he always kept his promises to himself.

He knocked.

No answer.

He knocked again. This was strange because he had heard that scraping noise. It had to have come from here or from Ed's apartment below, but it was more likely that Ed was away. Maybe they just weren't answering the door. Maybe they were the so-called meth-heads after all and were passed out now.

Peter thought about knocking a third time but decided against it. He shrugged and turned to Pippin. "I guess it's just number 7, and then we're done."

As they turned to head diagonally across to the last apartment, the door to number 5 opened and a short, round-bodied, elderly woman with pink hair looked out.

"You knocked?"

Presumably not a drug user or a heavy metal drummer, and certainly not half of a young, blond religious couple. This was the previously unknown tenth resident of the building. The map was complete, assuming the odd girl in apartment 6 was a drug user and not part of the religious couple, putting the latter in apartment 7. This contradicted some of Sam's information, but that did not come as a surprise. Peter smiled to himself. A completed map was deeply satisfying.

"I did. Sorry to disturb you!" Peter went on to explain the purpose of his visit, this time feeling he had finally hit his stride.

"Of course, I'll keep an eye out for the poor dear. And I might know something that could help your brother," she added, her voice lowered, but her eyes lighting up. "Did you want to come in for a minute?" She swung the door open wide, revealing an explosion of pink.

CHAPTER *Eleven*

Food lady was fine. Not exceptional, but fine. She remained as quiet and friendly as she had been when he met her. So that was good. But the food was not quite as tasty as from first food man or second food man. They had both given him and his brothers lots of crunchy food. He loved crunchy food. For some unfathomable reason, food lady counted each crunchy food piece one by one, out loud, in a singsong voice. He couldn't count past three or four, so he didn't know the number, but it wasn't a pile, like it should be. It was a few scattered pieces, like kittens in a litter. He had had a bunch more brothers and sisters before he left his mother to go live with first food man. It was a similar number to the number of food pieces. Maybe a few more pieces than siblings. But not many more. Regardless, it was not nearly enough. But the wet food that came out of a can was superior. So that partly compensated.

The other worry was that it was boring here. He did miss his brothers. Food lady wasn't around much, so she wasn't a proper playmate. And the room was mostly empty. He missed all of second food man's stuff. That had been fun. This room did have a window that faced a tree, and that tree had a lot of birds in it. He enjoyed watching them for a little while. He didn't get frustrated that he couldn't catch them. His brothers often got frustrated by that sort of thing. And he had noticed that first food man often watched little men running around in his noisy light box, which seemed to be some sort of special window, and he got frustrated sometimes too. So, it was probably more normal to get frustrated when watching something you couldn't catch, but fortunately that wasn't a feeling he had experienced himself very often.

This would do . . . for now. He'd just have to be alert for an opportunity to leave this room and go find his brothers and second food man.

CHAPTER *Twelve*

The walls were pink. The furniture was pink. The carpet was pink. All in different shades, ranging from quiet dusty rose to shrieking magenta.

Peter squinted, as if that would tone down the retina-searing assault. Pippin was lucky. Dogs can't see red or pink, so it would look beige to him. He sniffed the carpet with great interest, though.

The woman was beaming. Clearly, Peter was expected to say something.

"Wow," was all he could muster at first. He knew a compliment would help foster trust. He looked from side to side, nodding, thinking hard. "You have quite a flair for decorating!" was the best he could come up with on the spot.

"Everyone says that!" the woman said, still beaming.

Then Peter noticed what was on the walls. There were about a dozen framed photographs of cats. The frames were all ornate, some gold, some red, and some white. The whole scene reminded him powerfully of Dolores Umbridge's office in the Harry Potter books. He hoped the similarity ended there.

The woman noticed Peter taking in the pictures. "My babies," she said, almost purring. "But I'm being rude. Won't you take a seat?" She indicated an exceptionally poofy-looking pale pink armchair. "And what can I offer you? Coffee? Tea?" She paused and winked. "Gin?"

"Tea would be wonderful, thank you. Decaf if you have it." Peter settled cautiously into the chair, as if he expected it to swallow him whole. He sank so deeply that, because of his long legs, his knees ended up almost level with his chin. Pippin settled down beside him, resting his chin on his forepaws. He raised an eyebrow to Peter before half closing his eyes.

While the woman hummed and clattered about in the kitchen, Peter looked around him, trying to pinpoint what, besides the shocking colour, seemed odd. Then he realized what it was.

No cat.

Despite the welcome mat and the photos, there was no sign of a cat — not a hint of fur, scratched furniture, or litter box smell. Not that any of these had to be present in a clean house with a cat, but after years of house calls, Peter had seen very few where there wasn't at least some subtle clue. Most tellingly, though, Pippin was napping and not on alert for another animal lurking somewhere.

The woman returned with a tray with two mugs on it, a sugar bowl, a small carton of cream, and a plate of cookies. Peter had expected fancy China cups, but these were mugs decorated with the logos of local casinos.

"You don't have a cat anymore?" he asked.

"Oh no, I do," she said, shovelling sugar into her mug. "Biscuits is around here somewhere. He's shy with strangers, and he's so clever at hiding."

Pippin must be off his game today, Peter thought. But it had been a long, strange, and tiring day for both of them so far, and it was far from over yet.

Peter took a cautious sip of his tea. A superior English breakfast blend. It was surprisingly good. In his experience, 90 percent of people either had terrible tea on hand, or, if they had good tea, didn't know how to brew it properly. He made a minor adjustment in his appraisal of the woman.

"So, you think you might know something that could help my brother?"

"Yes," she said, widening her eyes. "I told the police this too, but they didn't seem very interested." She paused and leaned forward. "There was a ruckus the night of the murder."

"A ruckus?"

"Yes, a ruckus. From across the hall."

"The drug addicts?"

The woman frowned. "Oh, I wouldn't know anything about that. Is that what your brother said? They seem like a very nice couple. A tiny woman and a very large hairy man. A fairy and a bear, I always thought. Anyway. They're always so quiet. Sometimes I would think they had moved out. But then I'd see one of them in the hall or at the door. But never a peep from inside their apartment. Until the night that fellow was killed. That night there was a scream, some shouting, and then a door slammed."

"And you're sure it was from apartment 6?"

"Absolutely sure." She nodded emphatically. "After the scream, I opened the door to see what was going on. I thought it was in the hall. But then I heard the shout, and it was directly from over there." She pointed over Peter's shoulder in the general direction of the other apartment.

"And the police weren't interested?"

"They wrote it down and said thank you. That's it." She shrugged, sat back, and picked up her mug.

Peter considered for a moment, taking another sip of tea. "So, you think that makes them better suspects than Sam? It seems to me a murderer would be very quiet, like they would be trying not to draw attention to themselves."

"Yes, but," she said, drawing out the "but" dramatically, "what if one of them did it and the other found out and screamed?" She arched her eyebrows and gave a sharp little nod.

This struck Peter as highly improbable, but he didn't want to endanger the rapport by arguing. Also, he thought about the bang he had heard from that apartment earlier. In his brief experience, those people weren't as quiet as the woman indicated. "OK, I see what you mean. Good point. Was there anything else unusual going on then? Anything at all?"

"Only that Biscuits was on edge all that night. Cats can sense things, you know? And it wasn't because of the noises from across the hall. That sort of thing doesn't bother him. It's more that he can sense evil. I didn't mention it to the police because they were rude to Biscuits. Totally ignored him. I'm sure they wouldn't believe anything I said about his talents. But that doesn't help your brother. It only means that Biscuits knew that there were evil goings-on in the building that night. Such a very sensitive little darling, you know? But he wouldn't have a way of knowing who the evildoer was unless they were right in front of him."

"Or be able to tell us!" Peter chuckled. OK, so her eccentricity went beyond her passion for pink. No surprise there.

The woman shot Peter an odd look. But then she brightened up right away. "Speak of my charming little devil, there he is!" She pointed to a bare patch of the vivid salmon-coloured carpet. Peter briefly thought that she must have dyed the cat's fur so he was perfectly camouflaged: he couldn't see anything. He looked at her quizzically.

She ignored him and cooed toward where she had pointed. "Yes, darling, this guest is fine. He loves kitties too. Why don't you jump onto your favourite cushion and join us?"

Peter assumed she was referring to a cushion with the word *Biscuits* stitched on it on the couch opposite him.

"There, isn't that comfy?" Then she turned to Peter. "Now, be honest, I know I'm biased, but isn't he the most handsome cat you've ever seen?"

There was no cat.

Peter stood out in the hall, debating with himself whether or not that had been a complete waste of time. At least he had gotten her name, Maureen, as they said their good-byes. And at least he hadn't started laughing or made any snide remarks. He had enough eccentric clients to know how to play along and keep his tone calm and free of obvious judgment. He even bantered a bit with "Biscuits." Maureen seemed pleased. Pippin, however, ignored the phantom cat, which appeared to surprise the woman. "Puppies normally love Biscuits. Just go gaga over him. And he loves them. Your dog must be very tired." *Yes,* that's *it,* Peter thought. *Not that you're a complete loon and there is no Biscuits.*

He went over the whole encounter in his mind, trying to remember any telltale signs of lying. The invisible cat was technically a lie, but one she seemed to sincerely believe, so it didn't count. It was the rest of the conversation he was interested in. He remembered a few of the other clues detailed in the article, like the fibber being vague and using long preambles, but Maureen had done neither of those. He would write out the whole conversation when he got back to Sam's suite. That would help him process the information and perhaps extract something helpful from it.

Last stop, apartment 7, in the southeast corner. This would have to be the religious couple.

A middle-aged man answered the door. He was pale-skinned, blond, and blue-eyed as Sam had described. But he didn't give off any weird vibes. In fact, he had a warm smile, Peter thought. And he wore a Barn Hammer Brewery T-shirt, which didn't strike him as religious apparel.

"Well, my wife and I are really allergic to cats, but we'll do our best! That's why we have gerbils. We're not allergic to them." He smiled and gestured over his shoulder where Peter could see a large cage by the window. One of the gerbils was running on the wheel. He caught a whiff of cedar shavings. The man's expression switched to a frown. "I'm sorry to hear about your brother. That must be so stressful for both of you, but I'm afraid I can't help you. Like I told the officer, we don't go out much, and we didn't hear anything from inside our apartment." *Interesting*, Peter thought. *Either Maureen has better hearing, or this couple were sound sleepers, or one of them was lying.*

"OK, thanks. But if you happen to suddenly think of something, I'll be staying at Sam's tonight, and after that you can call me at the number that'll be on the reward posters we're putting up tomorrow."

"Will do. Best of luck. I'm Peter, by the way." The man stuck his hand out.

"I'm Peter too!"

"I know. Dr. Peter Bannerman. The vet and amateur detective," the man said as he shook Peter's hand vigorously. "Mia and I are big true-crime fans. And animal lovers. Except cats." He chuckled.

"Wow, OK. I didn't know my name was that well known," Peter said, thinking that true-crime fandom also didn't fit with alleged religious fanaticism, but then maybe he was allowing preconceptions to narrow his view.

The man shrugged. "Bannerman isn't a common name, and we like to know who our neighbours are, so when your brother moved in, we did some internet sleuthing and put two and two together." He winked and smiled.

"Well, Pippin," Peter said, once the Other Peter closed the door. "That was different, but I guess that's it for our investigations today. Back to the apartment for a quiet evening of contemplation."

He pulled the keys out, trying to remember which one was for the door of the suite. *Why did Sam have so many keys?*

"If the kittens let us, that is," he added, chuckling, as he found the right one and unlocked the door.

After a frenzied greeting, the kittens settled down quickly. Peter had bought some bagels and cream cheese for his supper. When he was on his own, he defaulted to very simple meals, and he didn't feel like rummaging around in Sam's kitchen, looking for pots and such. He wondered what Laura was eating at home. They kept a menu list posted on the fridge to help plan grocery shopping, but he couldn't recall what was intended for tonight.

A couple bites into the bagel, he realized that he wasn't very hungry, so he finished only half, minus the corner he gave to Pippin. Peter smiled to himself when he considered how Laura would have teased him about doing the opposite of what he told his clients to do. "Never feed them food from the table!" she'd say, wagging her finger and mimicking his voice. He tried to remember who had said "Consistency is the hobgoblin of little minds." Churchill? Twain? Emerson? Wilde? He couldn't recall, and anyway, in this instance, he disagreed. To be sure, consistency did make for a much more rational and predictable world. And many of the greatest minds had remarkably consistent habits. Darwin visited his greenhouse at noon every day. Kant went for a walk at precisely 3:30 p.m. every day. Beethoven's daily morning coffee was brewed from precisely 60 beans. And Hemingway counted every word he typed. However, when it came to pleasing Pippin, it was entirely appropriate and rational to be a little inconsistent. When nobody was watching.

Peter looked at his watch. It was only just after seven, so a full evening in this rummage sale of an apartment stretched ahead of him. Certainly, he should keep looking for anything that might help clear Sam, but first he wanted to write out everything he had learned so far. The act of writing always helped clarify his thoughts. Unfortunately, he had failed to bring his favourite notebook, or any notebook. Or even a pen. He would have to look for something in this anarchy.

"Where would you keep paper and pens if you were Sam?" Peter asked Pippin. Pippin looked up, eyes bright, probably appraising the chance that this question would somehow relate to more bagel and cream cheese. Apparently deciding it didn't, he lay down and closed his eyes.

Peter looked through a few kitchen drawers, which, somewhat to his surprise, only contained cutlery and kitchenware. Then he went into the living room and scanned the piles, hands on his hips. He spied the corner of a small black Ikea desk, hidden behind that armchair with the book stacks. That was a part of the room he hadn't investigated yet.

A desk! Bingo!

He manoeuvred over to the desk and glanced at the mounds of papers stacked on it. He thought that if there was nothing in the drawer, he could probably find a sheet in that pile that was blank on one side at least.

He opened the drawer. There was a pale green Hilroy school notebook and a few ballpoint pens on the right, but he barely noticed them.

The rest of the drawer was filled with *Star Wars* action figurines lined up, side by side.

Each one with a tiny plastic bag over its head, tied up at the neck.

CHAPTER *Thirteen*

Darth Vader, Luke Skywalker, Han Solo, Chewbacca, Princess Leia, C-3PO, and even little R2-D2.

Each one staring mutely back at Peter through a plastic bag.

Oddly, Peter's first thought was that the little bags looked like they might have been fashioned from the corners of bread bags.

Then his mind went blank.

He slammed the drawer shut and took a big step backwards, knocking over a stack of books on the armchair. They fell with a loud clatter against a pile of LPs, which in turn fell into a broken laundry basket full of brightly coloured tourist souvenir towels.

Pippin came running into the room. The kittens, who had been sleeping beside Pippin in the kitchen, came charging in behind him.

"Oh my gosh," Peter said as he staggered back to the old dining chair and sat down. "Oh my gosh," he repeated.

Pippin looked at him, ears down, mouth tense.

"It's OK, boy. Nothing for you to worry about right now." Peter patted him. The kittens discovered the tip of Pippin's tail, but he ignored them and kept looking at Peter.

"Oh my gosh," Peter said for the third time. What did this mean? Did it mean Sam was guilty after all? No, not necessarily. Given Sam's mental state, doing this to the toys could have been a stress response to the news of how Dženan had died. Sam had never been violent. Not even during his worst psychotic breaks. There had to be another explanation.

Peter exhaled loudly and shook his head vigorously, as if to rid it of something. "Speaking of stress responses, I wonder if he's got something to drink around here," Peter said, more to the room than to Pippin, who had finally stood up to make his tail less accessible to the kittens.

Peter decided that he was serious about the drink and made his way into the kitchen. He always described himself as a "s.o.s.o." drinker, meaning "social or special occasions." This counted as "special," although not in the usual sense. Special should be somewhere on the list of adjectives describing the occasion of finding out that your brother suffocated action figures, but it was well below a number of other, much sunnier, ones.

He recalled catching a glimpse of what appeared to be a liquor bottle in one of the cupboards. Would it be too much to ask for it to be Scotch?

It was too much to ask. It was absinthe.

What the devil is Sam doing with absinthe?

Peter shrugged and sighed. "Any port in a storm, I suppose," he said, more to himself than to Pippin, who had followed him into the kitchen. "Although I would prefer the port to be port." He found a clean tumbler and sat down at the kitchen table. He poured a narrow finger of the vivid green liquid and sniffed it. Anise. Now he remembered. Absinthe was one of those licoricey drinks, like ouzo, sambuca, and pastis. He thought about the hidden licorice in the teddy bear. He didn't recall Sam having such an interest in that flavour. Peter himself didn't mind it, but he didn't love it either. He sniffed the absinthe again and then pushed the glass away and sat back in his chair.

"What do we do now, Pippin?" Peter reached over and began scratching Pippin behind the ear. "Call the police? Call Kevin? Call

Laura?" He shook his head slowly, still scratching Pippin. "The police must have searched this place before taking Sam in, although he didn't mention that. Maybe they hadn't yet? But if they had, they would have seen the *Star Wars* figures and maybe that's why they arrested him. Maybe that was the key evidence? But wouldn't they have taken the figures back to the station and sealed the room? It makes no sense. More likely they haven't searched yet."

Peter sighed, stood up, and began pacing in the kitchen. Pippin, who had been lying down, sat up and watched him.

"I don't want to call the police until I've thought this through more carefully. There's nothing useful they would do with this evidence one way or the other tonight anyway. I'd love to call Kevin and get his opinion, but that would put him in an awkward spot, so I probably shouldn't." Peter felt a brief flash of pride at taking Kevin's perspective into account. He knew that he wasn't always the best at doing that. "And calling Laura would just worry her, especially since we have to spend the night here."

That question settled, Peter returned to his original plan and retrieved the notebook and a pen from beside the murdered toys. Han looked especially reproachful as he closed the drawer again.

Back at the kitchen table, Peter opened the notebook with trepidation. What if it was full of gruesome drawings further implicating Sam?

But it wasn't. The first half-dozen pages had been roughly ripped out, but the remainder was blank. The ruled pages with the vertical red margin line gave him a pang of nostalgia. The last time he wrote in a Hilroy, he would have been in high school, a quarter century ago.

After absentmindedly chewing on the pen's cap for a minute, Peter began to write. First, he titled each page with an apartment number. Then he wrote out the names, when he knew them, and descriptions of the occupants, including animals. He mentioned the imaginary "Biscuits" in his description of Maureen, rather than as an animal occupant. When he didn't know the names, he referred to the people by nicknames, such as Black Hair Man and Green Dress Woman. Then he crossed out Green Dress Woman and wrote Woman with Slavic Accent instead, so it wouldn't be confusing in case she wore other outfits. Under Black Hair Man, he wrote "pet?" because Pippin had been so intent on sniffing around the door. Unless he had been instructed to seek a specific scent, that kind of sniffing usually meant an animal was present. Peter chuckled to himself when he suddenly recalled what Sam had wanted him to use Pippin for.

"You weren't sniffing out ghosts at apartment 3, were you?" he asked Pippin, who was half-asleep and didn't bother to stir in response.

For apartment 4 he wrote out what he knew about Dženan Knezevic: that he was 70 years old and was born in Sarajevo, Bosnia-Herzegovina, and murdered by a suffocation made to look like auto-erotic asphyxiation. Then, looking at the picture on his phone, Peter carefully sketched the symbol with the U in the middle. He briefly considered putting it at the bottom of the page for apartment 3, but dismissed that as irrational speculation, given that he had no evidence that it had anything to do with Black Hair Man.

"Shoot, Pippin, I was going to look up that marking on Google Lens but got distracted by the *Star Wars* massacre." He pulled out his phone, found the photo, and ran it through the image search app.

It didn't return any matches.

"So much for that," he said, and put his phone back. "I'll show it to Laura tomorrow and see if it rings any bells with her. She's good with that sort of thing."

Once he was satisfied that he had written down everything notable about the tenants and the few known animals (really just the Other Peter's gerbils), he then set about reproducing each of the conversations as close to verbatim as he could recall.

He was so intent on this that without thinking, he reached out, picked up the glass, and took a swallow. The intensity of the anise flavour and the burn of the 60 percent alcohol made him gasp. He had to stop himself from spitting it out.

"Whoa!"

He quickly set the glass back down.

When he was done writing, he stood up and paced again for a few minutes. The clear floor area was only large enough to permit five steps in each direction, with sharp 180-degree turns, but it was as close as he could get to the walking he preferred to do when he needed to think. Something about letting both his feet and his mind ramble was often helpful. The main room, while larger, had too many tripping hazards. He had already stumbled over a pig's head made of welded scrap metal that was hiding under a sheet of newspaper. The thing must have weighed over a hundred pounds. And then there were the video tapes, many of which had at some point tumbled from their teetering stacks and were underfoot all over the place. In trying to shuffle them aside, Peter noticed that most were actually Betamax, not VHS, and all were of obscure horror and slasher films he had never heard of. He picked up one, *SATURDAY NIGHT SHOCKERS Vol. 4 Mesa of Lost Women*. With an inward shudder, he quickly put it back down. He tried to clear his mind as he took his five tight paces back and forth in the kitchen.

Suddenly, he heard a loud thud from next door, similar to before, but this time without a scream, so Peter decided to ignore it. *Such a quiet couple*, Peter thought, shaking his head.

"You know what I have to do now?" he asked Pippin. Pippin kept sleeping. "The walking isn't helping. Instead, I should write out the anomalies. The things we learned that don't fit or make sense. The key to helping Sam may be tied into those. Maybe, maybe not, but it's all we have right now."

He sat down again, opened the book to a fresh page, and began to write.

> *<u>Anomaly 1</u>: Scraping noise heard from apartment 2 or 6 despite both appearing to be empty, although right now there seems to be somebody in 6.*

Anomaly 2: Maureen is certain she heard loud noises from 6, including a scream, on the night of the murder, but the Other Peter reported that they heard nothing, despite the fact that they are almost as close.

Anomaly 3: Maureen has an imaginary cat that she talks to.

Anomaly 4: Strange marking on the wall near the door to the victim's apartment.

Anomaly 5: Sam has a collection of Star Wars figures with bags over their heads, like Dženan.

Anomaly 6: Dženan's door was apparently latched several different ways from the inside. How did the murderer get in, and out?

This last "anomaly" did not arise from the conversations with the neighbours just now. It was something Sam had told him, but it kept popping into Peter's mind. How could Sam, or anyone, have gotten into that room without breaking the locks? He wondered what theory the police had come up with for that. Surely, someone would have heard the sounds of a door being broken down. The only other way in would be through the window. When they walked around the side of the building looking for Mr. Bingley, Peter had noticed that the window to apartment 4 was intact and closed. He presumed it was latched from the inside. It was a classic locked room mystery, like in Sherlock Holmes. In that case, Arthur Conan Doyle had the murderer use a poisonous snake sent in through a heating duct. Peter thought about Black Hair Man's snake tattoo but quickly dismissed the notion because there was no ductwork in the building. The heat came through hot water radiators. Of course, Sam's solution to this locked room mystery was ghosts. Bolstered, allegedly, by Dženan's stories of being persecuted by malevolent spirits.

"Ghosts!" Peter said loudly, startling Pippin awake. "Do you believe in ghosts?"

Pippin stared at him. This was a very direct question in a tone that usually indicated something important was being communicated, but Pippin didn't recognize the word.

"No, I didn't think so. Although I suppose when you pick up the lingering scent of someone who's died, that's like a ghost for you, right? Because for you it's not 'seeing is believing,' but 'smelling is believing.'" Peter laughed at his joke. Pippin relaxed. Clearly this was Peter rambling on again without expecting anything from him, as he had been doing most of the day. It was kind of exhausting.

Peter picked up the notebook again, the thoughts of ghosts and strangulation having reminded him of something.

> *Anomaly 7: Why was the murder made to look like an auto-erotic asphyxiation?*

Like anomaly 6, this question didn't arise from his recent tour of the neighbours, but it was one that had been bugging him, and this was as good a place as any to write it out. Making a murder look like an accident was a time-honoured technique for sure, but this specific accident struck Peter as bizarre, and perhaps meaningful. If he could come up with a logical theory explaining why someone would choose to make the victim look, what? depraved? foolish? then he would be closer to figuring out who was behind it. And hopefully that wouldn't just lead back to Sam, Peter thought, the image of the suffocated action figures continually popping back into his mind.

He shook his head, flipped to the next blank page, and wrote, "main suspects" at the top. He paused, and then he underlined those words. He paused again, chewed on the pen cap, and then he wrote:

Black Hair Man

Short Pale Girl / Boyfriend (allegedly large & hairy)

Ed

Then he sat back and looked at this list. Normally, he made lists based on careful weighing of the available evidence and a calculation of the probabilities. It was the only sensible way to rank anything like this. But he didn't do that this time. He just wrote the names down without any conscious reasoning. Especially Ed, whom he hadn't thought about much at all. He wondered whether this was what people called instinct or intuition. Whatever it was, it was garbage. Angry at himself, he tore the page out, crumpled it, and shoved it into his pocket, lest someone find it in the apartment later and get the wrong idea.

Peter sighed and looked at his watch. Not even eight o'clock yet. Even by Peter's aggressive early-to-bed-early-to-rise standards, it was far too early to try to go to sleep. Einstein was right, time was definitely relative, and it was moving as if mired in molasses tonight.

Then he decided. He was getting nowhere with his so-called investigations. He needed a walk. A proper walk. Pacing the kitchen was an exceedingly poor substitute. And Pippin would love a walk too.

"Wouldn't you, boy?" he asked, as if Pippin could not only understand his words, but hear his thoughts.

However, this was the precise body language and inflection Pippin had been waiting for. The word "walk" may not have been enunciated, but nonetheless, it was unmistakable that this was the proposed activity. Pippin trotted to the door and looked back at Peter, tongue lolling, eyes bright.

CHAPTER *Fourteen*

Winnipeg's North End had a reputation for being unsafe at night, but Peter wasn't worried. He had studied the statistics before settling on a place for Sam to rent and found that most of the serious crime was between people who knew each other. And even those crimes weren't as common as the sensation-seeking news made them out to be. Also, crime was just as high or higher in some other disadvantaged neighbourhoods. The main negative interaction with strangers was panhandling and low-level harassment. Peter kept his valuables out of sight and maintained an alert, polite demeanour. He also knew that he benefited from being tall. Having a dog along didn't hurt either.

The hallways were empty, and the building was quiet. It would have felt abandoned if it weren't for the faint smell of cooking. Something fried. Chicken, maybe? Peter and Pippin stepped around boxes that had been piled by the front door. Somebody was moving in or out? Probably not. It wasn't near month-end, and nobody was around. It was almost eerie.

It was dark outside already, but Burrows Avenue was well lit. They turned right and headed toward Main Street. The air was cool and autumnal, redolent of fallen leaves and distant smoke. Despite being in the heart of a large city, the North End, and most of inner Winnipeg for that matter, was well treed and had the character of a forest that just happened to have a lot of houses in it, like giant boxy mushrooms sprouting among the trees.

Arriving at Main, Peter looked left and right. He decided to turn left, heading north up the storied street. Main was no longer the true "main" street of Winnipeg — rather just one of a number of large thoroughfares that radiated out from downtown like spokes on a bicycle wheel — but it was one of Peter's favourites. He loved how he could read the city's history in its mix of businesses and restaurants. Once the centre of Eastern European immigrant life, it now bore an ever-stronger Indigenous fingerprint, mixed with evidence that the city drew newcomers from every part of the world. It was not pretty in a tourist-friendly sort of way, but all the more interesting to Peter for that.

The street itself was busy, the four lanes each way thrumming with buses, trucks, taxis, delivery vans, and cars of all descriptions, while the sidewalk was quiet. Peter and Pippin passed a clutch of teenage girls who ignored them while they chattered and looked at their phones. In his opinion, they were underdressed for the brisk weather. A little further along they encountered an elderly man walking toward them, who, conversely, was overdressed in a full parka with the fur-fringed hood pulled up.

The man smiled at Peter, revealing a solitary tooth, and bent down to offer his mittened hand for Pippin to sniff. Pippin did so, tail wagging. The old man cackled, straightened up, and walked on.

After six short blocks, Peter decided to cross Main at Mountain to go into St. John's Park and have a look at the river. During the long wait for the walk light, he pulled out his phone to search the name origin of Mountain Avenue. While there were some very slight hills in Winnipeg, for example in River *Heights*, this was an especially flat bit, so it struck him as an odd name. It turned out it was named for George Jehoshaphat Mountain, the first Anglican Bishop to visit Western Canada. *How dull*, he thought. *They should at least have named it Jehoshaphat Avenue.*

Crossing the street, he admired the beautiful Holy Trinity Ukrainian Orthodox Metropolitan Cathedral, just to the south of the park. With the enormous gleaming mosaic above the front door and the five golden onion domes on top, it was easily the most striking building on this stretch of Main.

St. John's Park was quiet. A few figures lay bundled in sleeping bags on the benches. Dry leaves chased each other down the path as the breeze picked up. It was only 100 metres to the riverbank, so Peter and Pippin were soon there. Pippin was plainly delighted by all the novel urban park smells. Many, many dogs had been walked here and left scent traces behind.

They stood together, watching the wide river flow silently past, like a great gleaming conveyor belt. In daytime the Red River was brown, but at night its smooth surface gathered all the remaining light and shone in quicksilver grey. Peter heard a bicycle rattle by on the path behind them but didn't turn around to look. Pippin sniffed a gopher hole.

Then Peter noticed a glow in the east, above the trees and houses of Elmwood across the river. It hadn't been there before. It grew quickly until the edge of an immense silver coin slid into view.

"The harvest moon!" Peter whispered to Pippin.

The moon rose rapidly, as if pulled upwards by an invisible string. Peter knew he could calculate the actual speed relatively easily, but he allowed himself to just enjoy the view. Beams of moonlight played across the water as the moon climbed ever higher behind the trees on the opposite shore. Moon shadows steadily sharpened in the pearly light. The riverbank and the park were transformed. Everything was perfectly still. Even the breeze stopped, as if holding its breath.

"Dr. Bannerman?"

The deep male voice came from directly behind him.

Peter almost let out a yelp as he whirled around.

Pippin stepped between Peter and the man, his tail and ears low, his stance tense.

The man was in the moon shadow of an enormous elm, but Peter could make out that he was tall and wide. He had no idea who this was, or how they knew who he was.

"Hello? Do I know you?"

The man laughed. "No! Not yet. I'm Josh." He extended his hand. It was one and a half times the size of Peter's, but his grip was soft. He had stepped out of the shadow, so now Peter could see the large brown beard and bright blue eyes.

Big and hairy. This rang a bell.

Peter nodded. "Nice to meet you . . ." He looked at the man quizzically.

The man laughed again. "I'm your brother's neighbour. You met Claire, my girlfriend."

Ah. That's it. "The bear." Bizarre. What is he doing here? And how does he know who I am?

"Oh, OK." He didn't know what else to say. He reached down to pet Pippin, who was beginning to relax. Josh didn't say anything either.

"The moon is stunning, isn't it?" Peter then added.

"Fantabulous," Josh said, grinning. "That's why I came down here. Beautiful Artemis, the huntress, preparing to glide across our autumn sky again."

Peter raised an eyebrow.

"The Greek goddess. Diana to the Romans."

"I know who Artemis and Diana are, but you don't hear that too often!" Peter said, forcing a small laugh to cover his irritation at having something explained to him that he already knew.

Josh shrugged. "MA in Classics. Excellent qualification for sounding pretentious. And for working at Dollarama."

Peter chuckled. Maybe this guy wasn't so bad after all. He thought of a question he should have asked the others.

"Stressful times in the building, eh? Did you know the deceased very well?" Anomalies 6 and 7 hinged on who knew Knezevic and what sort of relationship they had. Although assessing the answer would mean bringing those lie-detection skills to bear again, and Peter was disappointed with how poorly that had worked so far.

"The old Bosnian guy? Just to say hi and stuff in the hallway. Would have liked to have gotten to know him better. Claire and I backpacked through the Balkans a few years ago."

Peter nodded, hoping that his silence would prompt Josh to say more. This was something he had learned from Kevin. Most people feel compelled to prevent lapses in conversation from stretching too long. And that's when they say the most interesting things. In their desperation to fill the void, they'll sometimes say something they weren't planning to reveal.

But that wasn't the case with Josh. He seemed content with the stillness. They both stared at the moon for a couple minutes. It was fully above the horizon now and looked twice as large as it did when it was high up in the sky, but Peter knew that this was an optical illusion created by the comparison to objects on the ground.

"For what it's worth," Josh finally said, still looking at the moon as he spoke. "I don't think your brother did it."

Aha. Something interesting after all.

"Thank you, I appreciate it. Why do you say that?"

Josh shrugged. "Just a feeling, I guess. He just doesn't seem like the type."

He was quiet again for a long moment. Peter waited.

"One time," Josh continued, "all three of us, your brother, the Bosnian dude, and I, happened to be getting our mail at the same time. The two of them were chatting up a storm. Seemed very friendly with each other."

"Did you mention this to the police?" Peter asked, feeling that this might actually be stronger evidence for Sam being the killer than against.

"Yeah. I didn't tell them that I thought he was innocent because I didn't know then that he was a suspect, but they wanted to know about all the interactions the victim might have had with other tenants."

"Any idea what Sam and Knezevic were talking about?" Both of them were still facing the river, watching the play of moonlight on the water. Pippin had gone back to sniffing the gopher hole.

"Funny you should ask, but yeah. The two of them were talking as I came down, and I didn't catch any of that. We said a couple things to each other about the weather, and then when I turned to open my mailbox, they started up again and were quite excited about something called 'X-22.' Your brother talks fast, and the Bosnian has, or had, I should say, quite an accent, so I didn't make much else out. And I wasn't really trying to eavesdrop anyway. But the X-22 thing stuck in my mind, so I Googled it later and it turns out to be a Russian cruise missile. Figured they were a couple of military geeks bonding over missile stats!"

Peter paused, feeling a puzzle piece slide into place. "Backgammon geeks, I think. Not military geeks. X-22 was the nickname of the world's best backgammon player. A guy named Paul Magriel. Kind of the Garry Kasparov or Bobby Fischer of backgammon. Sam used to play semi-competitively."

"Huh. That's cool. Cooler than cruise missiles anyway."

Peter nodded, lost in thought.

"By the way, any luck finding that kitten? Mr. Bonkly?"

"Bingley. Mr. Bingley. No, not yet. But we're ramping up the search. More posters and stuff." Peter was still thinking about X-22, so this came out flat and mechanical.

Josh rubbed his beard. "You might want to double-check with Maureen."

"The pink cat lady in five? I was actually in her place. No cats at all." Peter paused, unsure how much to tell him. "Not even the one she claimed to be talking to."

Josh chuckled. "Yeah, she's a bit of a kook. Which is my point. A crazy person who's crazy about cats . . ."

The implication hung in the air for a long moment while they looked at the moon. Pippin was sniffing a crumpled paper bag.

"We tracked his scent down the back lane until it just disappeared. I assumed he had been picked up in a car. Pippin would have been able to keep following the scent otherwise, even if someone was carrying Mr. Bingley. He's a champion sniffer."

Josh smiled at Pippin and shrugged. "Who's to say Maureen wasn't the person in the car?"

"That would be quite the coincidence, but not impossible. She has a car?"

"Seen that old pink caddie parked up the street? That's hers."

Peter shook his head. "But I'm forgetting the main thing. Pippin didn't pick up any cat scents at all in her apartment. Even if a cat was hidden somehow, he'd smell it."

"Oh, you don't know about the rescue? Maureen runs Miss Pinkerton's Pussy Protection Posse."

"What?"

"Yup. That's what she calls it. You can check it out online. They have a busy Facebook page. She has a network of people she places stray cats with. She doesn't take in any herself because 'Biscuits doesn't like other kitties.'" He used air quotes and made a wry face.

CHAPTER *Fifteen*

Peter and Pippin left Josh at the riverbank, where he said he planned to stay to admire the moon a bit longer. Peter glanced over his shoulder as they walked away, saw the flare of a match in Josh's hand, and then quickly picked up the unmistakable scent of weed, as the breeze had freshened out of the east again.

There's no way that Sam would confuse potheads with meth-heads, would he?

Increasingly, Peter wondered how reliable a witness his brother was. It wasn't entirely clear anymore who, if anyone, the "religious fanatics" or "meth-heads" were, as nobody seemed to fit these descriptions. But Sam lived there and may have seen and heard a lot more to allow him to arrive at those conclusions validly. Still, Peter had doubts.

The walk back was quick and uneventful. They came across the old man in the parka again, but this time he ignored them and walked past, muttering to himself.

The Lady Alice was absolutely quiet. *Too quiet*, Peter thought. It was as if everyone had left or was fast asleep, even though it wasn't even quite nine o'clock. He hadn't spent much time in apartment buildings, so he wondered whether that was normal or not. Somehow, he had expected more ambient noise leaking out of the suites. A too loud television. An argument. Pots being banged around in a kitchen. A phone ringing. Although he supposed the latter was rare now, with most people having gotten rid of their landlines.

The kittens.

Peter suddenly realized why it felt odd for it to be so silent. Shouldn't the kittens be yelling after having been left alone? Sam had said something about an evening snack. Judging by past behaviour, they should be going bonkers for that.

He took the steps two at a time to the second floor and jogged to the door. This time he had the right key on the first try. He swung the door open and stepped inside, Pippin right behind him.

The kittens were asleep on the bed. One of them opened his eyes and stretched. Then the other one.

Then the yelling began.

"Nine too early for bed, boy?"

Pippin had been half-asleep. He perked up at the sound of Peter's voice.

"I should keep looking for clues that could help exonerate Sam, but it's been a long day. A very long day. We've done enough for one day, haven't we?"

Pippin cocked his head and watched Peter.

"No, I'm sorry, boy. I'm not asking you anything interesting." Peter yawned and stretched. "I'm just suggesting that we both go to bed now. You've got a head start on me." He chuckled and reached down to scratch Pippin behind the ear. Then he gently nudged the dog's head back into a sleeping position. Pippin had various sleeping styles. When he was really relaxed, his favourite was to lie flat on his side, legs fully extended. But here he was more on alert in a strange environment, and there wasn't enough open floor space for the full sprawl, so he was curled up, his chin on his paws and his tail in front of his nose, like a fox in the snow.

Pippin relaxed but kept his eyes open while Peter stretched again and shuffled over to the bed. It was a narrow single bed in the corner of the living room with a rumpled Thomas the Tank Engine quilt on it. One of the kittens was sleeping beside the pillow, and he assumed the other was somewhere under the quilt.

Peter sighed. He loved cats, especially his own Merry back in New Selfoss, but he did not love having them in bed with him. He was a light sleeper, and any kind of wriggling or purring could be disruptive. It was a good thing that Laura slept like a stone. There wasn't a choice here, though. The only room with a door was the bathroom. If he locked them in there, they would just start yelling. And who knows what other trouble they could get into. The room was full of painting supplies after all. In fact, now that Peter thought of it, there were containers of linseed oil inside bins, and rags soaked in it. He had a dim recollection of some sort of hazard involving linseed oil and confined spaces. He should look that up. But his sleepiness had transformed into exhaustion. The sight and thought of the bed had an analogous effect on him as a waterfall has on someone with a full bladder. A vague want suddenly became a desperate need as he slid beneath the covers.

Flinders and Barry may or may not have purred and tried to cuddle. Peter had no idea. He was asleep with the suddenness of a dead weight hitting the floor.

It was dark when he woke up. Absolute coalmine black. He couldn't remember where he was. There were no sounds to give a clue either. Silence wrapped him tightly like a thick shawl.

Then he heard something.

A light thud, like a book being carelessly tossed onto a desk.

It was directly beneath him. He was sure of it. It couldn't be somehow from the kittens getting under his bed. No, the sound came from further down, from the apartment below.

The murdered man's apartment.

He tapped on the face of his watch to light up the time: 11:35.

His first thought was that it wouldn't be the police back in there, investigating, at that hour. His second thought was that it could only be one person. It had to be the murderer. Who else would be interested in poking around Knezevic's place? Then, in his mind's ear, he heard Sam's voice telling him that ghosts would be interested, that's who else.

Peter sat up in bed and listened intently.

It was so quiet that he could hear the faint tick of the Kit-Cat Klock in the kitchen. He could picture the eyes rolling back and forth, in rhythm with the swinging tail. He forced himself to ignore the clock and focus on any other sounds.

Nothing. Tick, tick, tick.

Then, when he was about to give up listening, there was another sound from below. A scrape this time. A wood-on-wood kind of scrape. Like a chair being moved on hardwood floor.

This was good. The presence of somebody at the murder scene was another piece of evidence that Sam was innocent. But how could he record that evidence or prove to the police that this was happening? Should he call them? He dismissed that idea right away. They'd take far too long for a non-urgent call like this.

Pippin was awake in the meantime. Peter hadn't turned any lights on, but he could hear the dog quietly panting beside him.

"Hey buddy. You up too?" he whispered. "What do you think? Should we go down there? Casual, like we're on a late-night walk? See if the door is open or something, or if there's some clue that someone's in there? At a minimum, whatever sounds they make will be clearer through the door. I can record that."

Pant pant.

"But we're not going into the actual apartment. Don't worry. I doubt they're armed, but confrontation can lead to emotional reactions, and emotions make people unpredictable."

There was a shuffling sound on the floor beside the bed, and then Peter felt the press of a wet nose against his hand.

"Besides, Laura would freak out if she found out I had deliberately approached a suspected murderer!"

Peter realized that if they were going to do this, they had better head down to take a peek and have a listen before whoever was in there left and covered up any evidence of entry.

But the room was pitch black, so the first step was light. Was there a bedside lamp? Peter couldn't recall. His phone was on the floor beside him. To the right.

No, that's a wall. To the left then, near Pippin.

His phone was dead. He had forgotten to charge it. That was so unlike him. He never forgot things like that. But it had been an extraordinary day.

Cursing, he considered whether it still made sense to have a look downstairs if he couldn't take any photographs or record anything. It couldn't hurt to gather more data, though, even if he couldn't pair it with solid evidence. Given his past help with criminal cases, the police would consider him a reliable witness despite his connection to their suspect, so him reporting what he saw or heard would still be helpful.

OK, but he still needed light first.

Peter turned around and aimed his watch at the shelf he remembered being above the head of the bed. What had been up there? He couldn't recall. Maybe there was a lamp?

The glow from the watch face was exceedingly dim, but it was just enough to allow him to make out the shapes of a jumble of objects on the shelf. Then he spotted it — better than a lamp, one of those emergency flashlights! What were the odds? But he supposed it made sense. Sam tended toward paranoia.

With the help of the flashlight, he found the main light switch and then dressed as quickly and quietly as he could. Clearly, sound travelled very well through these floors. He didn't want to spook the person down there.

Handling the door like it was made of finest porcelain, he stepped out into the hall, Pippin at his heels. He walked gingerly to the stairs, almost tiptoeing. The hall light was dim and flickering, but the full moon shone directly through the windows over the stairwell, adding a watery grey glow.

Once they reached the bottom of the stairs, Peter stopped and considered his options.

Approaching the door and looking for more clues would be quick and easy to do. And if the person happened to step out that minute, he'd know who the murderer was! Presto! Case closed. Aside from convincing the police. Moreover, there would be no confrontation because he would have an innocent explanation for being at the far end of the hall from the front door. He could say Pippin spotted a mouse. This place had to have mice, didn't it?

It was a brilliant plan.

The air in the hallways felt somehow heavier and denser late at night. It was a presence that unsettled Peter. There was also a faint smell of mould and maybe something metallic.

But Peter didn't stop to try to figure this out, and they were at the door in a few quiet steps.

The police tape was still in place, and the door was closed. Of course it was. What kind of brain-damaged intruder would leave the door open behind them? Nothing else was visible. It would take even more brain damage for someone to leave their shoes or some other telltale sign in the hall. Peter's own brain hadn't been firing on all cylinders after being awakened in the middle of the night.

The police tape was easy to duck under. Peter leaned in, self-conscious of his breathing, and listened intently at the door. Nothing.

He waited, continuing to strain his hearing, for as long as he dared. Still nothing.

He looked at the doorknob. Would the intruder have thought to lock the door behind them? Probably, but not certainly. If it wasn't locked, that was excellent proof of someone being in there who shouldn't be. And if it was locked, it didn't mean much either way.

He could think of no way to tell without trying it.

Could he reach under the police tape and turn the knob silently, just to test it, without the person inside noticing?

Probably. Maybe.

Then something occurred to him. A flaw in this plan. If the murderer did happen to leave the apartment while Peter was there, it didn't matter that Peter had an excuse for being on the other side of the door, it mattered that the murderer didn't have an excuse for being in a sealed apartment.

They would know that he now knew. And then what?

They'd likely scramble for an excuse. Or an emotional fight, flight, or freeze response would kick in. Flight or freeze would be OK, but fight, not so much.

OK, he'd very quickly test the doorknob and then they'd leave.

As he reached for the knob, Peter heard a sound from the other side of the door.

It was like a heavy sigh. It was right there. Inches away.

Peter ran. Pippin was right behind him.

Maybe the sighing intruder heard them. Maybe not. Peter didn't hear the door open as they bolted up the stairs, but then he was not sure that he would have. His ears were filled with the sound of his blood pounding.

Later Peter would muse about the irony of considering the intruder's potential fight, flight, or freeze response, when it ended up being his own that was triggered.

Back in Sam's apartment with the door locked and double-checked behind him, Peter tried to slow down his breathing.

Deep breath in. Deep breath out. Deep breath innn . . . Deep breath ouuut . . .

That had been irrational. Leaving was a good idea, but running was not. It wasn't necessary, and it could have added to any potential danger by making someone emerging from Dženan's apartment immediately suspicious of what Peter had been up to. It would have been much better to just casually turn around and saunter up the hall, not even looking if and when the door opened. If the emerging intruder was somebody from one of the other apartments on the downstairs hall, he'd know by hearing which door opened next, left or right, near or far. And if it was somebody from upstairs, he'd see them as he turned at the landing. Then it would just be a casual encounter between neighbours returning home. Nothing to see here. Nothing going on.

Running had been stupid. But Peter knew he couldn't expect to make optimal decisions a hundred percent of the time. The past had amply demonstrated that. But he still beat the average in the population. He was sure of that. And it hadn't really been a *decision* anyway. It had been a reflex.

It was funny to view this hoarding catastrophe as a welcoming home, but that's what it felt like now. Familiar chaos was more comforting right now than anything unfamiliar.

Now, it was time to try to sleep again. He assumed that the adrenaline would interfere, regardless of the unmitigated exhaustion of the day, but no sooner did he have that thought than he was fast asleep.

CHAPTER
Sixteen

Again, he was awakened by a sound in the dark.

This time it was even more disorienting because he had been dreaming about playing fetch with Pippin and Lucas, that golden retriever they had met in the forest. But in the dream, he knew he had to be somewhere else, and he was really late, so he felt anxious.

It was a soft rattle. And then maybe a footstep.

What? Where?

Then he remembered. Sam's place. Of course. And then the memory of recent events came back too.

Sounds from downstairs again?

No, these were nearer. And not below him.

He fumbled to tap his watch face to wake it up: 12:37.

Then there was a sharp click. It came from the same direction as the other sounds. But he was so befuddled, he didn't know what that direction was. Somewhere beyond his feet.

Pippin stirred.

He remembered that the watch had a flashlight function of sorts where the whole face would glow white. He pressed some buttons and found the feature. It lit up to reveal nothing more than the face of Percy, the green engine from the children's *Thomas & Friends* television program, on his quilt.

"Who's there?" Peter said loudly, voice thick with sleep. "Anyone there? Sam?" Maybe he'd been let out of remand.

Pippin growled. Pippin hardly ever growled. Something was wrong. Somebody was in the apartment.

Peter got up on his knees and grabbed the flashlight, which he had placed back on the shelf above the bed. He turned around and swept the beam in a rapid arc across the room.

Nobody.

But Pippin was staring hard at the door. Peter pointed the flashlight back that way and climbed out of bed. He took a couple of steps toward the door.

Pippin went ahead of him and sniffed the door jamb. He growled again.

This made no sense. At least not to his just-wakened brain.

Had someone opened the door?

But it was locked. He was sure of it.

Peter checked the deadbolt. It was indeed locked. He hadn't put the security chain on, though. He quickly did that now.

He turned on every light switch he could find and sat down in the armchair.

The sudden abundance of harsh light and the chaotic, mutant thrift store scene it revealed did little to calm him down. The only thing that stopped him from believing that someone was hiding amongst the piles of junk was that they couldn't do that without setting off an avalanche.

He checked his phone. Still dead, of course. He didn't have a charging cable with him. Sam probably had one somewhere. Somewhere. There was no landline evident either, but that was fine. This did not merit an emergency call. It was just silly. In a pinch he could charge it in the truck and make calls from there.

His truck. It was hard to believe that his New Selfoss Veterinary Services truck was out there on the street, just a few dozen steps away, representing a normal, perfectly sane world that right now felt like it could only exist on an entirely different planet.

Then, another sound.

A soft thump.

It came from near the bathroom door, to Peter's right. He whirled around and looked.

Nothing.

Peter tried to quell the rising panic. *Hadn't Sam said something about a katana? A Japanese samurai sword? Where would he keep that?* Normally that would be a ridiculous question in this environment, but Peter figured that Sam would want it handy for emergencies, but not obviously visible either.

Under the bed!

He crouch-ran the few steps from the armchair to the bed and fished underneath it.

Bingo!

He stood up and held the sword out in front of him, like Luke Skywalker with his lightsaber. Where was Obi-Wan when you needed him?

He felt simultaneously ridiculous and terrified.

Then there was another soft thump. This one a little closer.

And another.

But he still couldn't see anything.

He gripped the sword tighter.

Someone or something was approaching. But who or what? He couldn't see anything.

Silence now.

He scanned the room frantically. Still nothing. Why couldn't he see who or what was making those sounds?

Peter felt like his heart was going to pop out from between his ribs.

"Who's there?" This time his voice came out in a croak.

He glanced at Pippin. He was looking up at Peter but seemed otherwise relaxed.

Then he heard it. A delicate soft rumble at first, and then more distinctly a purr.

It was the kittens.

Of course it was the kittens. They had jumped down from wherever they had been napping — thump, thump — and then walked silently up to him out of sight under the junk.

It's amazing what high stress, disrupted sleep, and an unfamiliar environment and circumstances can do to your perception of reality, he thought.

Peter took ten slow deep breaths with his eyes closed. This was the best way to stimulate his parasympathetic nervous system and calm himself down so that he could try to think clearly. He felt the tension gradually ebbing and his heart slowing. That was much better. He lowered the sword and opened his eyes, still half expecting to spot someone hiding deep in the junk somewhere. But everything was the same.

Pippin had gone back to sniffing around the door. The kittens explained the thumps, but not that rattle and click earlier.

"Yeah, I think so too," Peter said, addressing Pippin. "It wasn't Bosnian ghosts. It wasn't the kittens. Someone must have opened the door. But they didn't come in because they must have noticed we were here. They're just lucky we were both fast asleep. Pretty bold risk to take. Someone in the building must be able to pick locks. Or they have a master key."

Peter set the sword down, slumped back into the chair, and absent-mindedly fiddled with one of the brass rivets on its arms.

He considered that this wasn't actually a bad development, aside from the ridiculous panic over innocent kittens. In fact, it was a gift. It proved again that someone other than Sam was involved in Knezevic's murder. Unless the police considered this attempted break-in of Sam's apartment to be an unrelated coincidence. Which was a ridiculous notion.

"OK, Pippin, this is good. The murderer just made another serious mistake. Put the security chain on, and I'll push this chair against the door, and then we'll find a charging cable for my phone and try to get a bit more sleep before morning. I'll call the police then. Maybe they can dust the door for prints, as well as all around the apartment downstairs."

Peter was considering how to manoeuvre the large chair through the narrow path between the piles of stuff when he heard another click. This was a different click than before. He was sure the previous one had been the door closing. This was softer.

Then a man's voice suddenly filled the room.

"Knezevic was a pig who deserved to die. You are also a pig. You also deserve to die."

He couldn't tell where the voice was coming from. It seemed to be coming from everywhere at once.

Then the lights went out.

He grabbed Pippin and bolted from the apartment as fast as he could.

The corridor was dark as well. Maybe the whole building had suddenly lost power. Peter didn't care. They were leaving. It may have been irrational, and Peter hated irrationality, especially in himself, but he wasn't a machine. He was just as subject to an acute sympathetic nervous system response to a threat as any creature. Fight was not an option, and between flight and freeze, flight was what his instinct had chosen. He wasn't going to question his instinct at that specific moment. There would be plenty of time for analysis later.

The moon was still shining through the stairwell window at the front of the building, so Peter was able to fly down the stairs without killing himself. Pippin had no trouble regardless. He seemed delighted by the sudden burst of activity.

When they got to the front door, Peter saw someone silhouetted on the other side. The light of the streetlamp was directly behind them.

Oh shit. What now?

The silhouette waved and turned slightly to reach for the door handle. Now Peter could make out its profile.

Laura.

CHAPTER
Seventeen

Peter flung the door open.

"What are you . . . !"

"You look like . . . !"

Their words tumbled and ran into each other like mountain streams surging together. They stopped and embraced. Pippin circled them, wagging his tail furiously.

Peter motioned that they should walk away from the building. Once they were on the sidewalk, Laura explained that she had become worried because Peter hadn't texted goodnight like he always did when he was away. Moreover, he hadn't responded to any of her texts, or her subsequent emails and phone calls. It just seemed so very weird, so uncharacteristic. Peter was the most predictable and reliable person she knew. She couldn't sleep anyway, so she thought she'd may as well drive into the city and have a look. However, she had forgotten that the building didn't have a buzzer system. She had been outside a little while already, hoping someone would be coming home late from a Saturday night out and let her in.

Peter nodded, knowing how persuasive Laura could be with strangers. He then told her about the loud, threatening voice, preceded by the door possibly having been opened briefly. He also told her about the noises from the apartment below.

Laura pursed her lips and shook her head slowly. "No little Bluetooth speaker by the door?"

"I don't know. I should have looked, but I wasn't thinking straight. I just ran."

"That makes sense. But nothing else does."

"No, nothing else does. And I won't have a chance of making sense of it until the adrenaline starts to leave my system."

"OK, let's go sit in the car for a bit before doing anything else," Laura said. "You look and sound like hell."

"Good idea. The half-life of adrenaline is usually only about three minutes, but I got a potent dose, so the effects may last longer than the half-life suggests. But not that much more."

Laura laughed. "Now that's the Peter Bannerman that I know and love." She gave his shoulder a gentle squeeze and led the way to where she had parked near Main Street.

"Power's on everywhere else on the street," Laura observed once they had settled into the car. Pippin was on the back seat, chewing on a toy Laura kept there for him.

"Somebody must have thrown the main breaker in the apartment block," Peter said. His voice was steadier now, but it was quiet.

"Same someone who tried to enter the apartment and somehow projected that voice to scare you?"

"Safe to assume," Peter said. "But why? Why scare *me*? Because I asked some softball questions? Isn't that just going to draw suspicion away from Sam and make it more likely the real killer will be found?"

Laura was quiet for moment and then reached over to rest her hand on Peter's leg. "Now don't get mad, but I'm going to play devil's advocate here for a moment."

"OK . . ." Peter replied, uncertain where this was leading.

"Isn't it possible that Sam planted speakers to say that scary stuff at some random interval? It's his place after all. It would be a way to deflect suspicion. A weird way, mind you. And a weirdly complicated way. But a way. And isn't it possible you imagined the sounds by the door, or that they meant something else?"

Peter shook his head. "I appreciate the critical thinking. It's good to test a theory against challenges. But no. Pippin clearly reacted as if someone was at or near the door. He's never wrong."

"Agreed. He's a clever and talented boy. But as you said, at or *near* the door. The hallway's not wide. What if the neighbour across the way was having trouble with his keys and made some noises? And Pippin would have also picked up on your anxiety."

"Hmm. I doubt it."

Laura patted his leg and smiled at him. "I'm not saying that's what happened. I'm saying it's a plausible theory that the police will almost certainly consider."

"And what about the lights? They're back on, by the way." Peter gestured through the windshield at the Lady Alice. One bulb was now glowing feebly under the tattered entryway awning, in addition to dim light from behind the curtains on the bottom right.

"Decent point. But coincidence is possible. It doesn't look like maintenance is a high priority. Maybe the electrical is wonky."

"Maybe. But that particular coincidence seems like a stretch. Probability-wise."

"Of course, probability-wise." Laura grinned. "But not zero probability."

"And what about the person moving around in the dead guy's apartment earlier in the night? That bolsters the case that there is someone in the building still who is involved in the crime. Logically, it would be the same person who tried to enter Sam's apartment."

Laura nodded. "For sure. But just to play devil's advocate again, the police will probably also consider the fact that it is difficult to localize sounds in a building, so you might have been hearing those 'downstairs apartment' sounds from elsewhere, especially as they were relatively quiet and indistinct. Do you see?"

"Yeah, I suppose. But I'm sure they were from directly below."

Laura put her hand on his arm. "I believe you. One hundred percent. But they're also going to consider how stressed you've been, the disrupted sleep, and the fact that you are motivated to clear your brother . . ."

They were quiet for a long moment, Peter looking at his lap, Laura looking at him.

Then Peter glanced up. He squinted, peering across the street. "By the way, it looks like Ed's back."

"Ed?" Laura asked.

"Room 2." Peter pointed at the one suite with visible light. "Ed's Sam's friend who was out of town but was supposed to come back tomorrow — sorry, today now. Sam said he could look after the kittens once he got home. Maybe we're in luck. Because otherwise we'll have to take the kittens back to the clinic."

"You're sure he didn't just leave a light on when he left?"

"I suppose . . . I guess I'm not one hundred percent sure. But I've got to go back inside anyway to get the kittens, so I can knock on his door and see. It's late, but it looks like he's up, if he's home."

"Unless he just leaves the light on all the time, even when he's sleeping. Some people do that. Accidentally or on purpose. I'm coming with. You'll need help carrying the kittens, and if you end up waking up Ed and pissing him off, you'll need my smile." She smiled her biggest, toothiest smile and flicked her red hair in a way that was supposed to look winsome but ended up looking silly. They both laughed.

"Knock softly," Laura said.

Peter nodded and rapped lightly on the door to apartment 2, feeling both silly and nervous as he did so.

No response. They waited. Laura glanced at Peter. He wondered about knocking again. Then the door suddenly opened.

"Yes?" the man said, looking back and forth from Peter to Laura with narrowed eyes. He was short and thin with a pointy white goatee, unruly white hair, and small round glasses. He was wearing a bright green vest over a loose white dress shirt. The overall impression was that of a latter-day leprechaun down on his luck.

Peter was about to introduce himself and Laura when the man suddenly broke into a big smile. "Hang on, I know who you are! You're Sam's brother, Peter! The vet."

"I am, yes. And this is my wife, Laura. Do I look that much like Sam?"

"A little, but I mostly recognize you because I looked you up online before. But come on in, please! I think I know why you're here."

He swung the door open wider and gestured into his apartment. "I'm Ed, by the way." He thrust out his hand. "Ed MacDougall."

Ed's living room was dominated by several large aquaria lining two walls. That was the odd smell from the time he knocked and nobody was home! Another wall displayed a large banner with a blue circle, in the middle of a maroon background, containing the gold letters *VP* and a gold crown above them. He didn't appear to have a couch. He invited them to sit around a big square table in the centre of the room. Elements of a board game Peter didn't recognize were scattered across it. It featured a map of the world.

Ed smiled. "Yup, fish and games and the PPCLI. That's me!"

It took Peter a fraction of a second. "Princess Patricia's Canadian Light Infantry?"

"You bet. Twenty-one years reg force."

"Cool. Nice fish tanks too. What game is this?" Peter asked.

"Twilight Struggle. It's a two-player campaign game covering the Cold War. Very cool."

"And what kind of fish?" Peter asked. Sam had mentioned something about the fish, but he couldn't recall.

"Loaches. Five kinds. Kuhli, Clown, Yo Yo, Zebra, and Dojo. I breed the Kuhlis."

"That's interesting," was all Peter could think to say. He didn't know much about aquarium fish, and he knew even less about loaches specifically. He hated demonstrating ignorance.

Laura was examining some of the Twilight Struggle cards. "This does look cool. We'll have to get a copy, eh Peter?"

Peter nodded.

"But it's late and we don't want to keep you, Ed," Laura went on. "As you've probably guessed, we're here about Sam and the kittens. We saw your light on and took a chance that you came back from Gimli early and were still up."

"I did! As soon as I heard about Sam, I made arrangements to come back."

"How did you hear?" Peter interrupted.

"Oh, from Ted. Ha ha. Ed and Ted. He's the Filipino kid across the hall."

"The drummer?"

"Yeah. You've met him? Don't let appearances fool you. He's a good kid. Smart too. Anyway, we get along, and he thought I'd want to know about your brother. So, I got a ride back a couple hours ago, knowing that he wanted me to look after the kittens. I was relieved when I saw your New Selfoss Veterinary Services truck parked out front. I would have popped up to introduce myself and offer to take over cat-sitting duties, but it was late. Figured you were sleeping."

"I was until the —" Peter stopped himself. "Until the power failure. I mean, I woke up to go to the bathroom and the power was out . . ." Peter realized that it would be hard to explain why he was out of the suite in the middle of the night and how Laura ended up there. He hoped that Ed wouldn't notice or care.

"Yeah, I thought we should maybe take the kittens home in case the power stayed off for a long time. In an old building, you never know," Laura said. "And honestly, I'm guessing you know what Sam's place is like. Once I had an excuse not to spend the whole night there, I took it! Then we saw your lights on."

Ed nodded. "Makes sense. Where are those frisky little critters now?"

"Still in the apartment. We went down to the truck first to get . . . some stuff," Peter said. "By the way . . . I don't know whether you heard, but Mr. Bingley is missing."

"Oh no! Mr. Bingley's my favourite! Any ideas where he is?"

Peter explained how the search had gone so far.

"Well, at the first light of dawn, I'll take up the hunt too. Now, let's go get Barry and Flinders!"

As they were leaving, Peter glanced back at the game on the table. "Did you play Twilight Struggle with Sam?"

"No, he doesn't have the patience for this kind of game. It takes most of the day to play. He and I play backgammon, though. Dženan too. The three of us had a little Lady Alice backgammon club going." Ed chuckled. "That's how we met. I saw Dženan carrying an issue of *PrimeTime Backgammon* magazine, so I asked him about it. I never played it much, but I found I had a knack. He and your brother already had a regular game going, so that's how I met Sam. A friendly three-way rivalry!" He chuckled again.

Peter didn't reply to this. His train of thought had moved on from Cold War games, to the end of the Cold War, to the collapse of Yugoslavia, to the Bosnian War, to the PPCLI's deployment there.

CHAPTER

Eighteen

As is common for many people, most of Peter's dreams had no easily discernible meaning.

For example, black parrots the size of Labradors brought to the clinic for surgery.

Or, the layout of their house slowly morphing with that of his childhood home and the mixture of excitement and dread at maybe running into his parents, who had been dead for years.

Or, going with Laura on vacation to a cottage in Whiteshell Provincial Park but ending up in London instead, where they watched a private performance of a famous play that Peter could no longer remember the name of when he woke up.

But that night, his dreams had an obvious connection to his thoughts before falling asleep. He dreamt he was sorting a pile of Lego bricks into eight boxes. Then he dumped them out and sorted them again. He did this several times until he was satisfied. Then he stacked the boxes so that there were two layers of two by two. After he woke up, he lay quietly in bed for a long moment trying to recall which Lego ended up in which box, but the only one he could retrieve from the mists for his conscious mind to examine was the box in the bottom back right corner. He had filled it to the brim with red bricks.

"I figured this might be more of an espresso morning than an Earl Grey morning," Laura said, after giving Peter a good-morning peck on the cheek. She pointed to the freshly ground beans and espresso machine, ready to go.

"Thank you." Peter knew that most people would say something more effusive like, "you're amazing" or "what would I do without you," but that would probably worry Laura more than please her. Peter reserved his effusive remarks for elegant solutions to math and science problems. Laura had long experience of this and didn't expect anything different. Or even, at this point, want it.

"Sleep OK?" she asked.

"OK enough. Had a weird dream about putting Lego in boxes that I think might tie into my thoughts about the situation at the Lady Alice."

"Coffee first, thoughts after," Laura said.

Peter made his espresso while Laura fed Merry, their tortoiseshell cat, who had been winding around her legs. Pippin must have been as tired as Peter was. He was sound asleep in the far corner of the kitchen, flat on his side, legs stretched straight out. He almost always woke up when Peter got up, but not today. Peter sat on a stool with his coffee and smiled at Pippin. Laura had gone into the living room. She called out, "Gorgeous day!"

It certainly looked that way. The low morning sun lit the aspens and made the dewdrops on the grass sparkle.

"Don't forget that it's the last Sunday of the month," she added.

Right. Last Sunday of the month. He and Dwayne Lautermilch had a standing arrangement to meet once a month to go out with their metal detectors. This began at the time of the incident with the ostriches last spring. Prior to that, he hadn't seen Dwayne in decades, not since high school when he was part of a pack of bullies who tormented Peter. That he had come back into his life and then somehow became a friend continued to astonish Peter. It made no sense. But over the years, he had gradually come to understand that not everything that was good in life needed to make sense from a rational, analytical perspective. Laura was always good at gently opening his eyes to that truth.

Peter glanced at his watch. "Thanks for the reminder. I would have forgotten. We're meeting in front of The Flying Beaver at nine, so I still have quite a bit of time."

He finished his espresso and decided to throw caution to the wind and make a second one. He already felt a lot more alert, and the peak caffeine effect wouldn't even be for another half hour, so normally it would make sense to wait and decide at that point if he needed more. But he had enjoyed this cup so much and, objectively, two espressos were not an excessive amount of caffeine for the morning.

Laura came back into the kitchen. She smiled when she saw Peter making his second cup.

"Feeling better?"

"Yes. Yesterday feels like a fever dream now. I can't believe any of it. The murder. Sam's arrest. What happened during the night . . ." Peter wanted to say more, but he paused while waiting for the machine to finish the crema. It was always loudest then. He took a quick sip. "But what really stumps me right now is the fact that we couldn't find a speaker when we went up to get the kittens for Ed."

Laura sat down on a stool opposite him. "Yes, strange, but not that strange. For starters, we were in a hurry. Given the state of the place, it would take days to make absolutely sure. And have you seen how tiny some of these Bluetooth speakers are?" She held up her left hand. "Like the size of my thumb."

"True."

"And secondly, if someone was able to sneak in while you were sleeping to place it, they could just as easily sneak in again while we were out and collect it."

Peter nodded. She was right, of course. "Good points. But you also suggested last night that it could have been set up by Sam himself, in which case I suppose your first point is especially valid, as he could have taken the time to hide it god knows where. Of course, I disagree that Sam would do that, but the logic is sound otherwise. I like your second point, though. It doesn't involve Sam, and it makes some sense."

"But none of it answers the question why," Laura said. "Why bother scaring you? You said yesterday that you spoke to the other residents. Do you want to go through those conversations? Maybe we can figure out if there was something you said that might have been alarming to a possible perpetrator?"

Peter smiled. The fact that he was so powerfully drawn to these sorts of amateur investigations had always worried Laura, but she had gradually shifted from trying to stop him to accepting that he was going to do it anyway. She would have just as much luck getting Pippin to stop sniffing everything new in his environment or getting Merry to stop seeking sunbeams. It was simply in their nature. But in that acceptance, Laura had decided to adopt a "harm reduction" approach, meaning that if she could do anything to make his curiosity safer and more productive, then she would. Peter suspected that this was also part of a strategy to minimize the risks of irritating Kevin, her brother. He could tell that Laura tried to subtly channel his energies in directions that would be the least likely to interfere with police work.

"That would be great, thanks," Peter said. He looked at his watch again. "I still have plenty of time. If you've got the time too, I'd love to go through not just the conversations with you, but the whole day, right from when I first arrived at the Lady Alice. I've told you bits and pieces, but maybe you can see something I'm not seeing when you get the full picture."

"Of course! Just let me get a fresh mug of tea and a banana, and I'm all ears."

It took the better part of an hour for Peter to describe everything, from the search for Mr. Bingley, to Sam being taken for questioning, to his arrest, to Peter's visit with him at the remand centre, to his conversations with the other residents of the building, to finding the *Star Wars* figurines, to the walk to the river and meeting Josh there, and, finally, to the events of the night. Laura listened with full attention, leaning forward, asking questions for clarification from time to time, jotting notes on the message pad they kept on the kitchen island.

"Wow," Laura said when he was done. "That's . . . a lot. You know how New Selfoss is 'Canada's Quirkiest Town' according to *Maclean's* magazine? The Lady Alice must be 'Winnipeg's Quirkiest Apartment Block.' What a bunch of characters in there!"

They both laughed. "From what Sam's told me, the places he stayed in Toronto make the Alice look like Dullsville."

"Fair enough. But seriously, if Sam is innocent, and I agree, he almost certainly is —"

"*Almost* certainly?"

Laura pulled her face into a mock frown. "Who are you, and what have you done with my husband? The Dr. Peter Bannerman I know and love would never profess certainty in the absence of irrefutable hard data."

"OK, OK, you're right!" Peter laughed. "I'm letting feelings get in the way of logic. But go on."

"So, if he's innocent, then the murderer is *almost* certainly" — she paused to wink at Peter — "one of the other residents. But none of them stands out as being likely, or, for that matter, especially unlikely."

"Agreed. I made a list of my top three suspects, but then I tore it up because it was not based on data."

"But the key to clearing Sam is finding data that could be shared with the police to point them toward someone else."

"Exactly. The circumstantial evidence against Sam is strong, but it probably wouldn't hold up in court. The problem is that the whole process up until then is going to drastically set his mental health back." Peter paused and played with his empty espresso cup for a moment. "It might even kill him," he added quietly.

"Let's not get ahead of ourselves." Laura reached out to hold Peter's hand. "One step at a time. Let's see what we have so far. How about . . . Shoot! Don't you have to go? It's five to nine!"

"Yikes! Thanks! I'll leave right now. But what were you going to ask?"

"That symbol with the *U*. You said you sketched it?"

"I did. It's in that Hilroy notebook by my bedside."

"Let me see what I can figure out. For sure it could be a coincidence that it was drawn near the victim's door, especially given that that's also right across from Ted the drummer's apartment, but then again, maybe not. Have fun with Dwayne! Say hi from me."

Right then, Pippin finally woke up. The fur on the side of his face was smooshed. Canine bedhead. He scrambled to his feet, took a wobbly step forward, and then looked back and forth between Laura and Peter, his facial expression seeming to ask, "What's up, guys? What'd I miss?"

CHAPTER *Nineteen*

Peter arrived at The Flying Beaver at 9:02. He hated being late, even by two minutes. But he knew that Dwayne wouldn't care. Sometimes Dwayne was early. Sometimes he was late. Sometimes he was right on time. No matter when he arrived, he never seemed flustered in the slightest. He was one of the most relaxed people Peter had ever met. Completely the opposite of what he had been in high school. Peter couldn't help but wonder, figurative tongue in cheek, whether perhaps Dwayne had had a teensy tiny lobotomy while he was in prison.

This time, Dwayne had been on time or early. He was standing outside the pub with his metal detector, waving at Peter as he pulled up. Not for the first time, Peter considered how much his friend looked like a sasquatch that had been shaved down, leaving only a shaggy mullet on top. Same bulk. Same stooped shoulders. Same dangly, long arms. Same goofy vibe. He even walked like a sasquatch in an easy, ambling lope.

New Selfoss had slim pickings for detectorists, at least compared to the metal detecting nirvana of England, where Peter's cousin David pursued the hobby. David had even found part of an Anglo-Saxon era sword once. It was thought to have been lost during the Battle of Hatfield Chase, in 633, between the Northumbrians and Mercians.

Peter was thrilled to no end when David told him this. But New Selfoss, and Canada in general, offered little that was both very old and had the types of metals these devices were designed to find. So instead, they contented themselves with more recent history.

In particular, Paavo Jarvinen's story captivated Peter and Dwayne. According to local legend, the Finnish-Canadian lumber baron, and New Selfoss's first millionaire, hid a large amount of gold when he lost his mind and tried to canoe home to Finland in 1915. His departure from New Selfoss was an established fact, as was, to nobody's surprise, his failure to arrive in Finland, or anywhere else for that matter. But the gold was a matter of speculation, most of it quite wild. The Icelandic Canadians, who made up the majority of the town's population, were mostly of the opinion that Jarvinen was a braggart who had spent his entire fortune on building the mansion, which still dominated New Selfoss and that he left more or less penniless. Others weren't so sure. There were tantalizing newspaper photographs from his departure that showed two wooden trunks in his canoe, one partly opened, revealing what appeared to be mounds of coins. The reportage was appropriately breathless. The Klondike Gold Rush had only wrapped up 15 years prior. Gold fever was not difficult to stoke.

Peter counted himself in a third camp, reasoning that yes, Jarvinen did take a lot of gold with him, but no, it was likely to be unfindable as he was known to have been a good canoeist and surely got pretty far north into the bush before suffering whatever terminal misfortune stopped him from reaching Finland. The gold and Jarvinen's bones were probably at the bottom of one of the numberless, often nameless, lakes of Northern Manitoba. Peter sometimes wondered whether he should bring his detector with him next time he went up to Dragonfly Lake. Needle in a haystack, went the cliché, but even an actual needle in an actual haystack would be easier to locate with his Fisher F22.

But Dwayne was keen and optimistic, and Peter found that, in spite of himself, he enjoyed these outings. And occasionally they turned up a cool old implement of some sort, or a coin old enough to be mildly interesting. Once they even found Alice Richter's engagement ring, which she had lost on a mountain bike ride. It was distinctive because of the skull pattern etched in the band. She was immensely grateful. Over their protests, Alice gave them each a gift certificate for her shop, Krafts 'n' Things, on Linnaeus Street. Neither of them had used his yet. Not so much because she ran a BDSM dungeon in the basement of the store — thus resolving the question of what the "Things" were — but more because neither were interested in crafts.

"Head out to the end of Galileo and work our way along the edge of the bog there?" Dwayne asked.

"Yeah, that makes sense. If we had more time, I'd say we should drive across the Yellowgrass First Nation and check out the east shore of Little Otter Lake, but that's a whole day's expedition."

"Maybe if there's no snow by the end of October?" Dwayne suggested as he adjusted the shoulder strap of his detector.

"Sure, let's plan for that. But bog today sounds good. Maybe we can get an early lunch at the Beaver after. I think it still opens at 11 today?"

Dwayne was standing closer to the door. He leaned in and peered at the sign. "Yes. Sundays, eleven to ten, until Thanksgiving."

Peter checked that he had locked the truck and adjusted his gear. He was just about to say "OK, let's go," when his phone buzzed. He was inclined to ignore it as he wasn't on call this weekend, but he realized it might be Laura with a question about the case.

It was Sam.

Peter stifled a groan. He really craved a break from the situation, but he was planning on talking to him soon anyway. Eat the frog.

"Good morning, Sam. How was your night?"

"Where the hell are you?" Sam was shouting into the phone at his end.

"Um, out with Dwayne. About to go metal detecting."

"What?" Sam screamed. "It's ten after nine! You were supposed to be here at nine!"

"Be where? At the remand? To visit you? I didn't say that. We didn't discuss the next —"

Sam cut him off. "The hell we didn't! You said, very clearly, 9 a.m., Sunday morning. I can picture you right in front of me, opening your stupid mouth, saying that. Today. Not next Sunday. Or some Sunday in friggin 2035 when I'll still be here if you keep this up!"

Peter was at a loss for words. He scrambled to formulate some sort of response that wouldn't just further aggravate his brother.

Dwayne glanced at him and raised a quizzical eyebrow. Pippin, who had been padding along beside them quietly, looked at Peter as well.

After a brief pause, Sam started again. "I have it in my notes! Last night at 8:25 p.m. you came into my cell and after giving me some more lame-ass excuses as to why you still hadn't found Mr. Bingley, you promised you'd be back at nine this morning with better news. So now it's —"

"Whoa! Whoa!" Peter interrupted. "Sam . . . I . . . I wasn't there. In your cell last night? I absolutely, positively was not there. I was in your apartment, doing everything you asked me to when I visited you in the —"

"Bullshit, Peter! Why are you trying to mess with me? At a time like this! I was worried I couldn't count on you and now —"

"No, no, no! Sam. Listen. Think about it. How could I be in your cell? They don't allow that. Do you have your meds there? Can you pass me over to one of the officers?"

Click.

"He hung up," Peter said quietly. He was shaking. They had stopped walking now. Dwayne and Pippin both looked concerned.

Peter dialed the number Sam had called from. It went to the remand centre's voicemail system. "My brother, Sam Bannerman, just called me from the remand centre, and he sounded delusional.

I'm worried he's having a psychotic break. Please have someone assess him and call me back as soon as possible."

"I'm sorry, Peter. That sounds pretty rough," Dwayne said, and put his hand on Peter's shoulder. Peter didn't normally like to be touched, but this was comforting.

"Thanks."

"Does your brother often hallucinate?"

"He goes through periods. He's been much better lately, but stress seems to bring it on."

"Hyperphantasia?"

"Hyperphantasia? Imagining too much?"

"Kind of. It's having unusually vivid mental imagery," Dwayne explained. "It's on a spectrum, so people on the extreme end see things so clearly and sharply in their mind's eye that it starts to mess with their perception of what's real and what's not."

"OK. Makes sense. Yes, he might be that way. It probably would overlap with his passion for painting."

"Totally. Many artists have hyperphantasia." Dwayne paused and then added, "I have the opposite, aphantasia."

They had been walking again and were approaching a fork in the road. Peter pointed right.

"Really? So, you don't have any mental images? None at all? Not even hazy ones?"

"Nope. Nothing. I just think in words. No pictures ever. I was shocked when I first found out that most people can see things in their minds. I was upset about what I was missing. But it's the only thing I know, and I think it might give me an advantage."

"Pure thought with no distracting pictures." Peter had never considered this before. It felt like a door opening into an undiscovered room. Not really of practical use to him, but fascinating, nonetheless.

"Exactly."

They fell into an amiable silence as they turned off the road onto a woodchip trail leading north of town through a mixed forest of birch and spruce. It was a good year for mushrooms. Peter spotted three different kinds within the first hundred metres or so. He wished he knew more about mushrooms. Maybe someday he would make a proper study of them. Something to add to the list.

Peter kept Pippin on his leash as coyotes had been reported in the area, but the leash was long and loose. Pippin ambled along just ahead of them, nose always to the ground, tail slowly wagging.

The forest was very quiet. The air was cool and still. Peter loved it. He allowed himself to forget Sam for a few minutes. Trees. Mushrooms. Pippin. Dwayne. Coolness. Stillness.

This reverie was broken by Dwayne asking, almost in a whisper, "Should we start?" He was fiddling with the dials on his metal detector.

"Yeah, sure. Let's start. The bog is ahead on the left. I can smell it."

Without further discussion they began sweeping opposite sides of the path with their devices. This slowed them down considerably, so Pippin slowed down as well, occasionally stopping to sit and watch Peter.

They didn't find anything. Not even a rusty nail or lost penny. But it was beside the point. It was an absorbing activity regardless of success, and it created a pleasant state of flow for Peter. To a point, at least. After half an hour he could feel a fidgetiness rising in him. He checked his phone, which he had deliberately put deep in a zippered pocket to reduce the temptation. He had the ringer on, though, in case remand phoned him back.

Nothing. No emails. No messages.

Dwayne was humming something that sounded like a blend between "Hotel California" and "Shallow." He swayed to the beat as he swept his metal detector back and forth. With his bulk and mullet, this looked faintly ridiculous. It made Peter smile.

"Hey, Dwayne? Is it OK if we start heading back?"

Dwayne looked up and smiled. "Sure thing. Worried about your brother, I bet."

"Yeah. This is a perfect break from the craziness, but I'd better see what's going on with him."

"No worries. My mom has a ton of raking for me to do today anyway. Rain check on the Beaver then?"

"You bet. I'll see you there anyway on Wednesday night for the first pre-season Pointsmen warm-up."

The New Selfoss Pointsmen, sponsored by The Flying Beaver, was the darts team Peter belonged to with Dwayne, Laura, and an old friend, Chris Olson. They had lost the championship last season to their cross-lake rivals, the Gimli Bullseye Gliders. Chris, the team captain, was hoping that more practices would help. Peter thought that the real problem was that none of them, other than Chris, took it very seriously. But he managed to stop himself from saying so.

Laura was in the living room when he got home. She was putting the finishing touches on the *Matrix* sweater she had been working on.

"Wow! You made fast progress on that."

"It's pretty much all I did yesterday. And being worried about you last night made me work faster. Hyperfocus anxiety avoidance!"

Peter laughed. "Silver lining, I guess."

"Also, I think I figured out that symbol." Laura beamed. She loved cracking a puzzle almost as much as Peter did.

"Great! I had a crazy conversation with Sam an hour ago and was going to call remand again, but I want to see what you found first."

Laura set her knitting aside and pulled out her phone. "It's one of the symbols used by the Ustasha, a Croatian ultra-nationalist organization."

"Really? I wasn't expecting that." Peter was standing beside Laura, peering over her shoulder. He made his way over to the couch and sat opposite her. Pippin, who had been noisily slurping from his water bowl in the kitchen, came over and lay down between them.

"They were most active before and during the war, when they led the fascist Croatian government that was allied with Nazi Germany. Now it's more of a slur to call someone a Ustasha. But elements of the movement still exist. Croatian soccer fans sometimes use a chant associated with the Ustasha. FIFA has banned it."

"Huh." Peter rubbed his chin. He had forgotten to shave that morning. He never forgot, but everything was topsy-turvy right now. He enjoyed the rough sensation, a bit like a cat's tongue. "So, it is connected. That can't be a coincidence. We know that the victim, Dženan Knezevic, was born in Bosnia. He was 70, so too young to have anything to do with World War Two. But he came here during the Yugoslav civil war. Were the Ustasha active then?"

"I'm not sure. Easy enough to check." Laura scrolled while she spoke. "Do you think Dženan would be more likely to be a member, or an opponent?"

"No idea. Do you know what ethnicity the name Knezevic is?" Peter asked.

Laura tapped quickly. Peter was always impressed by the speed and precision of her typing.

"Knezevic name origin," she mumbled to herself. "Ha!" She looked up at Peter. "Knezevic is a Croatian, Serbian, Bosnian, and Montenegrin surname. Not super helpful."

"No. But the Ustasha connection is. Thank you. And happily, there's no way to tie Sam into that. On the other hand, there's also no easy way to tie it into the murder, but the reference to a violent organization adjacent to a murder site is worth looking into."

"You'll let the police know, or should I?" Laura grinned.

"I will. I should report that weird threat last night anyway. Although I'm sure they'll just nod and smile."

"You don't know that. And the *Star Wars* toy suffocations?"

"They've got to have seen that already."

"You don't know that either. Best to report it." Laura stood up and gave Peter a peck on the forehead. "If you're heading back into the city, don't forget that Kevin and Stuart are coming early for dinner tonight to show us their surprise."

Peter suppressed a groan. There were only so many surprises he could absorb in one weekend.

CHAPTER *Twenty*

The opportunity came in the morning, a few hours after breakfast. The food lady had gone out. When she came back, she was carrying many bags. He thought this might be his chance. That had worked with the second food man, but the food lady spotted him lurking near the door.

She put her bags down quickly and picked him up. She hugged him and made a lot of noises at him. Possibly his name was now something that sounded like Pritteeboy, or maybe those were just noises she liked to make a lot.

He hated the hugging. Really hated it. He would have loved to sink his teeth into her arm. He wondered whether it would taste more like chicken, fish, or liver? Or maybe like a luxury turkey dinner with gravy? That would be wonderful. But finding out would make things worse for him. He knew that. Patience was hard — *so* hard — but it was important.

The real opportunity came right after. She put him down and then made different noises and fanned her face with her hand. She opened the window to let fresh air in. This was nice. It was especially nice because he noticed that the screen was loose.

Oh, please, please, please . . .

It was as if the world read his mind and responded. The food lady went into the room that had the large water bowl that sometimes made sudden, alarming noises and sometimes had bad smells. She closed the door behind her.

Yes!

He climbed onto the window ledge and hooked the nails from his left forepaw around the loose corner. At first it wouldn't budge, but then it suddenly popped loose. The screen hit the floor with a loud clatter.

The food lady made shouting noises from the water bowl room.

He jumped through the window. The ground was right there. He noticed now that there were windows much higher above the ground. He had been lucky.

He ran as fast as he could toward bushes where the food lady wouldn't see him. She would not fit out the window herself, but he knew she would soon come through the door to look for him.

In the bushes he was invisible. He was free again.

CHAPTER
Twenty-One

This time Peter got straight through to reception when he called remand. He was passed along to an officer who apologized for not returning his message. It had been "a lively morning," not just regarding Sam. They were well aware of his erratic behaviour and had put him on suicide watch because he had repeatedly and loudly exclaimed that he couldn't live without Mr. Bingley, whom they had assumed was a boyfriend. In any case, Peter was welcome to come right down.

The call with the police was no less surprising. A detective had been happy to speak to Peter and said they would look into an Ustasha connection and would search the apartment for a speaker. These sounded like automatic, polite responses. But her tone changed when he told her about the figurines. No, they had not seen those. They had been able to lay the charges based on other evidence, so searching the apartment had not been an immediate priority. Because they planned to go through Sam's place thoroughly and would likely have to remove a lot of material in order to inspect everything, they would need to block a good amount of time for the search. She thanked him for the information and said they'd be in touch if they had questions.

Peter looked at Pippin, who had been sitting beside him while he made his calls out on the deck. Pippin was briefly distracted by a squirrel before he returned Peter's attention. Pippin must have thought there was the possibility of a second morning walk. It did happen occasionally, especially on days where he didn't put on those boots that smelled of cows, horses, and pigs.

"I better go now. Sorry, buddy, I don't think you should come with this time. I'm going straight to see Sam at remand."

The tone of voice and body language said it all. No second walk. But it was a perfect morning to nap in the yard — warm enough in the sun not to have to wear a jacket if you weren't blessed with fur. And that squirrel was bound to show up again soon.

Peter was ushered directly into the visitors room. Nobody else was there as it was outside normal visiting hours. He waited nervously, drumming his long fingers on his knees for a good ten minutes before Sam appeared.

Sam looked even more haggard than he had the day before, which was saying a lot. His hair was sticking out at odd angles, and he had heavy purple bags under his eyes. He wore grey coveralls and was handcuffed this time.

Peter, unsure of what tone to take, settled on an uneasy blend of concerned and cheerful: "Sam!"

The guard stepped back but remained close by. Sam adjusted his seating position and scowled at Peter. "About time! You said you were coming right down this morning!"

Peter decided to ignore that. "Look, Sam, I have two pieces of good news for you. First, we have a solid lead on Mr. Bingley." He hoped that Sam wouldn't be able to detect the white lie in Peter's nervous delivery. Sam continued to scowl at him, making odd chewing motions with his mouth. Peter expected him to interrupt and ask for more details, but he didn't. "And second, I found a symbol beside Dženan's door that appears to link to a Croatian paramilitary organization. Laura and I think this may be a clue pointing to the real killer."

Sam still didn't say anything. He continued to move his jaw in a slow, circular way that reminded Peter of a cow working on its cud. His scowl had turned into a smirk.

Peter waited. He was tempted to babble on but thought it was better to see what Sam would say in response to the news.

The room was silent except for the hum of the HVAC system.

The smirk became a grimace. "They're here, Peter. Right in my cell. Maybe in this room. But hiding."

"They?"

Sam lowered his voice and spoke in a kind of hiss. "The ghosts of course, you moron. Who else? The Vienna Boys Choir?"

This was not the direction Peter had expected the conversation to take, but he was learning to let go of all expectations as the weekend went along. "Ah . . . Dženan's ghosts. Here? At remand now? Not at the apartment?"

"They're frigging ghosts!" Sam had reverted to his usual bombastic delivery. Peter glanced at the guard, but he wore an impassive expression. Peter supposed he had seen it all. "They can be lots of different places. Bosnia. The Lady Alice. The remand centre. The effing moon, for all I know. Here and there and wherever they friggin want to be. Remember the science bubble we talked about yesterday? Anyway. Whatever. The ghosts are going to murder me here. Just like they did with Dženan. They said I am next. Even though I didn't do anything to them. I didn't do anything wrong. I've never been to Todorovo, or Bosnia, or anywhere in the effing Balkans. But maybe ghosts aren't logical, right? I mean, I don't know how the thinking works when you're dead and pissed off and no longer have anything to lose. But who am I asking? You?" He snorted. "You have no idea.

You don't care. But it doesn't matter. It doesn't change the bottom line. You have to get me out of here. Out. Of. Here. And now. Like right friggin now."

Peter sucked his breath in and briefly closed his eyes. He exhaled. "Yes, we're working on it. The lawyer, me, Laura, the police even, we're all working on getting you out." He paused and weighed whether to say what he wanted to say. It was probably a bad idea, but he couldn't help himself. "But Sam, when you get out, where can you go to get away from the ghosts? I mean, if they can find you here, how are you safer somewhere else?"

Another change came over Sam's face. He looked like he was going to cry. Peter struggled to remember when he had ever seen Sam cry.

"You're right. I'm not safe anywhere." His voice quavered.

Another first. Peter couldn't recall his brother ever changing his mind and agreeing with him. "I think you're safer here. I honestly do," he said. "The guards are keeping a close eye on you. I'm sure they've" — Peter hesitated — "seen this kind of thing before and know what to do."

Sam now looked stern. His mood changed with a frequency and speed that made it feel like the glass between them had a time-lapse feature. "Then what we need to do is satisfy the ghosts. They got Dženan, but there's obviously something more they want. They're not satisfied yet. But I can't be the right target. It doesn't make sense. I think there's some ritual that needs to be performed to placate them. Or maybe some object in Dženan's apartment that needs to be destroyed." He was talking faster and faster. Peter feared what was coming. Sam's accelerated speech usually led to wilder and wilder ideas.

Peter tried to shift the conversation. "Yes, but —"

Sam ignored him. "That must be it. I was so stupid before. I assumed they just straight out killed him for whatever reason that made them follow him from Bosnia, but I see now why they're not satisfied. They needed him to do this ritual or destroy this thing, or" — Sam's eyes widened in a cartoon of sudden insight — "*destroy this thing in a ritual!*" It looked like he was going to slap his forehead, but the handcuffs stopped him. "Fuck," he muttered.

"So," Peter began carefully, "they mentioned this ritual to you? The ghosts, I mean, when you see them, what do they say?"

"No, dummy, they're just in the phase of scaring me first. Getting me to believe in them and be shit-scared of them so that I'll do whatever they say when they get to the next phase."

"The ritual requesting phase?" Peter looked at the guard again. He was staring into the middle distance with a professionally neutral expression.

"Yes, yes. That phase. But I won't know how to do it! That's the thing! They don't understand that. Bosnian ghosts won't get what Canadians can and can't do. Then they'll kill me. Then they'll effing strangle me."

Peter wished fervently that he was back home, reading a book, with Laura maybe making tea for both of them, Pippin and Merry snoozing nearby, and possibly some nice quiet Chopin on the stereo. But he wasn't. He was here, listening to his brother go right off the deep end. A swan dive from the high tower into a bottomless pool of madness.

Peter suppressed a sigh. "Ah, all right then. That buys us some time at least, right? How long is this scaring phase? It can't be pleasant for you, but it doesn't sound like it's dangerous."

"Glad to see we're finally on the same page. I'm going to mark the time, date, and place. Banner day for the Bannerman brothers. Brother Peter finally sees what Brother Samuel has been trying to drill into his thick skull." Sam leaned forward and lowered his voice. "Hard to say about ghost phases. Dženan complained about them for weeks. But maybe they're impatient now. Maybe they're frustrated and will accelerate the scaring phase. Maybe they'll move immediately to the choking Sam phase."

"But you'll have at least a little time between, er, phases two and three because in phase two they'll ask you to do the ritual first. That's kind of a final warning. They'd have to give you a bit of time, what with you being in jail."

"That's live human logic. Live *scientist* human logic. I don't know how ghost logic works. But it doesn't matter because you're going to get into his apartment and figure out what object needs to be destroyed and how the ritual goes. Do that, and I get to live. Assuming that outcome is of interest to you."

Peter opened his mouth to reply, but Sam went on. "By the way, I should let you know that you are *not* in my will. So don't go thinking that letting me die gives you access to all my stuff."

"Sam, come on . . ."

"No offence. It's not against you. It's for the animals. It's all going to the Toronto Humane Society. Although I need to talk to that lawyer about cutting the Winnipeg Humane Society in now that I'm living here. You're a rich doctor, so you don't need anything. The animals are poor — they need everything."

Peter pictured stray dogs playing with Sam's weird collection of Russian fur hats, and litters of kittens batting backgammon pieces around.

"No, really. It never crossed my mind. And I don't want you to die. Of course not."

"Then you'll get into Dženan's apartment and" — Sam dropped his voice to a whisper again — "do the thing? The ritual — you know. Promise me."

Peter was about to tell him that it was exceptionally illegal to break into a crime scene, but he realized it was pointless. Sam would just get agitated and argue. So instead he said, "OK," and quickly changed the subject. "How are things here anyway, like the food?"

Sometimes distraction worked. Sometimes it didn't. Thank goodness it worked this time. Sam seemed to accept Peter's "OK" and was excited to answer his questions. "The food looks better than I expected. I guess all the prison shows are from the US, where the food always looks like goop. You know, piles of brown stuff on those metal trays. But it looked decent. Not that I could eat with all the stress and everything. But it looked good. And it . . ."

Sam didn't seem to need a response, and Peter zoned out. He thought about what he should do next. Probably go back to the apartment and have another look for a little speaker and anything else that might be of help. The police said they were coming to have another look, but it didn't sound like it would be right away. But Peter wanted a break from all this too. He wondered whether Whodunit Books was open on a Sunday. He had been supplementing his usual literature and history reading with mysteries lately, ever since Kevin suggested that his amateur sleuthing was like something out of a badly written murder mystery.

". . . and then last night the guys and I were watching —"

"The guys?" Peter hoped that he hadn't missed the explanation of who they were.

"Oh yeah, the guys. You'd think this place would be full of walleyed neck-tattooed gangbangers, but there's all kinds. So anyway, a group of us bonded over *The Bear*. You seen it? You gotta. Although season three is weaker. Anyway, Michael, Trevor, Ivan, Jason, Cory, and I binged it. Good guys. Not like major criminals. They might look sketchy, but each and every one of them is innocent. Totally innocent. Framed. Just like me. It's crazy how much that happens. Total scandal. I had no idea. Nobody does, unless they're on the inside."

The guard caught Peter's eye and tapped his watch.

"Looks like time's up," Peter said.

Sam nodded and then leaned in as far as he could. He spoke in a barely audible whisper. "You notice that I didn't mention Mr. Bingley, or Flinders, or Barry. That's on purpose. If the ghosts figure out that they're important to me, they'll know my weaknesses."

CHAPTER *Twenty-Two*

Whodunit was open. Peter was relieved. He wanted to go back to the apartment, but at the same time, he wasn't in a great hurry to do so. And if he did not have something specific and attention-grabbing to do in the meantime, he'd just wander around and obsess about the weird conversation with Sam. The wandering around would have been fine as Whodunit was in a beautiful neighbourhood, the streets golden cathedrals of overarching autumnal elms. But the obsessing would not be fine. There'd be no new data to be gleaned, and he could not foresee any useful analysis of the existing data. Normally, walking helped, but Sam's weirdness lay like a heavy fog over Peter's brain. He didn't think it would lift without a significant distraction. A mental Ctrl-Alt-Del, so to speak.

The bookstore break was, however, too brief to be of much help in that regard. Peter already had a specific idea of what he was looking for, and the clerk was helpful and efficient. He had been curious how many mystery novels were published, so he dug through the net for that statistic, but it proved impossible to find the specific number. By his estimate, however, it had to be thousands and thousands. Consequently, he decided to focus on Canadian authors, which narrowed things down considerably. He read some reviews in advance of his visit and made a short list on his phone. With the clerk's guidance, he quickly picked out novels from Deverell, Kalteis, Emery, and Bidulka. He hoped he had chosen well, but there was no obvious way to improve the odds beyond what he had already done. That accomplished, standing around afterwards and just vaguely looking at the displays, or worse still, trying to make small talk with the clerk, were not viable options. So, he left with the four books tucked under his arm. The whole visit hadn't taken much more than ten minutes.

He was very much looking forward to sitting by the fireplace tonight and reading the first chapter of each book before deciding which one to tackle first. But he would not read them all back-to-back. He wanted to learn more about private investigators, as imagined in fiction, but he also needed to leaven this with the reliably soothing facts of solid non-fiction. Too much fiction made him feel unmoored from reality, like a ship drifting before random winds and currents. Consequently, it had always been his habit to alternate fiction and non. Often with history. Sometimes with science. A historical fiction or science fiction novel, followed by some actual history or science, and then back again. He was very pleased with this system.

For non-fiction on the theme of investigative work, he had already picked up a biography of Eugène-François Vidocq, the 19th-century Frenchman who was arguably the first detective, experimenting with fingerprints and disguises. Peter also had looked at *The Complete Idiot's Guide to Private Investigating* but rejected it as he realized it would probably alarm Laura. Even with these books, he would have to work hard to reassure her that he had no intention of becoming a PI. He was very happy being a veterinarian. He just felt that he needed to know more about the world he found himself repeatedly stumbling into. If he was honest with himself, it was a world that intrigued him enough that he didn't mind these accidental exposures to it. And regardless, more knowledge about anything was always a good thing. Always. He couldn't think of an important exception to that rule.

He mused about all this as he walked to his truck, but the pleasant reverie was broken when he remembered that it was Sunday, and that Kevin and Stuart were coming over. And they were bringing a surprise that they were obviously excited about, so there would be no way to cancel.

"Shoot," he muttered under his breath. So much for cozily leafing through a stack of books by the fireside tonight. Oh well, there was always tomorrow, so long as the situation with Sam didn't spiral into some direction that required even more of his time. He climbed into the truck and set the books down with care on the passenger seat. He didn't press the ignition button, though. He just sat, staring out the windshield at the leaves wafting down.

What now? His brain was still buzzing with Sam's exhortation to break into Dženan's apartment, and with all the associated nonsense about ghosts. He really worried that his brother's mental health was deteriorating and that self-harm was an increasing risk.

Peter sighed. No amount of distraction was going to do the trick. He was going to have to allow himself to think about Sam, whether these thoughts were productive or not. He had been wrong. Going back to the apartment now was the best next step after all. His mind could whirr away on the conversation in the meantime, but as soon as he started to dig for more data in the apartment, it would shift to analyzing that. Somehow, progress had to be made. The status quo was unacceptable.

He just wished Pippin were with him, but it would be a two-and-a-half-hour round-trip to collect him. Somehow he felt even farther away from home.

Sam's place seemed different without the kittens. There was no way a hoarder's lair like this could ever truly feel empty, but the absence of life made the space feel oddly hollowed out. Even though he had only known them a short time, Peter missed Flinders and Barry. He wondered how they were doing at Ed's. And he reminded himself to check in with Laura on any progress in their advertising for the still-missing Mr. Bingley.

But it was time to do something concrete. His first action should be to look more carefully for the source of the threatening voice last night.

He stood with his hands on his hips and ran his eyes over the piles of stuff. Laura was probably right — whoever placed a speaker would likely have removed it again while the apartment was empty overnight. Unless the theory was correct that it had been Sam. But that still didn't make any sense to Peter. So he was probably looking for nothing. Nonetheless, another examination of the contents of the apartment couldn't hurt. There was so much there that you could search a hundred times and still find something new every time. Any search was necessarily limited by the state of the place, unless you removed everything as the police suggested they might do, but a speaker couldn't have been buried, or it would have been muffled, so Peter concentrated on open, but out-of-sight, spots.

The tops of towers of boxes were the first places he checked, not having looked there previously. Some towers were tall enough that, despite his height, Peter had to stand on a chair to be able to see. But all that revealed was a deep layer of grey fuzz and a couple of dust-encrusted rubber bands. Peter smiled to himself, picturing Sam trying to shoot ghosts with rubber bands. Not highly probable, but certainly not out of the question either.

Having inspected all of these, he moved on to the bookcases, all of which were jumbled full. Looking at them was like looking at a page from one of those Richard Scarry's Busytown picture books he and Sam loved when they were kids. Peter was always very good at quickly spotting the hidden Goldbug character, but even back then, he marvelled that it was not instant. Everything in his field of view would have hit his retina and been transported down the optic nerve to his brain, so Goldbug should have registered immediately, on first seeing the page. Yet sometimes he still had to systematically work his way through the picture to find him. The hold-up must have been in his brain, and this annoyed him. Although he had learned the meaning of "retina" and "optic nerve" at a young age, it would be a few years yet before he understood how attentional bandwidth worked.

These bookcases were even busier than Busytown, so it was going to take a systematic approach right from the start. Start in the top left corner and begin scanning along, as if reading a book.

He reached a heap of small Ookpik owl souvenirs when suddenly he heard a loud shriek from outside the apartment. It came from his floor, he thought. But maybe more toward the front of the building.

Peter stopped looking for a moment and strained to listen. Maybe he heard the sound of knocking? He wasn't sure. But not on his door anyway.

He waited a minute or two longer before deciding that he should probably go and see if there was an obvious need for help somewhere. The shriek sounded painful or distressed. And it was broad daylight, after all, so there shouldn't be any danger to him associated with it.

Peter committed the Ookpiks to memory so that he knew where he had left off, and he exited the suite.

The Other Peter from across the hall and Claire from next door were standing in front of the door to apartment 5.

"I think we should go in," Claire was saying to the Other Peter as Peter stepped toward them. She was half facing away from him, so it wasn't clear whether she had seen him.

The Other Peter nodded. "If it's not locked."

"What's going on?" Peter asked.

"We don't know," the Other Peter answered. "But the scream sounded terrible, so I came over and knocked to see if she needed help. She hasn't responded."

"I've got her number, so I called her just now, but it went to voicemail," Claire added, holding her phone up. Peter noticed that it had a cute teddy bear case.

The Other Peter tried the doorknob. It turned, and the deadbolt wasn't engaged. He swung the door open.

Maureen was lying on her back on the floor, legs and arms akimbo. Her face and whole body had the unsettling rigidity of a wax figure. Her eyes were open, fixed on something in the middle distance above her.

CHAPTER
Twenty-Three

"Is she dead?" the Other Peter asked.

Claire ran into the apartment and grabbed Maureen's wrist to check for a pulse.

Peter was right behind her, scanning the room as he entered. He saw a shattered teacup on the floor to Maureen's right, with brown tea staining the pink carpet around it. Otherwise, everything looked like it did when he and Pippin were there before. *Why was the door unlocked?* he thought.

"I've got nine-one-one!" the Other Peter shouted. Peter heard him describing the particulars of the situation to the operator.

"Dead?" he asked, squatting down beside Claire.

Claire nodded sharply. She elbowed Peter aside and began to perform chest compressions.

"One, two, three, four, five . . ." she counted out loud, pushing down on Maureen's chest with remarkable power at each number. She was quick and precise. At 30 she paused, tilted the old woman's head back, and gave her two deep breaths mouth-to-mouth before returning to another round of compressions.

The Other Peter was off the phone and standing beside them now. "They're on their way," he said, breathing hard. "They'll be here in ten minutes. What do you think?"

What Peter thought was that it was another murder, possibly by poison. But this was an instantaneous reaction without a thorough consideration of the facts. Also, he couldn't immediately think of what specific poison or other means would cause the victim to shriek and then die, without any other signs. But he didn't say any of this. Instead, he said, "No idea. Heart attack, maybe?"

The Other Peter nodded.

They watched Claire performing CPR. The room had an unearthly sense of deep quiet to it, despite the counting. It was as if the air itself had become denser and was pressing all around them, muffling everything.

"Good job, Claire," the Other Peter said. His voice sounded like it was coming from a great distance.

Peter heard a siren, also muffled and distant, but steadily becoming louder.

He glanced around again. But there was nothing. Just all the pink, a broken teacup, and a dead woman.

Firefighters came first. They took over the CPR from Claire, who immediately slumped back against the side of a chair. She put her head in her hands, knees up, quietly sobbing. The paramedics arrived shortly after. In total, perhaps 20 minutes had passed between when Claire had started the chest compressions and when one of the paramedics said there was no hope. Peter recognized the tone of professionalized compassion. It was the one he took when someone he didn't know rushed in with a dying cat.

Questions were asked about who the Peters and Claire were, and what they knew about Maureen's next of kin. The Peters knew nothing, but Claire blew her nose, stood up, and said that she knew Maureen had a sister in the city. The contact information should be on the fridge.

In the meantime, a crowd of other residents had gathered in the hall. Ed was talking to Josh, the bear, in low tones. Josh leaned in to hear Ed. He caught Peter's eye, and they nodded at each other. Peter briefly considered joining in, and then also chatting with the Other Peter's wife and the Filipino drummer kid — he forgot both their names in the excitement of the moment — but he wanted to get back to Sam's apartment to process what had just happened. Besides, he was becoming unsure of his ability to spot lies after all, despite how well he had studied the subject. Not well enough, it seemed. Or perhaps it was just very difficult to do successfully, even with the best techniques.

Everyone stopped talking when the stretcher was taken out. It was hard to believe that the rounded hump under the blanket had been a living woman a few minutes ago. One of the firefighters had found Maureen's keys and locked up after they all left the apartment. There were no sirens as the ambulance and fire truck drove away.

"Will the police come?" Peter heard Claire ask behind him. He had already taken a step toward Sam's door. He turned around. She was facing him and had obviously directed the question at him.

"I assume only if foul play is suspected. I don't know under what circumstances an autopsy is ordered to rule that out, though. There were no visible wounds, but —"

"But that doesn't mean it wasn't murder. Like the man in four, downstairs." Claire's eyes were still red-rimmed, but she said this in a flat, matter-of-fact way.

"No, I agree." Peter wasn't sure how much he wanted to speculate with her.

"And they still haven't said what actually killed him. Everyone here assumes someone suffocated him with that plastic bag, but with his pants down and everything, that was probably a set-up to humiliate him after death. Destroy his reputation."

Peter nodded.

The rest of the crowd had dispersed, except for Josh, who now stood beside Claire, listening.

"And choking someone, even with a bag, is noisy," Claire went on. "And usually, the victim ends up with bruises on their neck because it's hard to hold the bag tight on someone who is resisting."

"She watches a lot of true crime," Josh interjected.

"So, I think he was poisoned first. And that could be what happened to Maureen just now."

"Without setting up something to embarrass her?" Peter said.

"Yeah, without that. The killer probably hated that guy but just offed Maureen because she found something out."

"Mm hmm," Peter said, and rubbed his chin unselfconsciously. "Maybe instead of poisoning Dženan, the murderer drugged him so he couldn't resist and then killed him with the plastic bag. That seems to be the police's theory. And poor Maureen was just the victim of an unfortunate, coincidental, catastrophic myocardial infarction."

"Do you believe in coincidences?" Claire asked. She twisted a hank of her long purple hair around her finger and looked him directly in the eyes.

"Yes and no. I don't like the word because it implies something inexplicable and strange. I prefer to think about probabilities. Most events that people call coincidences are just low-probability events, but not zero probability."

Josh laughed. Claire and Peter looked at him.

"The way you guys talk! Claire like you're on *CSI*, and Peter like you're on . . ." Josh paused, obviously searching for the name of a program. "Like you're on *Sherlock*, that one with Cumberbatch. All logical and stuff."

Claire snorted. "There's a murderer in the building who may now be a serial killer. What do you want us to be like we're in? *The Simpsons*?"

Josh gave Claire an affectionate squeeze on the shoulder. "I dunno, that Lisa Simpson's pretty sharp."

Peter wondered how best to exit this conversation. He needed to be alone to sort through the new data. External input usually just confuses matters. Discussing *The Simpsons* had no chance whatsoever of being helpful. Claire, although obviously smart, did not have any useful additional information. At least not any that she was sharing.

"Ha!" Claire said. "Actually, come to think of it, Martin, Dr. Hibbert, and Sideshow Bob are all pretty damned smart too." She enumerated these characters on her fingers. "And some would argue that Bart himself is brilliant, as is Marge. So, I take it back. We can be *Simpsons* characters and crack this case just as well."

Josh's hand was resting on her shoulder, and he gave it another squeeze. "Let's leave the case cracking to the police and let the good doctor here get back to his day."

Whew, Peter thought. "Yeah, I suppose I should get back to . . . organizing stuff in my brother's apartment."

"OK, but let's compare notes if either of us thinks of anything," Claire said. She looked him directly in the eyes again. A brief hard stare. It was unnerving.

"Will do," Peter said, reaching for the doorknob.

"Whatever we can do to keep everyone safe and clear your brother." Claire's expression softened, and she flashed him a thumbs-up.

Back to the Ookpiks.

Peter had decided to finish scanning the shelves first before turning his thoughts to analyzing what Maureen's death might mean. It took a moment to fully regain his focus and return the hunt for a miniature wireless speaker to being uppermost in his mind.

Pencil cases, stacks of blank writable CDs, agriculture and philosophy textbooks, a toy log home building kit, several broken soldering irons, novelty mugs — lots and lots of novelty mugs, mostly featuring cartoon animals — a broken electric juicer, a stack of programs for a Toronto theatre Peter had never heard of, a bag of plastic fruit, the 1978 *World Book Encyclopedia* volumes A, D, M, N, and T, a Sasquatch doll, several broken microphones, and . . . a speaker! But on closer inspection, it was a broken wired computer speaker.

Peter sighed. He looked at the other shelving units. He sighed even deeper. He would have to take breaks in order to be able to maintain his focus. And in order not to start screaming obscenities and throwing everything into trash bags with the wild energy of a dervish. Not that he would ever do such a thing, but occasionally he fantasized about being a less controlled person. Those were fleeting fantasies, though, as he quickly reminded himself that such people did not make good decisions and consequently led unhappy lives.

Tea would be perfect now. But that awful blend Sam had? Then he remembered that he had brought a box of decaf Yorkshire. He smiled.

Tea brewed and chipped cup selected — this one had some kind of small blue flowers on it, possibly forget-me-nots, rather than roses — he sat down in the kitchen and took a deep breath. Peter was about to take his first sip when he realized that he should probably call Laura and update her. Normally he would just text, but a message saying something like "a woman just died in the building, but don't worry" would definitely make her worry. Better to explain in more detail, leaving out any speculation about poisoning, and field the questions immediately.

Laura picked up right away and was predictably taken aback but seemed satisfied with Peter's explanations. She thanked him for not poking around Maureen's apartment or asking the other residents more questions. Let the authorities handle it. And just a heart attack anyway. Happens every day. Come home as soon as you can. That was about the gist of it.

After Peter hung up, he pictured Pippin watching Laura talk on the phone. He usually paid attention when someone was speaking, whether to a visible person or into that mysterious little glass slab humans carried with them everywhere. For about the 20th time that day, he missed his dog.

Peter looked at his watch. He'd give it another hour here, and then he'd head home, regardless of what he had accomplished.

So, Maureen. Peter pulled out his phone and searched for fast-acting poisons. This really seemed like a long shot, but it was not impossible. He thought it more likely that Dženan had been rendered defenceless first by drugs or alcohol and then been suffocated afterwards. He wished he had access to the autopsy report. He wondered whether Kevin could . . . Peter stopped that train of thought. Foolish. Of course not. Kevin probably couldn't, and he certainly wouldn't. And it wouldn't provide Peter with any information he could act on. It would just be to scratch a curiosity itch, which is hardly enough of a justification. Plus, if Laura found out that Peter had asked, and she definitely would find out, then . . . Well, it didn't bear thinking about.

Peter gave his head a little shake as if to physically rid himself of that thought. He turned his attention to the search results. The top-five fast-acting poisons were arsenic, atropine, strychnine, cyanide, and thallium, although with the latter, by "fast-acting" they meant a few days. That ruled that out, at least for Maureen. Strychnine caused seizures, so not that either. Of the remaining three, atropine and cyanide were quite bitter. So that left arsenic, unless the tea was so strong that it could disguise bitterness. This was unlikely. Chinese "bitter nail" kuding tea might do the trick, but he would be shocked if anyone here had heard of it. Nor would the drinker welcome it. No, cyanide and atropine were better for suicide than murder.

Arsenic, then, if it was murder by poisoning. But he doubted it very much in both cases. Maureen's death looked a lot more like a garden-variety heart attack. Yet, the low probability of two sudden deaths in the same small building within a week of each other unsettled him a little. He shouldn't dismiss the idea. Especially since there was the question of why Maureen's door was unlocked. He was sure it had been locked when he visited her. As far as he knew, all the residents locked up all the time anyway. Maybe Claire's theory about Maureen having learned something that would threaten to unmask the killer wasn't so far-fetched. But why would she have tea with this person? That made no sense. And where was the other cup? He supposed a killer could have taken it or hidden it.

Peter finished his tea and sat back. That had been an unsatisfying bit of analytical thinking. He hadn't made much progress other than to identify which poison was likely, on the off chance there had been a poison. And Google had done that, not his brain.

He stood up, stretched, and looked balefully at the next over-stuffed set of shelves.

Then he heard a loud knocking on the door. And a quiet yip, like that of a small dog or a puppy.

CHAPTER *Twenty-Four*

He waited until the food lady gave up. She had made a lot of noises and had walked back and forth and then gone around the corner of the giant box with windows, disappearing for a while. He had been tempted to leave his hiding spot then, but something told him to stay still just a little longer.

That something was right. The food lady returned and made more noises. She even peered into his bush once, but he was well hidden behind the leaves and the bits of paper and plastic the wind had blown in. Eventually she went back into the giant box.

When he was confident that the food lady was going to stay in the giant box, he came out from behind the bush and sniffed the air. One of these giant boxes would have the second food man, but which one? He was sure it wasn't the one the food lady was in. It didn't smell right on the inside. The outsides of these giant boxes all had a similar mixed-up smell of squirrels, and pee, and garbage, and strange people, and decaying leaves, and a hundred other things all constantly changing and stirred up by the annoying moving air.

To figure this out, he would need to be able to smell the insides of the giant boxes. The nearest giant box looked familiar. It was very similar to the one the food lady was in, but there was something about it that made him think he should check there first. He wished he had paid more attention when he left the second food man's place. He should have tried to memorize something that could serve to guide him back. But he had had no idea that it would be so large and so confusing out here. And he had been excited. And in a hurry. Those were all good reasons.

The door to this giant box was in the same place as the door to the food lady's. It faced a hard-looking grey stripe where more of those noisy rolling boxes were. He'd stay well away from those. He didn't want some other food person to trick him or scoop him up and roll him away somewhere else.

He was about to approach the door when an especially loud rolling box raced up. So fast and so loud. It was making screaming noises, and it had bright flashing lights. He didn't like this. Not at all. People came rushing out.

He ran back to his bush and hid again.

CHAPTER

Twenty-Five

"Peter!"

It was Kevin, and behind him, smiling shyly, Stuart. Stuart was holding a wriggling Shetland sheepdog puppy.

"Kevin . . . Stuart . . ." Peter stammered. He was comprehensively confused. A host of questions contended for priority in his mind. He settled on, "A puppy?"

"You bet! Can we come in?" Kevin took a step into the room.

"Yes, of course. A warning, though —"

Kevin held up his hand to cut Peter off. "We know, we know! We've heard all the stories about Sam's place. No worries, Pete. It can't be half as bad as we've been imagining."

Peter shrugged and stepped aside to let them in.

Kevin stopped cold after a couple of steps. His eyes panned side to side and up and down. He sucked his breath in and snorted. "Christ on a bicycle! OK. I was right, it's not half as bad — it's twice as bad!"

Stuart stood quietly behind Kevin, clutching the puppy who was now struggling mightily to jump free.

"Here, let's go to the kitchen," Peter said, pointing to his right. "It's not quite as catastrophic in there, and there are a couple chairs and a crate that can work as a third chair."

Kevin sidled through the piles, chuckling, shaking his head as he went. Stuart stepped gingerly, eyes glued to the floor ahead of him, as if trying to find stones to balance on while crossing a river.

"You can let him go now," Kevin said to Stuart once they had settled in the kitchen. The puppy had started whining and was wriggling even harder.

Stuart raised his eyebrows. "Here? Is it safe?" he asked, his normally faint Nigerian accent coming through strongly. Peter had noticed before that it was more pronounced when Stuart was stressed.

"Oh, yeah." Kevin waved his hand, as if effectively dismissing all concerns with a flick of the wrist.

"What's his name?" Peter asked.

"Orbit," Stuart answered while carefully placing the puppy on the floor.

"Orbit?"

"Yeah, Orbit," Kevin answered. "Watch this."

As soon as Stuart released the puppy, it began to careen in circles around the table, tail wagging, an expression of pure undiluted delight on its face.

"See? He orbits!" Kevin laughed. Stuart smiled, but he watched the puppy intently, his hands at the ready to grab him.

"He's pretty big for, what? eight weeks?"

"Yes, eight," Stuart said. "The breeder took one look at Kevin and said that we should take the biggest, most rugged puppy."

Kevin beamed. "I took that as a compliment."

Stuart and Peter exchanged glances.

"Well, he's beautiful. Congratulations. I had no idea you were even looking for a puppy."

Kevin shrugged. "We weren't, really, but then lately we were thinking Atlas could use a friend. And although we consider Atlas *our* dog, he lives with me most of the time. And Stuart's been wanting one that would bond to him more closely —"

"And one that I could raise from a puppy," Stuart interjected. "I always loved this breed. When I was a boy in Nigeria, I dreamed of having a beautiful, fluffy northern dog. A smaller one, but not tiny. Orbit will be perfect. I have already sent pictures to my family. They are very jealous!"

"That's great." Peter could ask more questions about the dog, but the unexpected nature of their visit was uppermost in his mind. "And what brings you guys here?"

"I texted Laura that we were in the city and asked if we could pick up anything for tonight," Kevin said.

"She replied that no, don't need to bring anything, but by the way a woman died unexpectedly in Sam's building and that you were there."

Peter pursed his lips and gave a short nod. Orbit was still running in circles around the kitchen with Stuart watching him. He looked like a parent with their toddler getting ready to hurtle down the big playground slide for the first time.

"So, we had some spare time, and thought we'd check in on you, Petey boy. See how you're getting along with all this weirdness," Kevin concluded.

"I'm doing OK, thanks. It's nice of you guys to stop by." Peter was going to try to think of another pleasantry, but something occurred to him. "How did you get in the building?"

Kevin guffawed. "Some joker jammed a piece of wood in the front door to prop it open. I guess they were coming and going a lot. Maybe moving."

"Oh? Who was there?" Peter asked.

"Nobody. Just speculating. Anyways, the door was open sesame."

"It's not a high-security building," Peter said, hoping he had made the irony obvious.

"Ha! Nope. In my considered professional opinion, I would have to agree with your assessment, Dr. Bannerman." Kevin chuckled. "So, how's your brother holding up?"

Orbit darted for the entrance to the living room. Stuart leapt from his chair and snatched him up into his arms. The puppy squirmed and protested. "You must stay here in this room, Orbit," Stuart said, his voice firm but soft around the edges. "Stay. Here." He pointed at the floor. He put the puppy back down. Orbit bolted straight for the living room again. Stuart was on him immediately.

"Maybe I should take this little troublemaker for a walk outside on the grass. Then you two gentlemen can continue your conversation in peace."

"Good idea," Kevin said. He reached over and ruffled the fur on Orbit's head. Then he poked Stuart lightly in the arm. "Off with both of you troublemakers. The serious adults have serious adult things to discuss."

"In which case, I should stay, and you should take Orbit out," Stuart said evenly. He grinned at Kevin.

"High-larious," Kevin replied, rolling his eyes for dramatic effect. "When did you take up comedy? You're very good. Maybe you should chuck accounting for a stand-up career. Anyway, he's technically your dog. So, off you go." He flicked his fingers at Stuart in a pantomime of a royal dismissal.

Stuart kissed Kevin on the forehead and left with the quivering sheltie puppy under his arm.

Without preamble, Peter launched into a description of Sam's paranoia about ghosts and his insistence that he enter the crime scene. Peter made it clear to his brother-in-law that he had no intention whatsoever of following through with that demand, but Kevin nonetheless raised a bushy red eyebrow and cleared his throat loudly when the subject came up. Peter also mentioned the strange symbol by the door and what Laura had found out about it.

"Croatian ultra-nationalists? What is it with you and the right-wing wacko crowd anyway? Who were those Nordic goobers in New Selfoss again? Elvis's Circle?"

"Eivor's Circle."

"Close enough. No offence, Pete, but you're some kind of bad luck charm, like the opposite of a rabbit's foot. Like a, I don't know . . . a rabbit's nose."

"That doesn't make any sense."

"Whatever. Point being, you're weird, and this is weird."

"If by weird you mean unusual, then I agree. But I'm unusual in a good way. Politically motivated murders are unusual in a bad way."

"So, you think the dead guy, what's his name? Zenon?"

"Dženan."

"Yeah, Dženan. You think he was murdered for political reasons by this Stashum?"

"Ustasha. Maybe? Or maybe he was a member of the Ustasha and was murdered because of it by whoever opposed them."

"OK." Kevin rubbed his beard. Peter could tell that he was struggling with whether to pursue this any further or change the subject away from police matters. One thing he had learned over the years about his brother-in-law was that if he just allowed a little silence to grow, which was very difficult for him, Kevin would crack first. And when he did, more often than not, it would be to say something unguarded or ask a question to satisfy his curiosity. Kevin couldn't help himself. At least not around Peter. He assumed he was more restrained when questioning suspects.

"So, you're thinking that if the perp isn't Sam, then it's someone connected to Bosnia or Croatia?" Kevin finally said. "Not that it's any of our business. The WPS knows what it's doing. We're just brothers-in-law shooting the shit here. Off the record."

"Totally. Yes, that's what I'm thinking. I mentioned the Ustasha symbol to the police . . ."

"Good."

They exchanged the briefest flicker of a look. It summarized a world of feelings about the numerous times when Peter had not spoken to the police as promptly as Kevin would have liked.

"So, I'm sure they're looking into it," Peter went on. He tried to keep skepticism out of his voice, but he doubted Kevin was fooled. "It's another piece of evidence that will help clear Sam. He's led a strange life, but he has no connection to the Balkans."

"Unless Sam drew the symbol to throw the scent off," Kevin said, shrugging as if to indicate that this was a casual, throwaway remark.

"Laura said something like that too, regarding the mysterious voice. Sure, it's possible. But is it probable? I don't think so. I mean, my brother's smart, but this is too elaborate and obscure."

Kevin raised an eyebrow.

"Yeah, yeah. I get it. 'Elaborate and obscure' kind of describes him. But not when he's scared. If he killed the guy — *if* — it would never be in cold blood. He just doesn't have it in him. I promise you that. It would have to be an accident, and then he'd panic and not be able to cover his tracks in such a sophisticated way."

"OK, sure. Just for the sake of argument, and you're right about Sam, this Ubashik —"

"Ustasha."

"Whatever. This weird little marking on the wall is hardly enough of a clue for the local cops to have cause to haul in every Croatian and Bosnian in Winnipeg for questioning."

"They wouldn't have to. Just the ones in this building."

"Ha! Didn't I just demonstrate the crapola security here?"

"That's the first time I've heard of the door being propped open. Normally someone has to let you in. But more critically, Dženan was killed by someone he knew and trusted enough to let in and to allow them to give him a drink or food that was spiked with something to knock him out. There were no signs of a struggle, right? And no signs of forced entry."

Kevin squinted and held his hand up to shade his eyes as the sun had suddenly broken through the clouds. It was lined up perfectly with the kitchen window. "Move your head a smidge to the left, Pete."

Peter did as he was asked.

"So, you're saying this dude had no friends outside the building?" Kevin said, still squinting a little.

Peter paused. Kevin had a good point. In fact, it was an incredibly obvious good point. He hated little more than missing incredibly obvious good points. This was embarrassing.

"Um, right. No, I wasn't saying that, but I assume the police checked all his contacts from his phone and address book. Someone in the building wouldn't necessarily be in his contact list. But decent point, Kev, thanks. I hope they went back and looked again for contacts from the Balkans after I told them about the Ustasha." Peter was pleased with himself for his face-saving reply.

"Can you do something about the sun? Maybe close the blinds? Your head is pretty damned big, but it's not big enough."

Peter smiled and got up to change the angle of the greasy Roman blinds. While he was up, he opened the window a crack to let in some fresh air. It was cool out, but not unpleasantly so. A warbly bugling sound filled the kitchen. It was loud and came from directly overhead. Peter twisted his head to try to see, but the windowpanes were grey with dust, and the glare of the sun made it impossible to see much from that angle. But he knew what was making the sound without having to lay eyes on it.

"What the hell is that?" Kevin exclaimed, leaning forward.

"Cranes! Sandhill cranes migrating."

"If you say so. Glad that doesn't happen all the time. They sound like geese who swallowed broken trumpets."

"They're beautiful birds, Kev."

"Sure. But anyway, this local Balkan killer — I imagine you have a short list?"

Peter returned to his chair. "Yes, as a matter of fact, I do."

CHAPTER
Twenty-Six

The food lady came out again. She joined several other people who had emerged from their giant boxes to stare at the rolling box with the bright flashing lights. Thank goodness it had stopped making its horrible screaming noises. He was smart to have gone back into his hiding bush. He'd have to remember it for future reference. It was a useful hiding bush. It might come in handy again.

The food lady and the other people chattered and pointed this way and that. After a little while they became quieter, but they kept standing there. This was annoying.

After much too long a time, the people from the rolling box came out again. This time they carried a board between them. The board had a very large thing on top of it, covered by a blanket. The food lady and the other people made sad noises when they saw this. Maybe a favourite toy or an important food source was being removed?

The door was held open now with a little piece of wood. He could maybe sneak in while all these people were distracted. But he was wary. There were too many eyes. He was hungry, but he could wait a little longer.

The rolling box went away without lights or screaming noises, but the food lady and the other people still stood around chattering some more. This was intolerable. He would be forced to make a choice between dying of starvation and running for the door and risking being snatched by the food lady or one of the other people. But he was very fast, and he did not want to die of starvation. What would that even feel like? Probably very terrible.

He tensed his muscles and was just about to dash when they all stopped chattering and left.

His luck had finally turned!

But then it turned again.

He had been so intent on watching what the food lady and other people were doing that he didn't notice another rolling box appear. Two people stepped out of it and walked to the door.

He'd have to wait again, but hopefully only a very short time.

And then he noticed something. One of the people was carrying a small animal. It was about the size and shape of a cat, but it was definitely not a cat. It had an ugly, fluffy tail, and its nose was way too long. The not-a-cat looked right at him. He froze. They locked eyes for a second. The not-a-cat squirmed and began whining. It wanted to jump from its person's arms and run to him. And then do who knows what. He was terrified. He wanted to hiss, but he was smart again, so instead of hissing, he shrank deeper into the bush. And fortunately, the not-a-cat's person held it tighter in response to the squirming.

The people and the not-a-cat entered the giant box. The other person, not the one holding the not-a-cat, kicked the little piece of wood away.

The door slammed shut behind them.

What was he going to do? His hunger was driving him mad. He was convinced now that this was the correct giant box. This was the giant box that contained the first food man, the second food man, and his brothers. He needed to get in there.

Finally, no people were around. He could approach the door safely and examine it. He wasn't sure how doors worked. It was worth trying a few things. But sadly, multiple attempts at pawing it and meowing at it did nothing. It remained closed. He turned around and began to groom himself out of frustration. That always made him feel better.

Then, out of the corner of his eye, he saw the door of the other giant box open. The food lady stepped out.

What was wrong with this person? Why did she keep going in and out of her box? Fortunately, she was staring at the black rectangle in her hand, so she didn't see him.

He bolted for the hiding bush. To his horror, she began walking toward him. He retreated as far into the bush as he could and made himself flat against the ground.

She walked right by him to the door of the giant box he had been trying to get into. She took a small silvery stick out of her pocket and stuck it into a little hole in the door. It opened! He wished he had a small silvery stick.

Please, please, please put the little wooden block back to keep the door open.

But she didn't.

He was doomed. Even if he got into the giant box, the food lady would catch him and drag him back to her box. He wouldn't starve there, but he would be a lonely prisoner.

He didn't know what to do. He was exhausted from all the stress, so he fell asleep.

He awoke to find the not-a-cat staring at him, nose to nose, its horribly pink mouth hanging open and its ridiculously long tongue dangling out like a wet cloth. His first thought was how disgusting its hot breath was. His second thought was, I'd better smack this thing, or I'm going to die and get eaten.

CHAPTER *Twenty-Seven*

"Hang on Pete, I'm all ears about your list, but I just got a text from Stuart." Kevin sucked his breath in. He looked up from his phone at Peter. "We've got to go down there. Orbit's been attacked by a cat."

"Attacked? What, how?"

"Don't know, but Stuart says there's blood." Kevin was already up and half jogging to the door, narrowly missing knocking over a teetering pile of old phone books.

"I'm right behind you."

"Good thing this happened with the family vet handy," Kevin said as they ran down the stairs.

Peter was struck by a thought. "Did he say what kind of cat?"

Kevin glanced at him. "Uh, no. Does it matter? Are some more dangerous?"

"No, not really. But I was thinking about Sam's missing cat."

"Uh-huh." Kevin had tuned him out after the "no" and was out the door before him.

Stuart was crouched with the puppy, stroking him and talking to him quietly.

"Let's have a look," Peter said, kneeling down beside them. Orbit was surprisingly calm. At first glance, he looked unharmed. "Where's the injury?"

"On his nose," Stuart said, and pointed to a spot at the edge of the puppy's nostril. Kevin hovered in the background, pacing.

Peter leaned in and peered more closely. He saw a tiny nick. "You mean this? Kevin said he was bleeding."

"Yes. But I wiped it. I hope that was the correct thing to do." Stuart showed Peter a tissue with a small spot of blood on it. "Is he going to be OK?" he asked. Kevin stopped pacing, and they both looked at Peter with their brows furrowed and their lips pursed.

"One hundred percent. It's nothing." He chuckled and adopted a faux British accent, "It's only a flesh wound." The Monty Python joke fell flat. They both stared at him.

"He won't need a tetanus shot?" Stuart asked.

"Or a rabies test?" Kevin added.

"No, dogs don't get tetanus. And no, rabies can't be transmitted through a scratch. And you don't want to know how we test for it."

Stuart did not look entirely convinced. Kevin took a deep breath and let it out in a loud whoosh.

"OK, that's great," he said. "Thanks, Pete. So, nothing else we need to do?"

"Nope, nothing. Just keep an eye on it and make sure it stays clean."

The puppy began to wriggle.

"OK, Orbit," Stuart said softly. "The doctor says you'll be fine. You can sniff around a little." He released the puppy, but kept a tight hold on his leash, an expensive-looking leather one. Orbit made a beeline for the bush.

"Is the cat still there?" Peter asked. "Did you see where it went?"

"I don't know. I haven't seen it since it attacked Orbit," Stuart said, reeling the protesting puppy back in.

Peter walked over to the bush, an unruly caragana, and crouched down. He made quiet pss-pss-pss noises, interspersed with "here, kitty" and "come, Mr. Bingley," although he doubted the kitten knew its name yet.

There was no response, nor could he detect any movement. But if the attacker was Mr. Bingley and he was in there, he might be very hard to see. Bengals are well camouflaged by their spotted tawny coats, and he was just a small kitten.

He had an idea. He stood up and walked back to where Stuart and Kevin were fussing with the puppy. "Hey guys, have you got any dog treats on you? Normally cats aren't too keen on those, but if it's who I think it is, he may be quite hungry."

Stuart nodded and pulled four bags of treats out of his coat pocket. Peter hadn't noticed before how much the pocket was bulging. "Please, take what you like."

Peter smiled and selected a soft one that claimed to have fish and lamb in it. He walked back to the bush and dropped to his hands and knees. He crawled around the perimeter of the bush, laying treats at intervals. Then he stepped away from the bush, sat on the grass quietly, and waited.

He was right. It only took a minute before he saw a pair of copper-coloured eyes catch the sun. The kitten crept cautiously forward, sniffing and glancing from side to side. It was a Bengal. It had to be Mr. Bingley. Peter was so relieved he almost shouted, "Right on!" But he kept quiet.

Orbit was out of his sight, behind Kevin, but Peter was sure the kitten knew that he was still there. Nonetheless, his hunger and curiosity appeared to overcome any fear, and he took a treat, munching on it loudly while obviously still on high alert, his ears erect, his tail puffed.

It took a few more treats and quite a few more minutes, but Peter was eventually able to approach the kitten, and then in one deft, lightning-fast move, scoop him up. He expected more of a struggle, but the kitten was relatively calm, still making wild animal chewing noises as he powered through more treats.

"Whoa, little man. We don't want to make you sick!" Peter chuckled.

Kevin came up to them, smiling. "So, this is the fierce marauder? Slasher of innocent puppies?"

"Looks like it. And it's Sam's missing cat. So, a big thank you to Orbit!"

"I'll pass that along." Kevin laughed. "Look, Pete, we'll have to leave the spine-tingling conclusion of another episode of *Inspector Bannerman Speculates* for another time. Stu and Orbit and I gotta head home and get cleaned up before dinner tonight."

"Sounds good. See you later."

Stuart headed to their car with Orbit, but Kevin lingered. He leaned toward Peter and whispered, "I do want to know. How do you test for rabies?"

Peter looked him straight in the eye. "We have to cut off the head and send the whole brain to the lab."

Kevin looked genuinely shocked. He didn't say anything. He just nodded and left.

After they were gone, Peter lifted the kitten up in front of him and dangled him from the armpits so they were looking at each other face to face, the kitten's forelegs stretched toward Peter and the rest of him hanging like a tiny sack of potatoes. This was his favourite behaviour test in kittens. It wasn't always accurate, but it was still a decent indicator of whether you had a relatively calm one or a relatively wild one. Mr. Bingley tested as relatively calm. He just hung there, staring placidly at him. But Peter considered that he was probably also exhausted.

"So, young fellow, are you ready to go to your temporary home and see your brothers again?"

This was going to work out well because Ed was on Peter's Balkan connection list. He had checked and confirmed that the PPCLI had been part of the peacekeeping force in Bosnia in the '90s. Maybe Ed had been deployed there. Maybe there was a link.

Ed beamed when he saw Peter and the kitten at his door. "You found him! Fantastic! Have you told your brother yet?" Ed was wearing a kilt. So Scottish, not Irish. Not a leprechaun.

"Ah, no. I just found him. I'll get a message through to Sam at remand right away."

Mr. Bingley began to meow in that characteristically loud Bengal voice, loud especially given his small size. Peter assumed that he must smell his brothers.

"Go ahead, let him go," Ed said. "There's fresh water there, and I'll grab some food for him in a sec. Flinders and Barry are in the bedroom. They'll come running right away." Seeing that Peter had noticed his kilt, he added, "Ha! Yeah, PPCLI pipe and drum band, Piper Sargeant MacDougall reporting." He snapped a comic salute and laughed. "Retired, that is. But the boys and I still get together in the park one Sunday a month."

"That's great," Peter said, thinking it actually was great, because it was the perfect excuse to ask him about his service. He set down Mr. Bingley, who immediately ran into the living room, tail in the air, meowing like he was making a major announcement. His brothers came running to him from the bedroom to the right, also meowing. Peter and Ed watched as the three of them sniffed each other. Then they all flopped on their sides, exposing their bellies, and began play fighting.

Ed chuckled. "Wanna come in for a minute? Watch the kitten show? I don't have to leave for a bit yet. Have a seat while I grab some chow for our adventurer."

Perfect. "Sure, I've got a few minutes too."

Ed motioned for him to sit at the game table again, like last time. The kittens continued to wrestle on the floor, occasionally making sounds like they were murdering each other, until Ed filled a food bowl. He held the other two back to allow Mr. Bingley at it first. The kitten attacked the bowl like a small hairy tornado.

"Yeah, I'm really enjoying these little guys. However long Sam needs to leave them here is fine by me. Dunno what the fish think, though." Ed laughed and inclined his head toward the large tank nearest where the kittens were playing.

"So, did you serve overseas?" Peter asked. He didn't mind changing the subject abruptly.

"Me? Yeah, several tours."

"Oh, like Afghanistan?" He didn't want to ask about Bosnia directly and risk spooking him. Most people were more familiar with the Afghanistan deployment than the one in Bosnia, so it was the more obvious first question to ask. Many longer-serving soldiers were deployed to both.

"Yeah, Operation Anaconda. But I don't like to talk about it." He looked down at his lap.

Shoot, Peter thought. He had missed his chance. Asking about Bosnia directly now felt inappropriate.

Ed looked up and smiled. "Sorry . . . didn't mean to make you uncomfortable. It's cool. But tell me about finding Bingley!"

Peter told him the story, all the while trying to think of a way to bring the conversation back to someplace where a Bosnia reference wouldn't be too far out of place. But he couldn't, so after a few more banal pleasantries, and seeing that the kittens had now collapsed into a napping heap, he thanked Ed for helping Sam and left.

As he exited the apartment and turned toward the stairs, he almost collided with a short young woman with a blond ponytail, wearing a Winnipeg Blue Bombers sweatshirt. She had just come from the room across the hall. That's where Woman with Slavic Accent lived, the one he had originally called Green Dress Woman. He had never seen this woman before, though.

"Oops, sorry," he said.

"No worries!" She smiled at him, but also seemed to be appraising him.

He noticed that she was carrying a large key ring. Odd. Best to be direct. "Are you new in the building?"

She tilted her head and gave him a peculiar look. "Nope. I'm the super. I live over in the Beatrice. And you are . . . ?"

"Peter. Peter Bannerman. Sam's brother. I'm checking on his place for him."

"Ah, right. Nice to meet you." She extended her hand to shake Peter's. Her grip was remarkably firm. "Rough few days here in the Alice."

"Yes. All very sad."

She shook her head. "We've got to be on the lookout. Things come in threes, you know."

Peter hated superstition, and the "things coming in threes" was especially annoying. It was so illogical. Didn't it depend on when you started counting and when you stopped? You could just as easily draw arbitrary circles around two events, or four. And you would have to define a maximum time period between events for them to be considered part of the set. But he didn't say any of that. He said, "Yeah, it's scary when one of them was a murder."

"Or two of them."

Interesting response. "You think so? I heard it was a heart attack."

"I don't know. Maybe. But it's fishy. I don't really believe in coincidences."

Back in Sam's apartment, Peter wished he had thought of a way to get more information about the Woman with Slavic Accent from the superintendent. Could her unusual accent in fact be from the Balkans? Maybe. And now he also wondered whether the superintendent should be on the radar as a suspect. She had access to all the apartments, after all, which would answer a few open questions. But on the other hand, she was blond, had a bog-standard Anglo-Canadian accent, and was too young to have been directly involved in the Yugoslav Wars. None of this precluded a passionate interest in Croatian or Bosnian affairs, but it made it less likely. Also, wouldn't the killer want to push the idea that Maureen died of a heart attack rather than cast doubt on it? Unless she was playing a clever double game of knowing he would think that.

Peter shook his head. The questions were increasing in number faster than the answers. He looked dolefully around the apartment, unable to summon any interest in continuing to search for that blasted Bluetooth speaker. If it was even still here. Or ever was.

He missed his dog. He missed his wife. It was time to go home.

CHAPTER

Twenty-Eight

Before leaving the apartment, Peter called the remand centre and left a message for Sam that Mr. Bingley had been found and was safe with Ed now. He felt a little guilty about not going and visiting again, but only a little.

He took the direct way home, up Main Street, and then across on the Perimeter to Highway 59. Sometimes he liked to take alternative routes for mental stimulation, but not today. He had had enough mental stimulation to last him a while. New Selfoss had been in his mind all day, the way an oasis is in the mind of a desert traveller.

Peter was relieved to see that Kevin and Stuart weren't there yet when he arrived. They weren't expected for another hour, but despite Stuart's moderating influence, Kevin could still be frustratingly random. Sometimes much too early. Sometimes much too late. Sometimes an unannounced visit. Sometimes a last-minute cancellation. But always with a belly-laugh, as if everyone else's adherence to schedules and calendars were a hilarious quirk. Peter wanted a quiet hour alone with Laura, Pippin, Merry, and Gandalf.

Thinking of Gandalf, Peter popped around the corner of the house to his paddock before going into the house. He hadn't gone to say hi to their goat yet today, something he normally did earlier.

All of Peter's routines were out of whack, like a bookshelf that's normally carefully arranged suddenly askew, with books upside down, spine-side in, stacked sideways, and generally jumbled. They didn't have to be alphabetized, or arranged by size or colour, just like his routines didn't need to be clockwork and always in the exact same sequence, but some readily graspable sense of order was necessary for him to not start forgetting things, like visiting Gandalf.

Gandalf came up to him and lowered his head for a scratch between the ears. This was the goat's second favourite thing. His favourite thing was eating treats. And among treats, fresh crunchy carrots — the crunchier the better — were at the top of his list, followed, oddly enough, by dried pasta. Peter had neither on him but made a mental note to bring him a carrot before the guests arrived.

"Hey, stranger!"

Peter turned around. Laura had opened the patio door and was smiling at him. He felt the last bit of tension ebb away. Laura was his safe harbour. Pippin, Merry, Gandalf, and even the house itself all played their role, but only Laura could make him feel this way.

He smiled back at her. "Hey! I couldn't take it there any longer, so I decided to come home a bit early."

"Perfect. Inside, you'll find a kitchen that's refusing to clean itself." Laura laughed and walked up to give Peter a kiss. "He looks happy to see you. Want a carrot for him before I put you to work?"

"Yes, thanks. And I'm going to have a half cup of Lapsang Souchong first too, if you think there's time."

Laura waved her hand dismissively at him. "Plenty of time! Treat yourself. Have a whole cup. I'll have one too. You can tell me what's new in the wonderful world of Sam Bannerman."

A half hour later, they were done their tea and were sitting quietly. Pippin was at Peter's feet, dozing, and Merry was on his lap, dozing as well.

"I guess I should start on the kitchen. They'll be here soon," Peter said, conscious that he was breaking a very soothing silence.

"I was half joking. It's in good enough shape for Kevin and Stuart. I just made a fall vegetable casserole, and there's not a lot of mess with that. No, tell me a bit more about what you're thinking with this Croatian connection. Nobody in that building is obviously from there, are they?" Laura was rooting about in her knitting bag as she asked this. Peter was unsure from the tone whether the interest was genuine or because she was fishing to find out how deeply Peter was becoming involved. He reasoned that, given her research on the Ustasha, it was more the former, but at the same time, he knew that he had to reassure her that he was not going to interfere with police work or put himself in harm's way.

"No, not obviously, but Ed served in an army unit that may have been stationed in Bosnia." Peter held up one finger. "And Josh and Claire backpacked in the Balkans a few years ago." He held up a second one. "And the woman in apartment 1 speaks with an accent that could possibly be Croatian or Bosnian." Third finger. "And finally, I've never heard Mia — that's the Other Peter's wife — speak, but she has a look that indicates she could be from Southeastern Europe." Fourth finger.

Laura put down her knitting and chuckled. "Really? Those are four pretty darned slender threads, Peter. 'May have been stationed there.' 'Was a tourist there.' 'Might have the right accent.' 'Might have the right look.'" She chuckled again and smiled at her husband. "Well below your usual standards of rational supposition!"

"I get your point, but I barely know these people, so it's all I've got to go on. Even if I can just get Mia's last name and the woman in apartment 1's names, then I might be on a little more solid ground."

"I'm sure the police have that and would have questioned them if they thought there was a relevant connection to the old country."

Peter shrugged. "But they have Sam in custody and apparently enough evidence to charge him, so it's easy for them to discount anything that didn't point that way. Confirmation bias. I'm not saying it's a conspiracy to lock him up. I'm sure they're professional and smart and honourable, but once there was strong evidence pointing to Sam, it would be human nature to orient more and more in that direction and begin to pay less attention to other possibilities."

Pippin woke up. He remained lying down, but he looked back and forth between Laura and Peter.

"Hmm, OK," Laura said, speaking slowly as if carefully considering each word. "But even if you find out that one of them has a potentially Croatian last name, what then? And the others, are you going to casually ask them for more details about their time in the Balkans? And where does that get you?"

Peter pursed his lips and nodded. These were good questions. He was just about to answer when a thunderous knocking rattled the front door. Pippin leapt to his feet and let out a sharp bark. Pippin was not normally a barker, but he must have sensed that dogs had arrived with the people at the door.

Before Laura or Peter could answer, the door swung open and Orbit, the Shetland sheepdog puppy, came racing in, followed by Atlas, the old husky, walking much slower, and then Kevin and Stuart. Stuart had a bouquet of flowers and a bottle of wine, which he gave to Laura.

"Puppy play time!" Kevin bellowed.

Normally Peter would be appalled at an uncontrolled dog introduction like that, but Pippin was especially good with puppies, and he and Atlas knew each other well. Merry, on the other hand, was having none of it and disappeared like a rocket into the master bedroom. Laura closed the bedroom door so that Orbit couldn't follow her.

"Should we let them play outside?" Stuart asked, eyeing lamps and other fragile objects as Orbit tore around in mad circles.

"The yard's not fenced," Peter said.

Stuart nodded. "Right, I forgot. I'll take him out on the lead if he doesn't settle down soon."

"Don't worry," Laura said. "He can't do much harm in here, and he's adorable." She scooped him up as he went hurtling by and hugged him.

Kevin settled into an armchair and waved to Peter. "Garçon, un cerveza s'il vous plait.'

"You're mixing up your Spanish and French, Kev, but sure."

Peter's phone buzzed. He fished it out of his pocket and, after glancing at the screen, said, "Hang on a sec, it's the remand centre."

He stepped out of the living room into the kitchen, where it was quieter. Pippin followed him.

After introducing himself, the officer cleared his throat and said, "Your brother hasn't eaten since he arrived here. At first, he said that he wasn't hungry because of the stress, but now he's calling it a hunger strike."

"Hunger strike? What are his demands?"

"No demands. He says he wants to die. We have him on suicide watch anyway, but we won't force him to eat. I should tell you that we caught him trying to choke himself by tying the sleeves of his shirt around his neck when he was getting changed. We were able to stop him right away."

"Jesus. Did you pass on the message that I found the cat?"

"Yes, and he said he was relieved, but he still wants to die because," the officer paused and cleared his throat, "and this is what he says, 'my life is hell, and my brother won't help me.' Do you know what he's talking about, or is it just delusional?"

"A little of both. There's something he wants me to do that's impossible." Peter sighed and sank down onto a kitchen chair.

"Oh? Well, he says he just needs you to bring a painting he was working on to ward off what he calls 'evil spirits.' I guess this painting doesn't exist, or you can't find it?"

Peter was impressed that Sam had restrained himself from ranting about Balkan ghosts. "Evil spirits" could be interpreted as simple superstition or even have religious overtones. In the latter case, the guards would be reluctant to openly voice skepticism.

"A painting? No, that's not what he asked me to do. What painting? Did he describe it?"

"He said it was very small, about the size of a paperback book. It has a blue eye in the middle."

Peter didn't remember seeing anything like that among Sam's paintings, only that large canvas with the horrendous purple intestines. "If I can find it, is he allowed to have that in his cell?"

"We'll have to check it over of course, but under the circumstances, sure." The officer cleared his throat again. "There's another thing I should mention, Mr. Bannerman. Your brother has also started saying that he is guilty, that he committed the murder. He has said so several times. He has asked his lawyer to be present so that he can make a formal statement."

"But he's obviously not in his right mind."

"At times, no. But he seems very lucid during these confessions. In any case, that's for the courts to determine, not us."

Peter went back into the living room. Pippin followed him again.

"Sorry, guys — I've got to go back into the city."

CHAPTER *Twenty-Nine*

This time Pippin was coming with. Peter would find the painting and then Pippin could stay at the apartment while he ran it over to remand and had a quick word with Sam. The officer had said that, given the situation, they would bend the normal visitation rules, but that it had to be brief. This suited Peter fine. He had no appetite whatsoever to subject himself to yet another session of wild rambling. With even just a little luck, they'd be back home in time for late dessert. He wasn't really a dessert guy, but Laura had baked his favourite, Varmahlíð apple cake, using her grandmother's recipe and her friend's excellent crabapples.

The traffic was light for early Sunday evening. During the summer, southbound 59 would be clogged with beachgoers and cottagers returning to the city after the weekend. The earlier part of September had been summery; this was the first weekend with proper fall weather, and the impact was obvious. Plus, many people were back into a different set of routines. Regardless of the reasons, Peter liked it. No impatient drivers tailgating him or making insane passing manoeuvres. Instead, just open road, golden aspens, harvested fields, and Mozart piano concertos.

This would have been lovely and soothing if it weren't for the unavoidable looping thoughts about Sam's confession. He had been so adamant before regarding his innocence. And Peter still firmly believed Sam was innocent. It was illogical to believe otherwise. But Sam's own brain did not have the same logic circuits, and clearly he was under enormous strain, so even those circuits that did exist would be misfiring. Maybe the ghost voices he was hallucinating told him to confess? That made the most sense. At a deeper level, perhaps it was a way for his subconscious to resolve tension and conflict. A confession could bring about a weird kind of clarity and resolution. The path forward would be much simpler this way. But Peter had no training in psychiatry, so he stopped that pointless train of thought. What he knew with greater certainty was that this made it all the more imperative that he quickly find concrete exonerating evidence.

The sun was low in the west already. Sunset was coming so much earlier. This close to the equinox, day length changed rapidly. It slanted through the aspens, lending them a deep glow, as if lit from within. Peter loved this kind of light. It often brought to mind the Joni Mitchell line "The sun poured in like butterscotch, and stuck to all my senses." Although "*all* my senses" was rather generous poetic licence. Vision mostly, and a bit of touch from the warmth, but definitely no smell, sound, or taste. However, he supposed that butterscotch itself had a distinctive smell and taste. So, as a metaphor, it worked that way; although sound remained unresolved. Neither the sun nor butterscotch made any sort of sound you could imagine hearing. He still loved the line, but he knew he'd never be a poet.

He was pleased that this little mental detour briefly distracted him from further unproductive speculation about Sam's confession. But now the speculation was back, unbidden, so he shifted his focus forcefully to how he should go about finding the necessary evidence. Obviously, he'd have to speak to each of the people on his list, but on what pretext? It would be different for each one.

"What do you think, Pippin?" Sometimes thinking aloud helped, and Pippin was a reliably good listener, even if not an especially responsive one. Peter chuckled to himself at the thought. He glanced in the rearview mirror and saw Pippin looking at him with a relaxed face, mouth partly open. He noticed for the first time a little crust at the edge of one of Pippin's nostrils. It was nothing, but it gave him an idea.

He smiled and turned up the Mozart. All he needed was one idea that put him one step forward. After all, even the most complex problem was solved one step at a time.

Half an hour later, they were in the city, headed south on Main. As Peter changed lanes, preparing for the right turn onto Burrows a few blocks ahead, he saw a familiar figure crossing the street. It was the bearded bulk of Josh. He was carrying two Dollarama shopping bags, but oddly, he was carrying them in the opposite direction of the apartment, crossing Main from west to east. Was he returning a bunch of stuff to the store? On a Sunday night? That made no sense. Peter pulled over into the parking lane and watched. After crossing the street, Josh headed into St. John's Park.

This was distinctly odd. Peter's idea would have to wait a moment. Here was a potential opportunity, handed to him by chance. What if Josh was getting rid of evidence? Maybe planning to dump it in the river, knowing that the police could more easily go through his garbage. So long after the crime was unusual, but maybe this was his first chance if Claire wasn't in on it. And maybe he even needed Peter to be away to get back into Sam's apartment and get rid of some incriminating evidence he knew was still there.

Peter stopped himself. Once again, this was pointless speculation. But nonetheless, Josh's activity was at least a little bit suspicious, so it made sense to follow him. Nothing was more natural than a man taking his dog for a walk in the park, right? They had met there coincidentally before, so why not again?

Pippin was delighted to be offered a spontaneous walk. He seemed to know they would be going into the park as he began to pull that way. Peter wished he had something with Josh's scent on it to get Pippin to follow, but they'd have to make do without. The sun had just set, but for the moment, there was still enough light.

He could see Josh's distinctive ursine shape silhouetted against the river. He was ambling north, along the riverbank. Peter and Pippin followed at a distance, trying to keep out of sight as much as possible without seeming furtive. Then Josh ducked into the dense bush in the northeast corner of the park.

This was even more suspicious. Why would someone take shopping bags into the trees in the half dark? Was there even a path there?

Peter and Pippin sped up. He didn't want to lose him. Pippin pricked his ears up and held his tail erect. Peter smiled, seeing that Pippin had clued in to the fact that this was not an ordinary walk. Pippin loved a bit of excitement.

As they approached the bush, Peter saw a narrow dirt path snaking in. Ah, he thought, this was one of those famous "monkey trails." The forests on the banks of the Red, Assiniboine, and Seine Rivers in the city were threaded with an extensive network of informal paths. Peter had walked Pippin on one of them near Assiniboine Park. There had been a couple mountain bikers and one bird watcher with a camera lens the length of a small piece of artillery, but otherwise it had been delightfully quiet — a little fragment of wilderness in the big city.

The trail was easy to follow for the first few steps, but then it split. Peter could no longer see Josh, but Pippin had his nose to the ground. He tugged toward the path on the left. Peter was uncertain whether Pippin had figured out they were following a person and had pointed them in the direction of the most recent human scent, or whether he was just having fun and wanted to follow something else that smelled interesting.

Bright scarlet dogwood crowded the path from both sides. It was beautiful, but it made it impossible to see more than a few metres ahead. Peter shortened Pippin's leash.

Pippin stopped.

A noise to their right.

It was in the tangled bush covering the slope down to the river. The river was not visible, but Peter knew that it couldn't be more than ten metres away.

Pippin sniffed the ground and the air.

The noise had stopped. Pippin remained still. Peter listened intently. He only picked up the hum of traffic from Main Street. And geese honking on the river.

The noise started again. It was a rustling. Someone was moving through the dense riverbottom forest. It was still on the right, toward the river, but now slightly behind them.

So, Josh was circling back through the bush to . . . what? Cut them off?

If Josh wanted to escape them, it would have made more sense to run ahead on the trail. It could only mean that he was trying to get behind them.

Shit.

Peter's heart began to thump loudly. He took a deep breath. *Stop these irrational thoughts.* There were a hundred more probable explanations. OK, maybe not a hundred, but a lot. *And look, Pippin is perfectly calm and collected.* This helped. But only a little.

Peter took another deep breath and held it.

Pippin's head slowly swivelled, following the sounds. Peter couldn't localize them himself, so he looked wherever Pippin was looking.

The rustling suddenly became much louder. It was almost directly behind them now.

Peter exhaled. He wheeled around and peered down the trail.

The rusting became a crashing.

A large shape emerged from the bush.

Oh my g—

It was a deer.

A young buck with small antlers. He looked at least as anxious as Peter felt. He bolted down the path away from them.

"Oh my god," Peter whispered hoarsely, bending down to brace his hands against his knees. "I really thought it was Josh coming to . . . Never mind. But now he's got a really long lead on us. Damn it."

Pippin panted and wagged his tail. He had enjoyed seeing the deer.

They continued down the path in the direction they had been going, only much faster now. It split several times, but Pippin seemed quite sure of himself. Often he picked the wider option, but sometimes the narrower. They were past the park now and below whatever street ran to the north of it. Peter was hazy on his geography here. He was unsure how far the monkey trails extended in this direction before they hit private backyards, or a part of the riverbank too steep to accommodate a path.

After a couple minutes, he heard something again. This time it was the murmur of voices. Probably other people walking on the path. Josh would be wanting to dispose of the evidence alone, if that's what he was doing. It didn't make sense for him to be meeting any sort of accomplice out here.

Pippin slowed down. He was sniffing more intently. Peter picked up something too. It was a hint of smoke.

Soon he could see flashes of blue and red ahead. The bushes had thinned, but the light was too dim now to make anything out.

The murmured voices were louder, but Peter couldn't make out any words yet. It was definitely a conversation between two or more people, though. And some laughter.

Peter sucked his breath in and wavered.

Was this risky? Maybe a little?

But he was just innocently out for a walk with his dog. Everyone could happily pretend nothing was going on.

They stepped into a clearing on a high riverbank.

Four faces swivelled to look at them. Josh and three other men were sitting and smoking on a couple of large elm logs. Beside them were three tarps strung like pup tents. This was the blue and red. The Dollarama bags were at Josh's feet.

Peter didn't know what to think or do. One instinct told him to run, and the other told him to stay.

Josh spoke first. "Dr. Bannerman! Hey!"

Peter stayed.

CHAPTER
Thirty

Afterwards Peter berated himself for being so jumpy. It had been irrational. The whole scenario with Sam was upsetting his steadfast emotional equilibrium. Being afraid of Josh based on his remark about backpacking in the Balkans and on carrying Dollarama bags to the riverbank did not meet his usual standards for rational threat analysis. In fact, Josh had just been bringing food and toiletries to a small homeless encampment. He had won the men's trust over the summer and now regularly checked in on them, bringing them necessities and occasionally staying to share a smoke. While this did not preclude him from also being a murderer, possibly due to some as yet undiscovered motivation related to his visit to the former Yugoslavia, it did make it less likely.

Josh dropped to the bottom of the list.

Peter was awkward around strangers at the best of times, and this was not the best of times, so he had declined to join them when Josh asked. He had made an excuse that seemed lame at the time, and now even more so. "Oh, look at the time . . ." Yikes. A 1980s TV sitcom cliché. Josh and his friends laughed.

They were back at the Lady Alice, having moved the car to park it closer. Peter stopped in front of the door, Pippin at his side.

"What should we do first? Look in Sam's room for that painting, or try out my idea?"

Pippin panted, tongue hanging out. His eyes were bright, and his head was cocked half to the side, evidently waiting for Peter to say something more interesting or recognizable.

"Idea first. That way, if they're not in now, we can check again after we're done at Sam's, but if we don't check now and they're gone later, we'll miss them." That sort of made sense, although if he was honest with himself, he was keener to talk to Mia and the Other Peter than he was to rummage about in Sam's apartment again.

They were home. This time Mia answered the door. She was a slender young woman with short black hair. Hadn't Sam said she was blond? Peter also took note of her Clannad T-shirt.

"Dr. Bannerman, hello!" No obvious accent, but a wide, genuine smile.

"Hi!" Peter suddenly remembered something. He glanced down at Pippin. "Shoot. I totally forgot that you're allergic. Sorry!"

Mia laughed. "No worries. It's much more to cats than dogs. It's fine so long as I don't rub my face on him and he doesn't slobber on me." She laughed again.

The Other Peter appeared behind her. "Hi! What can we do for you?"

"This might sound strange, but I have some veterinary advice for you."

"Oh?" Mia said. "For Jack and David?" She furrowed her brow but still had a friendly smile.

"I know it's weird to show up at your door with this, but I didn't have your number or email, and I happened to be back in the building. I don't know when I'll be here again." Peter had rehearsed this, and it came out in a rush. "But anyway," he tried to slow himself down and sound less manic, "what I wanted to tell you was that I noticed that you use cedar shavings in your gerbils' cage."

"Yes, we do. Is that a problem?" Mia asked.

"Do you want to come in?" the Other Peter added. "Don't worry about your dog. We'll be fine."

"Only if you're sure it's no problem."

"No, no. It's so nice of you to think of our boys and take the trouble to stop by," the Other Peter said.

Peter turned to Mia. "The scent of the cedar can be too strong for these little guys. It can be really irritating to their mucous membranes."

"Oh dear. We had no idea! Can you have a look at them and make sure they're OK?" Mia stepped aside and pointed to the cage. Still no accent. As Peter walked across the living room, he didn't see anything that resembled a clue. Not that it was reasonable to expect to see one, even if they were somehow involved in Dženan's death, but it wasn't wrong to harbour a little bit of hope for a low-probability event.

The gerbils were sleeping in a nest made from a partially chewed-up Kleenex box. Mia opened the cage door and woke them by rustling the shavings and making soft sounds.

One after another, two twitching noses and two pairs of beady black eyes emerged.

"Which is which?" Peter asked, crouching down.

"Honestly, it's hard to tell sometimes," the Other Peter said, laughing. "David used to be the chubbier one, but Jack is catching up. Too many sunflower seeds."

"How would we know if the shavings have been hurting them?" Mia asked, leaning in over Peter's shoulder as he peered into the cage. She smelled faintly floral.

"The irritation usually shows up around the nares — I mean nostrils — so I'll see redness and crusting there. Sometimes some discharge. Also, around the eyes. That lovely cedar scent can just be too powerful when they're immersed in it." Peter stood up again. "But these guys are fine. No signs of a problem. Nonetheless, you should change the bedding to something neutral and unscented, like shredded newspaper."

"Thank you! We really appreciate it!" Mia said. "We'll do that right away tonight."

"No trouble at all," Peter said. "Happy to help." He glanced around the room quickly again. Still nothing. "Nice place," he added.

"What do we owe you, Doctor?" the Other Peter asked.

"Nothing at all, really. Just being neighbourly on behalf of my brother."

"Are you sure?" The Other Peter had pulled out his wallet.

"Hundred percent. My pleasure, really."

"Well, thank you again," the Other Peter said, putting his wallet back in his hip pocket. "We really hope your brother's name gets cleared. He did not seem like the type."

"Thank you." Peter was about to turn and go but decided to take a chance now that they had made a connection of sorts. "Is there anyone here that does seem like the type?"

The Other Peter glanced at Mia. He looked like he was about to say something, but then Mia spoke up. "That Ed guy downstairs. The whole military thing and the war games."

"Yeah," the Other Peter said, "we don't mix with the other residents much, but we actively avoid him. Just the vibe, I guess." He shrugged.

CHAPTER
Thirty-One

Peter mentally updated the list. Mia joined her husband near the bottom, below Josh. No connection whatsoever to Dženan or his past was apparent, whereas Josh at least still had a tenuous one. Was Ed higher on the list? Possibly. He would have to ponder that.

First, though, Peter wanted to come up with a plan to approach the woman in apartment 1 — the one with the mystery Slavic accent — and find out more about her. While he thought about that, he figured that he may as well cross the hall to Sam's apartment and look for that painting. Also, he had to keep an eye on the time if he wanted to enjoy the Varmahlíð apple cake with his family. If he remembered correctly, he was scheduled to be done midafternoon at the clinic tomorrow, so he could come back then to talk to the woman with the accent. He felt a little nugget of guilt begin to pulsate just inside the edge of his awareness. Late tomorrow afternoon. Another delay in figuring this out. Another day Sam was in jail, and now not only in jail, but wanting to die.

Peter sighed.

What was more important, dessert or proving Sam's innocence?

The apartment was unchanged. Just before opening the door, a fear flashed across his consciousness that there would be something gruesome inside. Another warning from the murderer. But when he glanced around, nothing was obviously new.

It was, however, noticeably hotter than before. He'd have to check the radiators. But first, that painting.

Sam's canvases were all in the bathroom, stacked in the bathtub and against the walls amongst all manner of brushes, fluids, rags, cans, boxes, and other supplies. It was odd that he hadn't hung any of them on the apartment walls, but there wasn't much blank wall between all the shelving. The few potential spots were papered over in tattered vintage heavy metal concert posters. Whitesnake, Glasgow, 1980. Slayer, Japan Tour, 1990. Megadeth, Neuenkirchen, 1988. That sort of thing. Curiously, Peter couldn't remember Sam ever playing heavy metal or expressing an interest in it. Perhaps it was the design aesthetic? Made sense given some of the gruesome imagery in his artwork.

At least it looked like his paintings were all together in one place, so it would be easy to find the one with the blue eye.

But it wasn't.

The painting in question wasn't in any of the stacks. Peter sighed heavily. Pippin, who had been sniffing the licorice-stuffed teddy again nearby in the main room, padded over and looked at him.

There were several small plastic bins. The officer had said that the canvas was quite small, so Peter started rifling through them. The first two contained nothing but smelly rags and bottles of linseed oil. Peter supposed they were put in the bins because they didn't have lids, unlike the other bottles scattered about the room. The third one, however, held a half-dozen very small canvases. One of these depicted three wide concentric circles of dark blue, white, and turquoise with a black spot in the centre. This was the classic evil eye protection symbol, more commonly worn as a glass or ceramic amulet. Peter had seen them for sale all over Istanbul. It was crudely painted, as if in haste, and the background was blank.

"Bingo!" he called to Pippin. "OK, I'm going to run to the remand centre and hand this over. I won't be more than an hour."

Pippin looked at him, head cocked to one side. Peter knew Pippin would be fine by himself for however long he needed to be away. Pippin could be trusted not to get into trouble, even with all the stuff lying around, and not to begin howling out of loneliness. Atlas, the dog he had rescued from Dragonfly Lake, that Kevin now owned, had developed separation anxiety. He bayed mournfully whenever Kevin went to work. It got better with training, but Kevin had been an anxious wreck while it was at its worst, constantly calling Peter, blaming himself, despairing it would ever get better, asking about various weird advice he'd found on the internet. Then, when Atlas finally got over it, Kevin acted like it had been a trifle. But anyway, Pippin was thankfully rock-solid that way.

It was, however, too warm for him in the apartment. Peter tried to adjust the main radiator, but turning the dial didn't seem to do anything. He contemplated tracking down that superintendent, but he didn't have the time. He opened the window instead and pushed aside some boxes near it to give Pippin a place to lie down and enjoy the fresh air.

"I'll be back soon!"

Peter loped down the stairs, taking them two at a time. The woman with the accent from apartment 1 had just come into the building. She was carrying a familiar-looking small white paper shopping bag.

Bingo.

He couldn't believe his luck. This was the ticket. He could spare a couple minutes.

"Hi! I see you've just come from Cornelia Bean. One of my favourite places!"

The woman glanced down at her bag. "Yes, I have. One of my few little indulgences." She smiled at Peter. She was wearing the shimmering green dress again and that fleur-de-lys necklace. *Shoot,* he thought; he had meant to look that up. He also noticed half-moon glasses, like Dumbledore's, hanging from a chain around her neck. Her hair, black streaked with grey, was up in a bun, held in place with chopsticks.

"Life is hardly worth living without good quality tea," Peter said, smiling back at her. The shop sold coffee as well, but he remembered smelling Jasmine tea at her apartment before.

"Indeed, it is not." She was still smiling, but her tone hinted that she expected they were done and each would move on.

Peter decided that a bit of boldness was needed. He stuck his hand out. "Peter Bannerman, by the way. I don't recall whether I properly introduced myself when we last met."

"No, you did. But I may not have." She shook his hand. "Elena Baumgartner."

"German?" he asked. "I've been trying to place your accent, but I didn't think it sounded German."

"My husband was Austrian, and we lived there for a while, but I'm not from there, and I've lived all over. So, I suppose my accent is tricky." She chuckled.

He had been hoping for something more specific than "not from there" and "lived all over."

"I've never been to Austria but would love to go sometime. The closest I've been is Germany and Croatia. So, either side of Austria!" He laughed. Croatia wasn't true, but he hoped that it might spark a reaction. If she asked for details, he could fake it because he and Laura had been thinking about a trip to Dubrovnik and had read up a bit.

She nodded, but her expression was impassive.

"What brought you to Winnipeg?" Peter added, desperate to keep the conversation going.

She briefly narrowed her eyes and tightened her mouth. Peter knew that Europeans were much more reluctant to discuss personal details with relative strangers. He adopted the goofiest, most disarming smile he could.

She seemed to be considering her answer for a moment. "My husband, but then he died." She sounded more wistful than sad.

"Oh, I'm so sorry."

She shrugged. "Such is life." Her eyes darted to the door of her apartment, over Peter's right shoulder.

Peter cast around for another idea. He pointed at the bag. "So, what did you buy?"

She pulled a small packet of tea out of the bag and held it up for Peter to see. "It's an oolong. Iron Goddess. I can't afford the Lishan High Mountain, but this one is lovely."

"I bet!" Peter enthused.

"Would you like to smell it?"

"I would love to, thank you."

She unrolled the top of the packet and handed it to Peter.

He inhaled deeply through his nose. "A bit nutty? You're right. It is lovely. I'll have to buy some myself sometime. I'm usually more of a black tea guy myself. Boring, I suppose." He wasn't sure where he expected this tea conversation to go, but keeping her talking couldn't hurt regardless.

Peter handed the tea back to her. After sealing it up and putting it back into the bag, she said, "Have a nice day, Peter," and stepped around him.

"Enjoy your tea!" he called after her.

So, where did all this put her on the list? Maybe above Mia and Josh, roughly in line with Ed? That accent was definitely Slavic, and Austria was adjacent to the Balkans. But boy, that was a stretch. It was all a stretch. He sometimes prided himself on the belief that he was a talented amateur detective, but at times like this he had his doubts.

Good thing I have a day job, he thought, and chuckled wryly.

CHAPTER
Thirty-Two

The visit to the remand centre was remarkably efficient. Peter called ahead to say that he was coming. The officer he had spoken to earlier met him and took the painting for security inspection. Sam had already been brought to the visitors room, so Peter was able to go directly there without waiting. Perhaps because it was Sunday evening, it was busier than he had seen it before, with a mix of what he assumed were family members of various ages. Unlike before, the atmosphere was oddly a little festive. He even heard a bit of laughter.

In contrast, Sam was emotionally flat. Peter wondered whether he had been medicated. He expected anger, or sadness, or fear, or all of them mixed together in his brother's signature emotional roulette wheel style. But no, he was expressionless and spoke in a monotone. He didn't offer a greeting when Peter sat down. He just stared at him. Not a hostile glare, just a blank gaze.

"So, you heard about Mr. Bingley? You must be relieved," Peter said, trying not to allow false jollity to creep into his voice.

"Yes, thank you. I'm glad." He said that as if he were reading from a prepared statement.

Peter hadn't passed along any details regarding how Mr. Bingley had been found. He expected some questions about it, but as none were forthcoming, after a short pause, he forged on: "And I found the evil eye protection painting. They're just checking it over. It'll be in your cell when you get back."

"Thank you. That's good."

Peter wasn't sure where to take the conversation next. Given Sam's odd mood, was there any point in raising his confession and his apparent death wish? Or should he just wrap things up with a few pleasantries and leave?

Sam spoke again. "I killed him. We were playing backgammon, and I killed him with licorice."

What??

"Pardon me?"

"I killed him with too much licorice. It was too strong."

Licorice . . . The teddy! One mystery cleared up. But, what the heck?

"I'm sorry, I don't follow. He was found with a bag over his head and his pants around his ankles."

"We didn't talk about our sex lives, Peter."

At least there was a touch of the old Samuel Bannerman snark in that. As well as his reflexive obtuseness in clearly knowing what was meant by the comment but choosing to address some other aspect.

"Right. No, I mean, that's how they say he died. Auto-erotic asphyxiation. How would licorice play a role in this? Does it cause weird fantasies and impulses?" He knew he shouldn't have countered with snark of his own, but he couldn't help himself.

Sam appeared unfazed. "You wouldn't know this as a veterinarian because your patients don't eat licorice. High doses can cause ventricular fibrillation in vulnerable individuals. Also, it causes hypertension. Sometimes quite significant. A 59-year-old man in Boulder, Colorado, died from licorice toxicity two weeks ago."

"OK . . ." Peter was still unclear how this connected to the bag over Dženan's head. He wasn't surprised, though, by his brother's confident use of medical terminology. Sam had always been a sponge for learning. And despite his various paranoias and his susceptibility to conspiracy theories and oddball thought in general, he was scrupulous about using reliable sources when it came to anything science-related. Maybe Peter had a positive influence after all, at least in this limited way.

Sam went on. "Asphyxiation also increases the risks of ventricular fibrillation and high blood pressure. So, if Dženan was pleasuring himself, and already at risk, the additive effects of the licorice I pushed on him is what killed him. In other words, I killed him. Murder."

"Pushed on him?"

"I encouraged him strongly to take it. It's excellent licorice. Special from Sweden." His expression changed for the first time. He scowled briefly and muttered, "Effing Swedes."

"But surely if that's even what happened, it was an accident, not murder. You didn't mean to kill him. And anyway, I thought you said," Peter lowered his voice, "that the ghosts killed him?"

Sam's face was a blank again. "Yes. They did it through me."

Peter was about to rebut this, but he stopped himself. This contradicted what Sam had said on a previous visit about the supposed ghosts, but he shouldn't be surprised. Nor should he try to argue. It was as pointless as arguing with Gandalf or Merry. Sam had by now said so many different things. What was factual and what was fantasy was difficult to sort out. Other than that, the licorice-eating and backgammon-playing were almost certainly real, and the ghosts were not. Beyond those black-and-white landmarks, just a vast terrain of grey.

"I'll be dead by tomorrow," Sam went on.

"Come on, Sam!"

Abruptly, Sam stood up and walked to the door. The guard escorted him out. He did not look back.

Before driving back to the apartment, Peter sat in the car and took several deep breaths. There was no point in thinking too much about Sam's parting comment. He was already on suicide watch. Nothing would happen. Instead, Peter should turn his mind to facts, so he quickly read up on licorice toxicity.

At least, that's what he knew he should do, but "I'll be dead by tomorrow" kept loudly circling his brain like an aircraft looking for a place to land. Peter shook his head and tried to focus on the licorice search results.

He couldn't. He put his phone down and felt fear and worry wash over him. His stomach was tight, and he had a feeling of pressure inside his chest. He noticed how fast he was breathing and realized that he was terrified. And in realizing this, it oddly became a little easier to deal with. Just a little.

He gradually brought his breathing under control and then started the car but kept it in park. He picked up his phone again.

As Sam had said, licorice was not something veterinarians had to deal with. And it turned out he was right: it could cause a fatal rhythm disturbance in the ventricles of the heart. It was very rare, and only associated with high doses, but he didn't know how much Dženan had eaten.

OK, licorice *can* do this, but given the amount consumed around the world and the very small number of case reports, the probability was much lower than the probability that someone else killed him by other means. No doubt that news article about the guy in Colorado had set Sam off to research licorice poisoning. Like many people without a proper scientific education, Sam was unfortunately vulnerable to the availability heuristic — vividly remembered events tend to make you think they're more common than they actually are. For example, after hearing about a plane crash, many people are more nervous to get on an aircraft, even though it is an extremely safe mode of travel and had not become any less safe because of the event. Sam's apparent licorice paranoia was like that.

Also unfortunately, none of this could be disproved on autopsy — the active ingredient in licorice is not easy to test for, and ventricular fibrillation leaves no trace — so the police might buy his confession in the absence of another provable explanation. Peter pursed his lips and exhaled sharply. Everything always all circled back to the same point. He had to find evidence of someone else's involvement. And that evidence had to be more compelling than the evidence for the theories held by the police and now Sam. Peter felt the pressure rise in his chest again. He closed his eyes. It eased a little, but it refused to pass. He still couldn't shake the thought that Sam could be right. *Could* be. But how high was the probability?

Peter sucked his breath in and rubbed his temples hard, the friction of his fingertips briefly distracting him.

There was no point in speculating. He simply didn't have enough solid data yet for the case to be considered closed. Not nearly enough.

Pippin was waiting, and he was wasting time spinning pointless thoughts around his head like wobbly toy tops, but he'd have to live with them spinning for now while he got in with what he had to do.

Fortunately, it was just a ten-minute drive from Kennedy to Burrows.

As he pulled up to park, he saw whisps of smoke rising between the Lady Alice and the Lady Beatrice. In the few seconds it took for him to get out of the car and walk toward the building, the amount of smoke increased dramatically. Grey-black, it formed large pillows piling rapidly on top of each other.

Peter ran to where he could get a view of the space between the buildings.

The smoke was pouring out from the window of Sam's apartment.

CHAPTER *Thirty-Three*

The third food man was nice. And being with his brothers was nice too, although it was less nice when they pounced on him or swatted at his tail. He was so much more mature than they were.

The third food man was strange, though. The other food men did not move around as much. He didn't know about the food lady because he had only been with her for such a short time. This third food man kept moving. He was unpredictable. Sometimes one chair, then another. Sometimes standing here, sometimes standing there. It was a little bit annoying. But he was generous with the food and only fed them the good stuff, so him moving around all the time was tolerable.

Another good thing about this place was that the third food man had little colourful animals in glass boxes. They were fun to watch. It was confusing at first because it looked like they were flying, but very slowly. Then the third food man gave the flying creatures some food, and he could see that the glass boxes were actually full of water. That was cool! Animals living inside water. He had had no idea that existed. He'd pay closer attention to his water dish in the future.

But one thing the third food man did made him nervous. He took a long stick out of a box. It was dark and shiny and had a hole in one end. The other end was wider and not as dark. The third food man rubbed it with a cloth and held it up and looked at it from every angle. He seemed to really like this stick. Then he opened it near the wide end and put some small, smooth, shiny things inside it and closed it up again. Oddly, right away after he would open it and take these shiny things out again. Maybe it was a game. The part he didn't like was afterwards, when the third food man held the wide end of the stick to his shoulder and pointed the end with the opening at him and then his brothers. The third food man made some noises when he did this. These did not sound like the usual people noises. Then he laughed and put the stick away.

Somehow this made him nervous. But despite that, and the restlessness, he would have been happy to stay if the next thing hadn't happened.

The next thing happened because the third food man went in and out of the room often. Sometimes he could hear him talking to another person, maybe from another room, but sometimes not. It was never very long, but it meant that the door was open a lot. The temptation grew. Maybe it would be easy to find the second food man or even the first food man. The one that had stopped moving around at all and had been very lazy about feeding them. Maybe he was better now? It would be worth checking to compare all three food men. This time he wouldn't leave the giant box, though. That had been a very bad experience.

Then he heard a strange noise coming from above. It was not a people noise. It was an animal noise. But not a cat noise. It was loud. It got the attention of the third food man, who made some noises of his own. These were regular people noises, just a little louder.

Soon after he smelled something strange. It was not a nice smell. He had not smelled anything like it before. Even though he didn't know what it was, something about it told him to be cautious.

The third food man suddenly made much louder noises and ran to the door. He went out. He left the door open.

CHAPTER
Thirty-Four

Peter had always believed that he was someone who was good in a crisis. Calm. Efficient. Rational. Later, when he thought back about what happened over the next few minutes, he would come to question this belief.

He sprinted to the door. After a brief fumble for the keys, he tore it open. Ed and the woman from apartment 1 were standing there, talking, gesturing up the stairs.

Peter raced past them, almost colliding with Ed as he turned to say something to Peter. He didn't hear what it was. He was up the stairs and at Sam's apartment door in three or four seconds, although it felt longer.

Smoke was seeping in probing tendrils, like grey fingers, out from under the door.

Why weren't the smoke alarms going off?

Why wasn't Pippin barking?

Again, fumbling for keys. He flung the door open.

Pippin barked.

Thank god, he was alive.

Peter ran into a wall of smoke, which surged past him into the hall. He immediately tripped on something on the floor and went flying into a pile of something else. That pile tumbled to the ground in a hellish clatter.

Where was Pippin?

"Pippin!"

Pippin barked again. Several short, sharp yips from across the room, near the window.

Peter stayed on the ground, noting that the air was a little clearer there.

What to do? Find the source of the fire and put it out? Or get Pippin and leave?

The way ahead was blocked by a jumble of boxes, books, hats, games, video cassettes, and other junk. It was far more than could have come from the pile he knocked over. Probably Pippin had knocked some over too.

The smoke had an awful, rank smell that caught in his throat. Peter pulled his shirt up over his mouth and nose.

The air was probably better by the window.

"Pippin!" he called again.

Pippin barked back. He sounded normal, if somewhat anxious.

Peter didn't hear flames or feel much heat, so the fire must have been small. But somehow it produced a lot of smoke. Damp stuff? Like maybe in the kitchen? Or in the bathroom . . . ?

Hang on.

A switch flipped in his brain. Click.

The bathroom. The painting supplies.

Linseed oil!

Damn it!

How could he have been so stupid? Linseed oil can spontaneously burst into flames when exposed to air. He had opened those bins. In his hurry to leave, he hadn't closed them again. And then the heat in the apartment from the malfunctioning radiator made it even more combustible.

Peter felt his heart sink. He squeezed his eyes shut and opened them again. He had locked his dog in an apartment stuffed to the ceiling with potential fuel and with an ignition source in the bathroom.

Peter panicked.

His mind went blank. Some subconscious driver of action took over.

He stood up, swivelled to run to the bathroom, and ploughed right into a shelving unit. It was farther to the left than he expected it to be. It fell on him and knocked him hard to the side. Pain shot through his shoulder like a lightning bolt.

Righting himself, he tested the shoulder. Not broken. Not dislocated. But painful. Very painful.

The contents of the shelves had spilled onto the floor. Random stuff was all around him. He tried to jump over the pile but tripped again. This time he recovered his balance quickly.

Damn it, damn it, damn it. Where's the bathroom?

He was suddenly unsure of the exact layout of the apartment.

But somehow, a few steps later, he found himself standing just inside the bathroom door.

He was right. The linseed oil was in flames. All around it, various rags and canvases were smouldering, producing fat coils of greasy grey smoke that quickly spread across the ceiling, like a blind living thing seeking a meal.

It could all ignite in an instant. He knew this. An apartment filled with flames.

Flashover. Any second now.

Peter doubled over, coughing. So acrid. Grabbing his throat.

There's no way. I can't do it. He stumbled backwards, retching.

The flames grew. Curling around the edge of the Rubbermaid, they licked at a half-collapsed easel.

He heard Pippin barking again. Louder. More persistent.

A single word flashed across his brain: *no.*

Peter held his breath and threw himself forward. He reached into the bathtub and flung enough canvases over his shoulder to clear a spot.

He pulled his sleeves over his hands and, in one quick motion, grabbed the burning bin and tossed it into the tub.

He turned on the tap.

A tremendous whooshing and hissing sound hit his ears, like a geyser going off. White steam pushed into the existing grey smoke, causing eddies and swirls as they mixed.

Peter stepped back. He tripped over the paintings he had tossed behind him.

He fell.

He tried to get up but couldn't. The canvases kept slipping under him. His right shoulder was so painful. He cleared a bare patch of floor with his left arm. His hand encountered that ridiculous Japanese sword under all the junk.

Maybe not so ridiculous. He grabbed it and used it to help prop himself up. He tried to get to his feet.

A flash of bright orange caught his eye. Through the smoke he could see one of the smouldering canvases spout flames. And then the next one beside it. And the one beside that one.

He had been too late.

CHAPTER
Thirty-Five

This was the easiest escape yet. The door was open, and the third food man wasn't paying any attention. He was standing outside the door, looking up the stairs. He was making noises at an unfamiliar lady. She was making noises back at him. She was also looking up the stairs. Neither of them noticed him. Maybe he should go back and chase his brothers out too? This was a good chance. But it was a bad idea. Three kittens were more noticeable than one. Plus, the third food man was always restless, so this chance would not last long enough.

No, he would go ahead as a scout. He would find the other food men and then decide where it was best to live. He could get his brothers later. He was obviously an excellent escaper and could come and go from these food people as he needed to.

But there was a problem.

Seeing the stairs reminded him that when he escaped this giant box on his first exploring adventure, he had come down the stairs. So, the other food men were up the stairs. But the third food man and the lady were blocking the way. They would definitely see him.

He was getting nervous. The bad smell was getting worse. Everything was getting noisier. There was an especially loud noise now that was not like an animal noise or a people noise. He didn't know what it was. It scared him.

He froze in a shadow against the wall.

What to do?

Should he run back into the third food man's room and try again another time?

Then he saw something.

Another door was open a crack. Just a crack, but he was strong so he could push his way through. He was pretty sure the other food men would not be in there because they should be up the stairs, but he should check. And anyway, it would get him farther from the noises and the smell, which both seemed to be coming from up the stairs.

He was bold. He did it. In the blink of a cat's eye, he was inside this other room. He didn't think the people saw him.

He had chosen well. What a room of wonders this was! There were so many delicious smells and bright, interesting things. He had never been in a room like this before.

He was hungry again. He wanted to follow those delicious smells, but something told him he should hide first.

He hid just in time. The lady came back in and closed the door behind her. Why did people do that? Wouldn't it be easier just to keep doors open all the time? It would be less work for them. But people were strange animals.

He thought he was good at hiding, but apparently this was not always true. The lady walked right up to him and scooped him up.

He was too shocked to react.

She made very soft noises at him and stroked him exactly the way he liked it best, right behind his ears. Then she carried him toward where the delicious smells were coming from. She set him down while she opened some small doors. She found a small silver box, similar to the ones soft food came from, but this was longer.

It had a picture on it that looked like the little water animals in the third food man's room! And when she opened it, it smelled . . . like all his best dreams concentrated and put on a plate just for him!

He had found heaven.

CHAPTER *Thirty-Six*

Two things happened in rapid succession.

Before Peter could react to the growing conflagration in the bathroom, he noticed that Pippin's bark was much closer.

He whirled around. To his astonishment, Pippin was right beside him. How had he threaded his way through the smoke-filled, chaotic jumble of the living room?

But before he could properly greet him and process this, the second thing happened.

A dark figure stepped in front of him, wielding an object. It was too smoky to see anything clearly. In silhouette, it looked like a man. The object was a large cylinder, like a . . . Peter had no idea.

He didn't have time to generate a rational thought before the figure said, "Step back." It was a familiar voice.

Peter heard a loud whoosh. White foam shot out from the cylinder toward the flames.

"Mia! Get ready to hand me the other one!"

It was the Other Peter. He and Mia had come in with fire extinguishers.

Now Peter also heard the sound of a smoke alarm going off. But it wasn't in Sam's apartment. It was from across the hall. There were more voices too, from outside the apartment.

Things were starting to make more sense.

"Dr. Bannerman, why don't you get out of the smoke? The air's much better in the hall," Mia said. She handed the fire extinguisher she was holding to her husband and guided Peter toward the door. She smiled at him. "And you can put that sword down."

Peter sat on the stairs and tried to collect his thoughts. Pippin sat beside him, close enough that they touched. Normally, Pippin sought a little more personal space, but this was a special circumstance.

The fire department arrived shortly after. It was the same crew that had attended to Maureen earlier. The Other Peter had put the fire out by the time they got into the apartment, but it was still very smoky.

One of the firefighters asked Peter a few questions. First, about how he was feeling and whether he needed to go to the hospital to be assessed for smoke inhalation. He offered Peter an oxygen mask, but Peter said he was feeling fine, just frazzled. The firefighter shrugged but told Peter to wait for the paramedics before leaving. Peter's thought, although he didn't voice it, was that since his lungs had been fine after the insane forest fire adventure at Dragonfly Lake in the summer, they would probably be fine after this. Today's exposure had been much shorter. Then the firefighter asked him whether he knew how the fire started. Peter explained about the linseed oil. The firefighter nodded. It had happened before. Burnt a whole garage down in Linden Woods. Damaged the house and the neighbour's house. No injuries, though.

More people came.

First Ed. Then Ted the drummer. Then Claire and Josh. The Other Peter and Mia returned as well. Soon Elena joined them. They all crowded around, chattering, making sympathetic noises, asking questions. Then the paramedics showed up. And the firefighter captain, who wanted to speak to him.

Peter hadn't experienced a full autism overwhelm in many years. The last time might even have been back at vet school, almost 20 years ago. A classmate found him hiding in the bathroom, head down, hands over his ears, trying to centre himself, but failing.

It felt like, if it were ever going to happen again, it might be now.

He closed his eyes and tried to focus on his breathing for a moment. It wasn't helping.

Fortunately, one of the paramedics took charge of the situation and asked everyone to step right back and give them some space. This helped.

She gave him the time he needed to steady himself and then examined him carefully. His lungs sounded clear, and his blood oxygen was excellent. He was fine, she said. Surveying the chaotic scene, though, she winked at him and suggested he take it easy for the rest of the evening, and maybe the next day too.

The captain was next. He was a burly older man with a walrus moustache. He smiled at Peter and clapped him on the shoulder with his big, gloved hand.

"You were lucky. Another few minutes, and kaboom. Your apartment is a fire trap. So many —"

"It's not my apartment," Peter interrupted him. "It's my brother's. I'm just helping him while he's . . . away. I know it's extremely cluttered."

The captain gave him a hard stare. "That's an understatement, sir. There are so many fire code violations. Aside from the tonnage of flammables, the smoke detector is covered up, the fire extinguisher is missing or buried in the junk, and the escape route to the window is partially obstructed."

"Yes, I know. Well, I didn't know about the smoke detector and fire extinguisher, but the other stuff. The, er, tonnage for sure. I've tried and tried to talk to him about it." Peter was mortified to be associated with Sam's problem in the eyes of an official.

"We're going to have to declare it unfit for occupation until the issues are addressed."

"I understand."

"And we'll be speaking to building management." The captain frowned and swivelled his head around. "Is the superintendent here?"

She had shown up while the paramedic was assessing Peter and, at the moment, was having an animated conversation with a group of residents at the end of the hall. Peter could easily pick her out by her currently wildly swinging blond ponytail.

"Yes, that's her over there."

The captain thanked Peter and went over to speak with her. Her face was red, and she flapped both her hands as she spoke. Her voice was high pitched and carried, but Peter couldn't make out any of the words. Not that he necessarily wanted to. What he really wanted to do was go home and have Icelandic apple cake with his family, before Kevin ate it all. When he checked the time, he saw that only half an hour had elapsed since he had arrived at the apartment. It felt like half a day.

"So, Pippin? Home?"

Pippin had remained sitting quietly beside Peter the entire time. He glanced back and forth at people who spoke to Peter, but mostly he watched him. He did a happy pant smile in response to Peter's question. The tone of Peter's voice promised something good.

CHAPTER *Thirty-Seven*

Peter didn't think it necessary to say goodbye to everyone before leaving. He'd already thanked the Other Peter and Mia, hadn't he? In any case, he'd make sure to properly thank them again tomorrow.

Elena stopped him as he made his way down the stairs.

"Before you go, I think I might have your brother's lost cat," she said, gesturing down toward her apartment.

"Really? I don't think so. We found him earlier today. He's with Ed now. Is it a Bengal?"

"I don't know cats very well, but it's a young one, and it's a light golden colour with dark stripes."

"Oh. That could be him. That's strange." The adrenaline hadn't completely left Peter's system. He had a vague headache, and he was having trouble processing what she was saying. She had found a young cat that from the description could be a Bengal. But Mr. Bingley was in Ed's apartment. Could it be a coincidence? Multiple roaming Bengal kittens? Doubtful. He had escaped before, so Peter supposed he could escape again. Made sense. Or did it? It felt like molasses had gummed up the gears of his brain. He was self-conscious about this, as if the process were visible, sluggish machinery grinding away behind glass, but Elena showed no signs of noticing that anything was amiss.

"Why don't you come and see?"

"Sure, please. Can he come too? His paws are a bit sooty." Peter nodded at Pippin.

"Of course. It's not that fancy!"

But it was.

Given the low rent and the neighbourhood, Peter did not expect the Lady Alice to attract well-off residents. So far, what he had seen of people's apartments confirmed this. Elena's was different. Her green dress had already made an impression, as well as the expensive tea, both of which could easily be explained away as special treats, but the apartment was something else.

The walls were decorated with a tasteful mix of art prints and photographs. Peter recognized a Klee and a Kandinsky, both artists he was fond of. Oh, and a Chagall and a Miró! Peter was impressed. The photographs were moody, high-contrast black-and-white shots of ruined cities. The furniture was mid–20th century Danish teak. A couple of large Persian carpets covered the floor. The floor lamps might have been from IKEA, though. He wasn't sure. But nonetheless, wow.

Peter was so taken by the décor that he didn't notice the kitten right away. It came running up to him from where it had been sitting beside the couch. Then it noticed Pippin and stopped. It arched its back, puffed out its fur, and began to hiss.

Elena laughed. "Funny little guy! Don't be scared."

"Oh my gosh," Peter said, looking down at the frightened puffball. "You're absolutely right. It's Mr. Bingley! How the devil . . . ?"

He crouched down and held his hand out. "Mr. Bingley," he said, softly. "It's me. It's going to be OK. Pippin won't hurt you." Peter pivoted and held the palm of his hand out to Pippin, who was sitting behind him near the door.

"He must have snuck in when the fire started and I was in the hall talking to Ed. I think we briefly both had our doors open." Elena crouched down as well and reached out to Mr. Bingley.

He continued to hiss. She edged toward him, and once she was close enough, she began to pet him. Meanwhile, Peter sidled over to block Mr. Bingley's view of Pippin. The kitten's hiss turned into a purr. Elena picked him up.

"Let's maybe put you in the bedroom while I talk to your rescuer," she said in a quiet singsong.

"Oh, I should get going," Peter said. He did want to talk to her. The photographs of bombed-out buildings in particular piqued his curiosity. But more than wanting to talk to her, he wanted to get home. Even if Kevin had in fact already eaten all the cake, he still wanted to be there. This day had gone on long enough.

"Hang on a moment while I tuck this little troublemaker away."

While he waited, Peter looked more closely at the nearest photograph. It depicted two apartment blocks facing each other across a rubble-strewn street. The outer walls of both buildings were missing, making them look like cubbies for giants to put their mittens and hats in. It was beautiful in its symmetry, but also stark and cold.

"My husband was a war photographer," Elena said from behind him.

Later, Peter realized that he should have asked where the photo was taken, but he was overwhelmed with fatigue. He knew that the answer may not have made a difference to which step he took in the ever-forking paths ahead, but it might have. Instead, he turned to face her and said, "Can you bring Mr. Bingley back to Ed's place when you get the chance, please? I really need to go."

Her expression had been serious, but it softened now. "Oh, Dr. Bannerman, do you really think you're in any condition to drive, especially on the highway in the dark?"

"I've done it many times, even more tired than I am now. Those 3 a.m. calvings, you know . . ." Peter chuckled weakly. "I'll be fine."

He noticed that she was wearing the gold fleur-de-lys necklace again. He had meant to look that up. It stirred a distant memory now. It was like when you can't recall the name of an actor, but you know that you know. You just need to access that memory file. Patience. It would come to him.

"Why don't you at least sit down and have a cup of tea? That's always a good pick-me-up. Twenty minutes. Sit quietly. Sip tea. Collect yourself. I can probably rustle up a treat for your dog as well. Maybe a piece of sausage?"

"Thank you, but I don't know . . ." It did sound good. There were so many advantages to her offer. It made perfect logical sense. Only his silly feelings were pushing him to leave immediately. And Laura would not allow Kevin to eat all the cake.

"I know you're a bit of a tea connoisseur as well. I have quite a few options. How about an East Frisian, for example?" She smiled and indicated to the kitchen, where Peter saw eight or nine white canisters lined up, each with a hand-lettered label.

That clinched it. "East Frisian? I haven't been able to get that in months!"

"It is hard to find. And I have proper Kluntjes too."

Peter beamed. Kluntjes were lumps of crystalized sugar, commonly used in tea in East Frisia, which was in the far northwest corner of Germany, as well as in the Netherlands. Its slow dissolution was part of the East Frisian tea ritual. This very specific way of preparing tea reminded him of his paternal grandmother, who always insisted on doing it like this. Peter enjoyed telling people that the East Frisians drank more tea than the British. Obscure trivia delighted him, but that tidbit especially so.

"OK, you've twisted my arm in exactly the right way." Peter laughed. "But only one quick cup. I'm quite caffeine sensitive, so I usually switch to decaf after lunch."

"I'll make a small cup, and not too strong. Please do sit." She smiled again and pointed at one of the teak armchairs, upholstered in grey cloth.

Pippin ambled over and lay down beside Peter as he sat. Peter looked around and tried to figure out what was going on in some of the other photographs. One depicted an elderly woman wearing a headscarf, pushing a wheelbarrow past a graveyard. Another was of a perfectly rounded hilltop surmounted by three dead, burnt-looking trees. Yet another was a little more cheerful, showing a group of children playing with a deflated soccer ball beside the wreck of an army truck. They were all high quality, but not something Peter would choose to have on his walls. He turned his attention to the paintings. Much more relaxing to look at.

It had been very still in the apartment until he heard the whistle of the kettle. Elena was back shortly with a tray and two steaming cups. They were beautiful translucent white porcelain, set on saucers with tiny silver spoons. Beside them was a small porcelain creamer and a bowl heaped with fingertip-sized lumps of crystallized sugar that looked like chunks of ice.

"Wonderful," Peter said. "Thank you."

"You're very welcome. I don't get much company, and even less often company that truly appreciates fine tea, so it is I who should thank you." Elena set the tray on the oval coffee table and stepped over to where Pippin was. She set a piece of sausage down in front of him. "There, that's for you for being such a well-behaved boy." Pippin sniffed the offering but didn't eat it.

"Hmm," Elena said. "I have liverwurst in the fridge too. I don't imagine he'll be able to resist that. I'll get him some after."

"Don't go to the trouble. He's just really tired too, and he's actually not much of a snacker."

Elena nodded and sat down. "Please, help yourself."

"Are you having East Frisian too?"

"Yes, but I didn't make a whole pot since we're just having two cups."

Peter put two lumps of sugar into his cup and watched them sink to the bottom. Staying for tea was a very good decision.

"No cream?" Elena asked.

"No, thank you. I know it's traditional, but I find it clouds the taste."

"I agree."

They sipped their tea in silence for a moment. It was delicious. Perhaps not his very favourite, but top five for sure.

"I wanted to talk to you about something, but as you're so tired, perhaps I'll leave it." She smiled at him, but in a way that struck Peter as odd. "Shall I put on some music instead?"

"If you like, sure. But I should drink up and go. And actually, I should text my wife and update her."

Elena got up and walked over to a stereo cabinet, also teak, and selected an LP from the adjacent rack.

Peter felt a sudden cramp, and then a stabbing pain in his stomach. He winced audibly.

Elena glanced back at Peter. "Are you OK?"

"Yeah, I'm fine." But he wasn't. The pain had ramped up to the point of intensity where he couldn't think of anything else or do anything. He gritted his teeth, waiting for it to pass, which it surely would. Then he would definitely leave. But if it continued, maybe Laura would have to come and get him.

No, these things always passed.

The room abruptly filled with the sound of a stringed instrument he couldn't identify and a man's voice, singing in an unfamiliar language. It sounded mournful, almost keening.

An unfamiliar language, but Slavic.

Slavic song. War photos. Gold fleur-de-lys.

Peter suddenly felt very ill. He was going to vomit all over this nice woman's lovely tea service.

His vision was blurry, but he saw Elena smiling at him. Smiling, he thought, *That's strange. I must look like I'm ready to hurl, and she's smiling.*

"Do you like this song? It is called 'Kraj potoka,' It is an old Bosnian folk song. It means 'by the stream.' It's a sad song about death, but beautiful. We used to sing it in Todorovo." She began to hum, still watching him, smiling.

Yes, Bosnian. And Todorovo? Where had he heard that before? He was sure he had heard it, but he couldn't make the connection. His brain felt like it was strapped to the front of a lurching rollercoaster.

The track in front of that rollercoaster disappeared into a fog. Peter began to feel faint. His stomach felt like a volcano.

Sam. Dženan. Todorovo. Ghostly, shimmering figures.

Ghosts.

A thought began to form like words trying to arrange themselves and come into focus. Circling. Fading. Focusing. Circling again.

Then lining up.

Dženan . . . Dženan told Sam that ghosts from Todorovo were going to kill him. But ghosts aren't real. They don't kill people.

Peter's eyes widened. He looked at Elena. He was losing her in the fog too. His stomach began to lurch. "You . . ." he said, squeezing the word out with great difficulty.

"I need . . ." he whispered.

Peter vomited.

"I'm sor—"

He vomited again, and again, and again, until it was just dry heaves.

"No, I'm sorry," Elena said.

It was the last thing he heard before he blacked out.

CHAPTER
Thirty-Eight

Barking.

Shouting.

Peter felt an incredible pain in his abdomen, like he had been stabbed with a kitchen knife. So sharp and intense. So deep. His face was damp.

He was . . . where? On the floor somewhere?

Yes, the floor. But where?

Her apartment. That woman. Ellen. Helena. Alina. Elena. That's it. They had tea and then . . . He couldn't remember anything else. His mind was a confused blur of fragments of colour, sound, and smell, sometimes almost forming a memory, but never quite.

He blinked a few times and tried to see something. A grey film covered everything. For some reason, he couldn't move his head either.

He heard barking and shouting.

Pippin!

Where is he? Who's shouting?

The barking stopped, but the shouting became louder.

The pain was so intense, it was difficult to concentrate. But he heard two voices. One vaguely familiar, but the other very familiar . . .

It was . . . Laura! It was Laura!

He tried to say something, but he couldn't. Not even a whisper.

Laura was upset. She was the shouter. The other voice was quieter, calmer. But he couldn't make sense of any words. They were sea people speaking from the depths. Or he was the sea person, and they were at the surface.

He felt a hand on his shoulder.

Laura spoke to him. Something soothing. He didn't know what.

Then he blacked out again.

CHAPTER *Thirty-Nine*

He woke up again. This time the pain was gone. And he was lying on his back. In a bed? But he still couldn't see very well. Two shapes hovered over him. A slender, shorter one on his right, and a bulkier one on his left. And what was that smell? Sharp. Unpleasant. Familiar . . .

"Oh, you're awake!" It was Laura.

Peter blinked rapidly to try to clear his vision. It helped a little. Where was he? It didn't seem like home. Pale green walls. Painfully bright lights. An odd rhythmic beeping sound.

And who was the other person?

"Pete, buddy! Welcome back to the world of the living." Kevin.

OK, that was good. That made sense.

"Where am I?" The words came out thick and dry, like chunks of language gone stale in the back of a cupboard.

"The hospital. St. B." Laura answered.

Hospital smell! That's what it was.

Laura put her hand on his shoulder. He had a flash of memory to when she had done the same in that apartment, when he was on the floor, sick? He wasn't sure why, or what happened.

So many questions, but one was foremost. "Pippin? Where's Pippin?"

Laura smiled. "At home. He's fine."

"What . . . ? I mean, why? Am I sick?" He tried to sit up, but that did hurt, so he sank back down.

"Easy there, boy," Kevin said, putting a hand on his other shoulder.

Laura paused. "Are you sure you want to hear all this now? Maybe you should get some more rest first. There's plenty of time for the full story later."

Peter shook his head. "No. I feel . . . OK. You know, not great, but OK enough to listen. I won't get proper rest anyway if I'm left to speculate."

Laura looked at Kevin. Kevin shrugged.

"OK," Laura said. She leaned over and kissed Peter on the forehead. "We can give you the Coles Notes version."

She and Kevin each grabbed chairs from behind them and sat down on either side of the bed.

"Elena poisoned you. Arsenic. A whopping dose, according to the doctors. You're lucky to be here. You've been in the ICU for the last week."

"Arsenic . . ." Peter said quietly. "Tasteless and odourless. I researched a bit when I thought Dženan might have been poisoned."

"Bingo," Kevin said. "You were right for a change." He chuckled and gave Peter a light punch on the shoulder. "That's how she killed him too."

"And Pippin? Did she try to kill him with the sausage?"

"No. It was tested. He was either not hungry or just wary of her."

"And how about Maureen?" Peter grasped at the moments of clarity that were coming to him faster now through the fog of confusion.

"No, that turns out to be pure coincidence. Massive heart attack," Kevin said.

"Elena . . . she's under arrest?" Peter asked, realizing immediately that it was a silly question. Of course she was.

"Well, she would be if she wasn't dead, so, technically no."

OK, maybe not so silly.

"Dead?"

"When Laura found you, Elena acted like it was a shocking medical accident, nothing to do with her, but she knew the truth would come out, so she took an even more massive dose of arsenic herself."

"Wow. OK." Peter tried processing this, but another question immediately popped into his head. "How did you find me?"

"You hadn't come home well after we expected you," Laura said. "And you weren't answering my texts and calls, so I got worried and decided to come into town."

"Again," Peter said.

"Yes, again." Laura smiled and kissed him on the forehead again. "Pippin must have heard me or smelled me out in the hall, so he started barking. I knew it was him right away. Fortunately, Elena neglected to lock her door. Although I would have broken the door down if she hadn't opened up."

"I don't doubt that," Kevin said. "Which is a good thing. The docs have been saying that any more delay in your treatment, and I'd be writing your eulogy right now. Which I'm happy to do, but, well, you know."

Peter nodded, still processing. Arsenic poisonings. Saved by Pippin and Laura. Elena dead.

"Motive? Do we know why she did it?"

Kevin answered. "Yeah, more or less. She kept a journal, and the local cops have been able to more or less corroborate what she wrote. Lucky find, eh? The common sort of criminal I deal with never keeps a diary of nice, clean confessions. Only the high-class ones do, and we don't have enough of those in New Selfoss. But anyway, to your question, basically, this Croatian guy was a war criminal living under an assumed name, hiding out in Canada."

Peter interrupted. "So, he was Croatian and a Ustasha member? And she put the marking by his door to let him know that his cover had been blown?"

"Give the man ten points. Yes. His unit, under his personal direction, killed all the men of her family in some little town in Bosnia."

"Todorovo!" Peter said, loudly enough that Laura raised her eyebrows.

"You guys. Really?" she said. "This isn't *Reach for the Top* or *Jeopardy!*"

"Yeah, for sure not a game," Kevin said. "Sorry. Knezevic supervised the murder of her father, her brothers, her uncles . . . A massacre. So, she tracked him down to here, befriended him, and then started messing with his mind."

"She told me she moved because of her husband," Peter said, much quieter now.

"The Austrian photographer? No, he died back in Vienna. Natural causes, they say." Kevin paused and raised his eyebrows briefly. "But seriously, that sounded legit. Nothing fishy in her journal about that. They met when he came to take pictures of the war and the aftermath of the massacre."

"And you said 'messing with his mind'?" Peter adjusted his position in bed, while trying not to snarl the IV line. Laura reached over to help. "Like maybe that stuff about ghosts?"

"Yup. You got it. They drank tea together and played backgammon. Then, when he went to the can or whatever, she hid tiny Bluetooth speakers."

"And the bag over his head?"

Kevin cleared his throat. "They say that the only thing worse than death is a dishonourable death. After the arsenic killed him, she cleaned him up, yanked his pants down, and put a bag over his head. Post-mortem humiliation."

Peter shook his head slowly. It made sense, but it was still so strange, and sad. Killing a killer, and then killing yourself.

"About that bag," Peter began, and then paused, uncertain how to go on. "I mean, Sam . . . and those . . ." He faltered again.

"*Star Wars* toys?" Kevin offered.

"Yeah, that," Peter said. "I can't make any sense of it."

Kevin shrugged. "Beats me. I deal with a lot of, how shall I say, differently wired folks, and nothing really surprises me anymore."

Laura shook her head. "It's displacement," she said quietly. "Even mentally well people do this to some extent. When you can't process a troubling emotion, you might repress it, or, instead, you might act it out, or displace it, onto an object — working through it in a way that feels safer. For someone with a history of psychosis who is visually oriented, like Sam, it makes sense. He was so shocked by what happened to his friend, and especially how it happened, that he needed to do something physical to process the horrifying thoughts. I'm just surprised he didn't paint it. This was quicker, I suppose."

Peter and Kevin both nodded. The room was very quiet for a moment.

"And me? The motive for trying to kill me? I wasn't that close to figuring out that she murdered Dženan."

"Apparently, she thought you were. I probably shouldn't be telling you this, but in her diary, she said that you were extremely intelligent and were bound to crack the case. Might have been a mistranslation, though." Kevin laughed. "Anyway, that's why she tried scaring you in Sam's apartment. It was meant for you, not him."

"Could she have placed those *Star Wars* figures too? To bolster the case against Sam?"

"No. It looks like Sam did that . . ."

Peter sucked his breath in. He'd ask more about Sam after. First, he had one more question about what happened to him.

"And she'd just pass off my death as a mysterious medical event? Arsenic is pretty hard to detect on autopsy unless you're specifically looking for it."

"It looks that way," Kevin said, quieter now.

"You're probably wondering about Sam," Laura asked. Peter never stopped being astonished by her mind-reading skills. "His place has been condemned."

"Yeah, the fire captain told me that would be happening," Peter said.

"And he's been cleared of all charges, so he's in a transitional space now. Stuart's cousin has a few properties in the city and was able to rent him a room until he gets something more permanent. The stuff that can be salvaged is in storage for now. We'll figure something out. He's been up to visit you every day. He's quiet when he comes. He usually leaves you a book." She pointed to a stack on his bedside table. They were mostly histories. Some looked quite interesting.

The three of them were quiet for a minute while all around them the hospital hummed and beeped and bustled.

"One more thing, and then I probably should take a nap. How did she get into locked rooms, and how did she lock up Dženan's place after she left him?"

"Elementary, my dear Bannerman," Kevin said in the cheesiest British accent. "Keys. She made friends with the superintendent, swiped her keys one time, and had them copied. She locked up after she left his place but couldn't set the extra security latches inside. That's how the super got in to find the body without having to bust the door down."

"I feel so foolish," Peter said. "I just took Sam's word that it was latched from the inside. And Sam must have based this on Dženan telling him about the latches. And I didn't even think to consider that the murderer might have been invited in." Peter shook his head.

"Happens to the best of us." Kevin shrugged. They were quiet for a moment. Then Kevin added, "That Elena was one smart woman."

"A *very* smart woman, it seems," Peter said, beginning to close his eyes. "And that's how she made him believe in ghosts," he added in a groggy half-whisper. "When he went out, he couldn't set the latches, so that's when she snuck in to move his stuff around, or leave scrawled warnings, or maybe even use those Bluetooth speakers. Torture him mentally for a while before killing him. Smart. Not good . . . But smart . . ." He was fading out. "Not lucky, though . . ."

"There are all kinds of smart people. Good ones, bad ones. Lucky ones, unlucky ones," Laura said softly.

Peter fell deep asleep. He dreamed of three kittens dancing on the full moon.

CHAPTER
Forty

He didn't spend much time thinking about the past. Pointless and kind of hard to picture. But he did remember his brothers going away and not coming back. First Barry, then Flinders.

The second food man had come to the third food man's room. He thought he was coming for all three of them. He was very excited and happy. The second food man picked each of them up, made noises at them, and then set them down again. He looked at them for a short while.

Then he picked up Barry and left. Neither came back again.

The next day, a lady came. He didn't know this lady. She went directly to Flinders, picked him up and took him away. Neither of them came back either.

He was alone with the third food man and his water creatures for a long time. It was boring and sad.

That's what he remembered. But he thought about these memories less and less. Life was good now. The fourth food man was the nicest yet, and he had a much bigger set of rooms, full of interesting things.

Only one thing shocked him at first. When he was taken to the fourth food man's rooms, who do you think was waiting for him there?

The not-a-cat!

It was the same not-a-cat that tried to attack him that time outside of the giant box!

He hissed at the not-a-cat and tried to swat it again. Did the fourth food man not understand how dangerous this animal was?

But a strange thing happened. The not-a-cat turned out to be friendly. Probably because it knew it would be clawed to death if it didn't, but he didn't care why. The main thing was that this place wasn't boring anymore. It was the opposite of boring. The not-a-cat was in some ways a better friend than his brothers had been. More fun. Less annoying.

No, life was very good now. He was finally getting what he deserved.

Here's a sneak preview of the next
Dr. Bannerman Vet Mystery:

Five Icelandic Ponies

PROLOGUE

The wind had scoured a lot of the snow away from the top of a low hill, thinning it to a crust. She stopped. Maybe there would be grass here. She dug a little with her left hoof, breaking through the hard top layer. The others slowly walked ahead, heads down, tails to the wind. She could catch up easily. And it was not that she was hungry. They had plenty of hay back in the barn, but sometimes a bit of old frozen grass was just the thing. Just a few nibbles, mind you. Her friends had no interest. Only the freshest hay, thank you very much. But she liked the way the stiff, cold blades felt in her mouth as they melted and softened.

The wind was strong at this point. It was becoming unpleasant. The others had stopped moving on the lee side of a bush. She should probably go there too and get out of the wind for a bit.

Trotting over to join them, she noticed something out of the corner of her eye. Down the slope to the left. It caught the low winter sun. Something round and white, but not white like snow. A little bit more yellow and grey. Down there was where the farmer had drained the wet area in the fall and cut down some trees and shrubs that were around it. They lay in piles on the far side. She hoped he was making a new pasture for them. That would be nice once it was spring.

But she was curious about the round white thing.

She glanced at her friends. Still standing behind the bush.

Fine. Let them.

She turned and walked down the hillside. The wind now hit her fully on the side. It was strong and cold, but it didn't bother her. Not yet. She had a good winter coat. Perhaps thicker than any of them.

As she approached the object, she picked up a scent. It was faint, but she could see the telltale footprints now too.

Coyote.

She wasn't frightened. A well-placed kick would put an immediate end to any foolish ideas that the coyote might get. But nonetheless, it put her on alert.

From the pattern of footprints, it looked like the coyote had dragged this thing from somewhere in the old wet area. Then he abandoned it here. Bored with it? Got frightened off? Too awkward to carry further? She didn't know and didn't care.

She sniffed it close up. Then she nudged it with her nose to make it roll over.

The other side had two identical round black holes, side by side. Beneath those was a single triangular hole. And below that, a mouth full of teeth. Grinning at her, lipless.

CHAPTER *One*

"Orkney?" Laura asked, setting her mug down and sitting back in her armchair.

"Yeah," Peter replied. "I've always wanted to go. Check out the Bannerman ancestral lands. And since we're going to be in Iceland anyway . . ."

"A heritage tour, Gudmundurson and Bannerman, on top of the Scent Sport Worlds . . . ?" Laura chuckled. "This keeps growing and growing. Maybe I should look for a knitter's convention to throw in as well!"

"Right, ha. It's just a thought. And I don't know how easy the flight connections are. It'd be cool, though!"

"It would." Laura smiled. "But lots of time still to figure all this out." She reached into her knitting bag and pulled out a half-finished scarf. It was dark forest green with gold lettering on it.

"Tengwar?"

"Good eye. Yes. It's the most popular of Tolkien's Elvish scripts. And the easiest to knit!"

"Selling well?" Peter asked, only half paying attention to what he was saying because he was still daydreaming about Orkney.

"Like proverbial hotcakes. Believe it or not, I've got a half-dozen orders from Korea. Must be a word-of-mouth thing. Anne Shin bought one for her niece over there."

Peter nodded reflexively. He was picturing cozy stone cottages by the sea, weathered by winds off the North Atlantic. He assumed there would be lots of sheep on Orkney. He liked sheep. It's too bad he didn't have more as patients.

Pippin, their lab–huskie–border collie cross, stirred and opened one eye to look up at him. He had been snoozing at Peter's feet. Peter wondered whether he had read his mind about sheep and chuckled at the thought.

Peter's phone vibrated on the small table beside his chair. He glanced at the caller display.

"It's Bob Sigurdsson," he said, half to himself.

"Mm hmm," Laura said, also half to herself. "Hope you don't have to go out in this weather."

Peter looked out the window. The glass shook slightly with each gust of wind. The woods on the far side of the yard were blurry through the driving snow. It was like looking through dilute milk. There would be bad drifting. And the Sigurdssons were down a particularly exposed stretch of road. He didn't mind the cold or the snow, but the drifting would polish the road surface and make visibility terrible. The weather office said that the wind should be settling down any time now, but they were wrong as often as they were right.

He sighed.

Oh well, maybe Bob just has a question, he thought.

He picked up just before it went to voicemail. "Hi, it's Peter Bannerman."

"Hi, Dr. Bannerman. Sorry to bug you on a Sunday, especially in this weather. It's Elsie. She's cut her fetlock pretty deep. Must have snagged a wire in the snow. Happened this morning. I tried to bind it, but it's bleeding through."

Peter stifled another sigh. He'd have to go out there and suture this. It'd be a quick job, and they had a nice, heated barn for their horses, but he wasn't looking forward to the drive.

"OK, I'll be there in 30."

"That's terrific. Thank you. And again, I'm sorry to bring you out on a day like this."

"It's no problem, really," Peter lied, making a face at Laura as he said this.

"And by the way, your brother-in-law is probably going to be out here too," Bob added.

"Oh?"

"Yeah, I tracked the blood back to find out what Elsie cut herself on. I found the wire that I think did it, but you won't believe what I found nearby." He paused, apparently expecting Peter to ask what or maybe even guess. Peter disliked these kinds of conversations.

"No idea."

"A skull. A human skull. So, the Mounties are coming out to have a look. Probably be here around the same time."

After Peter hung up, he told Laura what Bob had said. She put her knitting down and looked at him.

"A skull at Sigurdssons'?" She sucked her breath in. "Remember about 20 years ago when Brenda Scheinbaum disappeared? One day, she just vanished. No trace of her ever found."

"Yeah, I think so," Peter answered. Twenty years ago. He was in vet school in Saskatoon then and didn't pay much attention to New Selfoss news. But it kind of rang a bell.

"Well, I don't remember which, but she used to date one of the Sigurdsson brothers."

Entertainment. Writing. Culture.

ECW is a proudly independent, Canadian-owned book publisher. We know great writing can improve people's lives, and we're passionate about sharing original, exciting, and insightful writing across genres.

Thanks for reading along!

We want our books not just to sustain our imaginations, but to help construct a healthier, more just world, and so we've become a certified B Corporation, meaning we meet a high standard of social and environmental responsibility — and we're going to keep aiming higher. We believe books can drive change, but the way we make them can too.

Being a B Corp means that the act of publishing this book should be a force for good — for the planet, for our communities, and for the people that worked to make this book. For example, everyone who worked on this book was paid at least a living wage. You can learn more at the Ontario Living Wage Network.

This book is also available as a Global Certified Accessible™ (GCA) ebook. ECW Press's ebooks are screen reader friendly and are built to meet the needs of those who are unable to read standard print due to blindness, low vision, dyslexia, or a physical disability.

The interior of this book is printed on Sustana EnviroBook™, which is made from 100% recycled fibres and processed chlorine-free.

ECW's office is situated on land that was the traditional territory of many nations, including the Wendat, the Anishinaabeg, Haudenosaunee, Chippewa, Métis, and current treaty holders the Mississaugas of the Credit. In the 1880s, the land was developed as part of a growing community around St. Matthew's Anglican and other churches. Starting in the 1950s, our neighbourhood was transformed by immigrants fleeing the Vietnam War and Chinese Canadians dispossessed by the building of Nathan Phillips Square and the subsequent rise in real estate value in other Chinatowns. We are grateful to those who cared for the land before us and are proud to be working amidst this mix of cultures.

ecwpress.com